W8-BW1-126

BY GEORGINA CROSS

The Stepdaughter

The Missing Woman

Nanny Needed

Nanny Needed

NANNY NEEDED

A Novel

GEORGINA CROSS

BANTAM BOOKS

NEW YORK

Nanny Needed is a work of fiction. Names, characters, places, and incidents are the products of the author's imagination or are used fictitiously. Any resemblance to actual events, locales, or persons, living or dead, is entirely coincidental.

A Bantam Books Trade Paperback Original

Published in the United States by Bantam Books, an imprint of Random House, a division of Penguin Random House LLC, New York.

BANTAM BOOKS and the HOUSE colophon are registered trademarks of Penguin Random House LLC.

LIBRARY OF CONGRESS CATALOGING-IN-PUBLICATION DATA
Names: Cross, Georgina, author.
Title: Nanny needed: a novel / Georgina Cross.
Description: New York: Bantam Books, [2021]
Identifiers: LCCN 2020057414 (print) | LCCN 2020057415 (ebook) |
ISBN 9780593355992 (trade paperback) |
ISBN 9780593356005 (ebook)
Classification: LCC PS3603.R6738 N36 2021 (print) |
LCC PS3603.R6738 (ebook) | DDC 813/.6—dc23
LC record available at https://lccn.loc.gov/2020057414
LC ebook record available at https://lccn.loc.gov/2020057415

Printed in the United States of America on acid-free paper

randomhousebooks.com

2 4 6 8 9 7 5 3 1

Title-page and page 6 art: © iStockphoto.com

Book design by Dana Leigh Blanchette

Dedicated to Nicole Angeleen,
who without your friendship and insight,
Nanny Needed wouldn't be the book it is today.
Thank you.

NANNY NEEDED

CHAPTER ONE

The children are chattering. Some sing softly to themselves while others look around the room, lollipops in hand, occasionally glancing at their mothers, who are moving beyond the double French doors.

The doors click shut.

For a moment, the children look worried: mouths downturned, lollipop licking paused. They're young, ages three and four, and their bodies stiffen with unease at watching their mothers go. But another woman enters the room smiling, and the children's faces brighten at the sight of her. She's beautiful, with diamonds the size of gumballs around her neck, a trail of heavenly perfume about her too.

The children look at her, awestruck, then confused. They've never seen her before. Until today, they've never had a reason to visit her Upper West Side apartment.

But I know Collette. I work for her, and not for much longer. After today, I won't be her nanny anymore.

Collette hands them more candy and the children's smiles widen, cherry-red flavoring sticking to the corners of their mouths. She points to a display of balloons and they giggle. She tells them about a birthday cake that is soon to come: four layers of vanilla sponge separated by strawberry icing, and the children settle into their seats, their mothers forgotten. For a short time, Collette seems happy too.

But then I see the way she looks at me and it feels as if ice has been dropped down my neck.

Collette wants to keep me.

The children face one another at a table, four girls and two boys plucked from a playground I stumbled upon several days ago. It was one of only a few parks I could find where the mothers would accept an invitation to a birthday party for a child they did not know.

They'd looked at me incredulously at first, asking, *Why? Doesn't the girl have her own friends from school?* They wanted to know if I was crazy. They thought it was a joke. But after turning over the invitation cards in their hands, they saw the address and promised to show up promptly at 3:00 P.M. I'm sure the cash I handed them helped too.

For the party, the children are seated in a room usually reserved for elaborate dinner parties, the occasional high-profile guest. But not today—those occurrences are fewer and further between these days, and never on July 10.

Today, only children are welcome at West Seventy-eighth Street.

My eyes tick around the table and I see that the children are fidgeting again. They're shifting in their seats, asking for cake. The patience of these preschoolers is waning by the millisecond, their shouts and sugar-high bouncing turning the room into a ticking time bomb.

Collette looks flustered too. She smooths the tablecloth with a snap, her hands trembling, an unmistakable twitch beneath her eye as she steals another glance at the door.

Where is the birthday girl? What's keeping her?

Collette bursts forward to fill juice cups and adjust centerpieces. When she moves like this—jittery, sporadic, nerves jangling with caffeine and God knows what else she popped in her mouth before everyone arrived—she reminds me of a small bird. Thin. Eyes flickering. Body perched before darting away again.

Collette Bird. She couldn't have married into a more perfect name for herself, and one of the wealthiest families in New York City too. Her wealth is what allows her to throw parties like this. It's what allows her to get away with them too.

I look at my watch. One hour to go.

The room quiets, overhead lights dim, and out comes the cake. The housekeeper wheels it on a table as the children erupt into cheers, their small hands clapping, and they toss aside their lollipops.

One of the girls counts the candles out loud, "One, two, three, four. Same as me. I'm four years old!"

She looks around. So do the others.

But where is the birthday girl?

Collette glances at the door. I can almost hear her heart racing, the children's eyes following hers. She rushes to the head of the table, a place setting she's purposely kept empty, and pulls out a chair. She peers into the light shining from the hallway.

"Wait for it . . ." she says, a sharp intake of breath as Collette whispers excitedly, "Any time now . . ."

And then . . .

A sharp noise from the next room pierces the air, getting closer. My eyes race to Collette, who looks as if her heart has just been ripped from her chest.

Nanny Needed

101 West 78th Street.

Call for interview: 212-555-0122 Paid weekly.

Discretion is of the utmost importance.

Special conditions apply.

CHAPTER TWO

===

"What do you think about me being a nanny?"

I hold up the flyer, the one I grabbed from the bulletin board in our apartment lobby.

Jonathan's eyes drift toward me. There's a layer of scruff on his chin from not having shaved yet this morning; his hair is a mess of thick waves across his head. In this light, I'm reminded of how handsome he is: rugged and sincere, the man who will be my husband. He rubs his chin, feeling my gaze landing there. I want to kiss that spot along his jaw, the one with the tiny white scar, and let my fingers trace the side of his face.

"Have you ever been a nanny?" he asks.

"I babysat in high school."

"And that makes you qualified?"

"I was certified in CPR."

He teases. "And when was that, ten years ago?"

I nudge him. "Don't be mean. The ad doesn't ask for any of that."

He plucks the flyer from my hands. "Let me see." We're lounging on our bed, which later we'll fold into a futon to make room in our tiny three-hundred-square-foot apartment. Two pillows are propped behind our backs, our legs stretched out in pajama pants, the coffee Jonathan makes for me every morning resting within arm's reach on the floor.

He reads over the ad, the four short lines. "What's with the *discretion is of utmost importance* part?"

"You mean the most interesting part?" I take back the flyer. "I think it must be a celebrity or someone important. I mean, the address is West Seventy-eighth."

"It doesn't say how many kids. It could be a dozen."

"I doubt it."

"Or an infant." He inhales sharply. "Do you know how to handle babies?"

I think of my childhood: solitary, except for the one aunt who raised me. The ten-year-old twins I babysat in high school. Jonathan and I are making plans for our wedding but we're still a long ways away from having our own children.

"I can figure it out," I tell him.

"Why do you want another job anyway? I thought you liked it at Hearth."

I sigh. I *do* like it at Hearth, the restaurant on the corner of East Thirteenth Street and First Avenue where we work. Jonathan helped me get the job a few months ago despite the fact that we were already engaged and didn't tell the owner. Paul found out anyway and sat us down for a "serious talk," warning us about arguing during shifts and said he didn't want any drama. We told him not to worry. Jonathan and I never argue.

"I'll work both jobs," I tell him. "Nanny during the day and keep nights and weekends at the restaurant."

"But you've already missed two shifts."

"That was last week."

"Paul keeps track."

"The man's all talk."

Jonathan throws me a look. "I got in trouble because I didn't set up my section correctly. He's one of those three-strikes-you're-out kind of guys."

"I'll make it work."

"You're talking as if you've already got the job."

"Thinking positive, right?" I turn to him. "Anyway, what are you so worried about?"

"Besides the risk of you losing a good restaurant gig—"

"Which I won't."

"—you don't know anything about this family. What if they're batshit crazy?"

"At least they'll pay me for it." I point again at the address. "Probably pretty well if I had to guess."

It's his turn to sigh. "What if the dad comes on to you?"

I choke on my coffee, my hand wiping the dribble at my mouth.

"Come on," Jonathan says. "You hear about that sort of thing all the time. Rich executive husband coming after the young, beautiful nanny."

"Aww, you think I'm beautiful?" I bat my eyelashes.

"Of course you're beautiful. And you're young, you're twenty-five."

I roll my eyes. "I appreciate the concern, but you're being a bit overdramatic."

But Jonathan isn't cracking an inch.

"Don't you think the extra money would be nice?" I ask. "You can't argue against that, can you?"

He tips his head. "Yes, the extra money would be nice—we need it, there's no doubt about that." His eyebrows furrow. He doesn't say another word but I know he's thinking about

our debt. The envelopes stacked on the counter with a gar-
ishly red Past Due mark stamped across each one. The wedding we'd like to have some time this year if only we had the
money. How we're constantly living paycheck to paycheck.

We sit in silence. I'm chewing my bottom lip while he
stares at the flyer and reads the ad one more time.

"You'd really work two jobs?" he asks.

"I don't think I have a choice."

"I could get an extra job too, you know."

I squeeze his elbow, my heart warming, knowing he would
do that in a heartbeat if he could. But he's already working
the most shifts anyone can have at Hearth and is always
picking up extras when he can. No, I tell myself, another job
for him is out of the question. I'm the one who needs to pick
up the slack. It's not his responsibility to pay my bills and get
us out from under the mountain of debt I've found myself
buried in. Filing for bankruptcy has come up more than
once—a distinct possibility, I may not have a choice about it
for much longer—and the thought of it makes me shudder.
In truth, when Jonathan's not looking, I bite my lip to keep
from crying. I don't want him to panic more if he doesn't
have to.

I tell him, "You already work so much. You're paying
most of the rent as it is and just about everything else. Besides, don't you want to go back to school?"

He nudges my shoulder. "Don't *you* want to go back to
school?"

I scrunch against the pillows. "Of course. We both do.
But that's on pause, you know it is."

Jonathan opens his mouth, closes it. This is an argument
he's lost many times before. We can't afford it because the

truth of the matter is, at this pace, living in the city, we're both on a hamster wheel, making just enough to cover rent, utilities, some groceries, and nothing more.

And even though I'd been close to finishing my degree, the one I started back home in Virginia Beach a few years ago, all starry-eyed and looking forward to the day I could bring my sketches to life in the great big fashion world, Aunt Clara's death changed all that—I had to give up and drop out. With the tidal wave of debt from her medical expenses, I couldn't justify paying for college anymore. I had to work, so I packed away my dreams and my sketchbook and left school.

But after a couple more years of handing out one frozen daiquiri after another to tourists at the beach, I convinced myself to move to New York, the city Aunt Clara had loved and always dreamed of moving back to.

She told me, "It's a place where anything's possible. I never felt more alive than when I lived there." And though I didn't know a soul, had no idea where I'd find a new job, that sounded like a much better prospect than sleepy Virginia Beach.

So I told myself, if I had to work, the money I earned slowly chiseling away at the invoices from St. John's Hospital, and the additional bills from Hospice Care, I could at least live in a place where I'd be surrounded by the fashion world, where the streets teemed with the latest designers and trends, with boutiques and showrooms on every corner, and I could find some inspiration again. Even if it took me years of waiting tables before I could afford to go back to school.

I just never realized how expensive living here would be.

Meeting Jonathan helped, not only with the apartment but with the job at Hearth. And he knows how precarious my situation is. He's seen how high the stack of bills is getting. He hears me on the phone several times a week begging the debt collectors for one more extension and how defeated it leaves me feeling afterward. He hugs me every time and reminds me to breathe. He tells me it's going to be all right, we'll figure out a way together even though neither of us has a solution yet—not until this flyer at least.

Jonathan says, "How much do nannies make these days anyway?" My eyes slide toward him, and I feel a small jolt of hope he might be coming around to the idea.

"I'm not sure, but it would definitely help, especially if I can stay at the restaurant."

"Let's hope so. I'd like it if we could keep working together."

I smile. Oh, my fiancé. The romantic. One of maybe only ten left in the city and somehow I managed to snag him.

Aunt Clara always told me not to settle. *Don't fall for a guy unless he makes you a priority.* And I've found that with Jonathan, I know I have. He's my everything, and I'm his everything too. We have each other's backs. How I wish Aunt Clara could have met him and seen how happy I am.

She'd been in love once too. She never told me much about it, only that it was a love she'd found while living in New York. I could tell from the flicker in her eyes how deep it was.

She never said much but I imagine Aunt Clara's relationship ended because of me. After my parents died, she was the only family I had left and I changed everything for her. She left New York, she left him, and she moved to Virginia to care for me. She told me all the time how I ended up being the greatest love of her life instead.

Now here I am, living in the big city where she had always

wanted to return and planning a wedding. I'm sharing my life with someone who wants the best for me. But by the way he's looking at me now, the way he's running the different scenarios in his head, I can tell Jonathan is worried about the pitfalls I might be overlooking.

If I lose my job at Hearth and work days as a nanny while he spends nights and weekends at the restaurant, we'll have little time together. We'll be like ships passing in the night and he doesn't want that.

I offer some hope. "Maybe I'll make enough from the nannying job that I can start paying off everything, or at least put a dent in it. I can go back to school, finally get a salary, do what I really want to do. You can go back to school too. Wouldn't that be great? Wouldn't you want that for me?"

"Of course." He turns serious. "Of course, I want that for you. For *us*." He takes another long look at the flyer. "So, Upper West Side, huh?" He mulls it over. "It does sound fancy."

I nod, picturing for the seven hundredth time what I think the apartment will look like: a doorman, Venetian marble, silk drapes with tassel trim. A glamorous family stepping out on the town with me following and children in tow, obedient and dressed to the hilt.

"You think anyone else in this building is going after the job?"

I blink, visions of the picture-perfect family coming to a halt.

"The flyer," Jonathan says. "How many were there?"

I stare at the copy in my hands. "This was the last one." I feel a tight squeeze in my gut.

I don't know why, but I don't tell him the copy I'm holding is not the last flyer but the only flyer left in our lobby. I've been waiting for him to wake up to tell him about it. Last night I was coming down the stairs as someone was pinning it to the bulletin board. I saw only the back of his head before he turned and walked out the door.

I'd tried looking up the job on my phone, hunting for more information than the brief description on the ad. But I couldn't find anything posted, not on Craigslist or any other job placement boards. From what I could tell, there was no public listing anywhere.

And that's when it dawned on me: this family is so discreet they sent a courier to walk the streets of the East Village instead of looking for a nanny online. It's their way of controlling how many people see it, reducing the number of respondents.

Making sure whoever does apply for the job can handle *Special conditions apply.*

CHAPTER THREE

===

Jonathan is in the shower when I call the number on the listing. A man answers, which surprises me at first—I'd been expecting the mother—and my eyes freeze on the wall. How old-fashioned of me.

Right off the bat, the man explains the nanny job is for his younger sister. *Oh good, only one kid.* That's a good start. He says he's the older brother, and a much older brother if I had to guess.

"I'm the stepson representing my stepmother. My father remarried and they had a little girl."

I appreciate the clarification and I think it's sweet he's taking such an active role in his younger sister's care. How many older brothers would do that sort of thing?

He introduces himself as Stephen Bird and sounds genuinely interested to learn how I moved to New York from Virginia Beach and am now looking for a new job. Of course, I don't breathe a word about waiting tables at Hearth. I want him to think I have all the time in the world to dedicate to his little sister.

After a few minutes, he asks that I attend the first round of interviews the next morning even though it's a Sunday, and I'm thrilled. He's giving me a chance, a real foot in the door, and not once does he ask if I have any nannying experience.

"Eleven A.M.," he says. "The doorman will show you the elevator to the top floor."

In the morning, I kiss Jonathan for good luck and he squeezes my hand twice—it's what we do. Whenever we leave for the day, he gives me one squeeze for love and one squeeze to say he'll be thinking about me. It's something he started at the end of our first date and I remember thinking how sincerely I knew he wanted to see me again, my heart warming at the touch of his fingertips.

From our building, I step onto the sidewalk and breathe in New York City, all one thousand smells of it. I love everything about this place—the rush. The energy. The sights and smells. Tommy's, the pizza place that sells slices of cheese and mushroom heaven twenty-four hours a day. The Jewish bakery with its warming loaves of mandel bread and babka. The coin-operated laundromat with its mountain fresh detergent mixed with the acrid exhale of someone's Parliament cigarette. The flower stall overflowing with pots of hyacinth and wisteria blooms.

On the corner, the bagel place where I ran in and out earlier for breakfast. Jonathan stayed home to make coffee while I fetched us egg sandwiches and a sesame bagel with avocado.

Almost two years living in the East Village and I still haven't been able to get over the noise: delivery vans, cabs, and Ubers filling the street, their horns blaring over the dings of bicyclists as they whiz past wearing their blazers and skinny jeans, shoulder bags strapped across their chests, ear-buds plugged in.

The subway is jam-packed too, with the never-ending clicking of turnstiles and beeping of card machines. A rush of wind smacks my face, the L train speeding along the track with a monstrous roar as it approaches the station.

All around me, heads seem bent in prayer, but really, it's people staring at their phones. Sunday shift workers mixed with tourists mixed with families and bright-eyed college students on their way to study. And me, traveling to a part of Manhattan I rarely visit, have never had reason to.

Several stops later, including a transfer to the 1 train, I emerge from the station, the quiet of the neighborhood set-tling upon me immediately. It's so unlike the East Village, with its gritty sounds and excitement of motion. Here on the Upper West Side, it's as if time itself has slowed down. The hushed crisscross of streets forms its own tranquillity away from the bustle permeating the rest of New York. I suppose money really can buy you sanctuary.

I count to ten before a car goes by. Another ten before someone else passes me on the street, an older gentleman smoking a pipe with a newspaper tucked beneath his arm. He's in no rush.

Trees shade the sidewalk. A woman steps from her apart-ment, in a row of classic brownstones, and locks a door that's been painted a deep maroon while a Maltipoo at her feet gently pulls on its leash and sniffs the air.

I take a breath too, finding I'm enjoying the quiet and calm. This neighborhood feels separate. Privileged. A place where people don't have to be bothered if they don't want to.

The architecture changes noticeably as I round the block,

quaint brownstones giving way to heavy stone façades and arched windows. I reach the address on West Seventy-eighth, and just as I imagined, a doorman is standing post beneath a green awning with his hands in pristine white gloves at his sides, his navy uniform–clad body swaying as he rocks on the heels of highly polished black shoes.

I tug at the scarf around my neck, fluffing my dirty-blond hair around my ears, and slow my steps in front of the building.

I look up toward the twelfth floor. The penthouse. The Birds' apartment.

The first wave of nerves hits my belly.

"Can I help you?" the doorman asks.

He's enormous: at least six foot four, more than two hundred pounds, with shoulders and a chest better suited to a linebacker. He could be a bouncer or champion bodybuilder instead of standing guard, probably bored, on this quiet street.

I cough to find my voice. "I have an appointment with the Birds."

He reaches for the door. "Apartment Twelve A, at the top."

I should be smart and pick his brain while I have the chance. After all, he must know the family. He can provide a few details. What's the mom like? The dad—is he a pervert like Jonathan warned? Is the kid a total pain in the ass? Do they run through nannies and throw them out like garbage?

But I don't say a word. Instead, I take a deep breath as he holds open the door, waiting for me to enter.

Come on, Sarah. Get a grip.

Moving forward, I feel the warm air of the building enveloping me. The door clicks shut and I'm in. Through the glass, I think I hear him say, "Good luck."

I nearly spin on my heels to ask him what's up, but then stop. Because when my eyes take in the lobby, my heart skips a beat. Floor-to-ceiling white marble with paintings in gilded frames on the walls, French and Dutch impressionism— originals, by the looks of them. Burgundy carpet leads to a vintage gold-colored elevator.

Against one wall, on a table of polished mahogany and walnut, sits a bowl of gardenias floating in fresh water, the scent filling the space until I'm positive if I stood here long enough, I'd get a headache. But I don't wait around.

Because if the lobby looks like this, I can't wait to see the apartment.

The elevator doors open slowly and I step inside, glancing back once more at the magnificent chandelier shimmering beautiful points of light. The elevator is surprisingly fast, and when the doors reopen, I peek out cautiously. The hallway is quiet. There's no one there, and I settle down, giving myself time to take in the exquisite ivory silk wallpaper, the antique pewter sconces lighting the corridor toward the one and only door at the end of the hall. The apartment address appears on the front in a large golden sign: 12A.

I knock on the door.

A woman opens it and I find I'm disappointed by how normal she looks—she's not in a maid's uniform holding an ostrich-feather duster. There's no sign of a butler with a white tie and matching white gloves.

An ostrich-feather duster—*seriously?* What's wrong with me?

Instead, she wears a light crew-neck sweater in robin's egg

blue and gray slacks, her hair tucked behind her ears in a no-nonsense manner, a few streaks of silver sprouting among the black at her crown. She's plump, a softness to her belly where her sweater is pulled past her hips, and I'm guessing she's in her fifties based on the small lines etched at the corners of her eyes.

She welcomes me with a warm smile. "Are you here for the interview?"

I nod. "Yes, ma'am."

Ma'am—there's that small-town Southern upbringing for you.

"Your name?"

"Sarah Larsen."

"I'm Pauline," she says. "Right this way." We step from the foyer to a hallway blanketed in Persian rugs. "I'm the housekeeper and have been working for the Birds for more than twenty years," she says, her eyes shining, undoubtedly proud of her impressive tenure.

And she should be. I can't imagine working at any one place for such a long time. I often wonder how much longer I'll last at Hearth.

"Very nice to meet you," I tell her.

We arrive at a room she calls the parlor and she instructs me to sit and wait.

I look around for any photos or personal effects that would clue me in a little more about the family. But I see none. While the room is elegantly furnished, gold and mauve striped wallpaper and a set of oval-backed armchairs, there are no personal details. I still don't know much about the Birds. I tried looking them up last night, wondering: Are they celebrities? Swedish royalty? Heirs to some giant fortune? From what Stephen Bird told me, his father has remarried and he has the one younger child. Is she an infant? Five? Ten? Is the mother a pop singer or is the father a diplomat? How active is Stephen Bird going to be in the care of his sister?

But to my disappointment, I couldn't find much to go on. Every Collette Bird listed was clearly not the right one. There's a woman living in the U.K., and a freelance graphic designer based in Singapore, but no Collette Bird living in New York City. *This* Collette Bird, the one hiring a nanny, doesn't have much of a digital footprint, something I thought was difficult to pull off these days. Either she doesn't know how to tweet, has been living under a rock, or is hell-bent on protecting her privacy.

But I did manage to find one link—just one. A website for a local children's hospital where she's listed as having been a board member for the last ten years, belonging to the Women's Committee of 100 known to have a half-million-dollar entrance fee. In the same article, she's named as the fundraising chair. And then, eureka, a picture. A single headshot where she is standing in front of the highly recognizable Corinthian columns of the Metropolitan Museum of Art. Wearing a ball gown, her blond hair pulled into a chignon, she's stunning—the epitome of what I envision New York City socialites to be. Sophistication and class. Beauty and grace. The power and peace of mind that comes with knowing you have gobs of money at your fingertips and all the luxury that comes with it: designer gowns, treasure troves of jewelry, upswept hairdos, vacations, and fancy dinners. Her lips form a kilowatt smile.

Somehow, I was able to discern all of that from one single

picture—she is radiating that much confidence. And while she doesn't appear to be a celebrity or singer, she seems to be heavily involved in philanthropy.

As for her husband, I discovered only a few details: his name is Alex Bird and he's a commercial property investor with his own firm and offices near Lincoln Center. I find more articles, but they're sparse, mostly ribbon cuttings and contract wins, photos taken with the mayor and city commissioner, several galas where he's wearing a tuxedo.

But nowhere can I find personal information about the family. No mention of the daughter, not even a picture. Though I do find a small amount of information about the stepson, Stephen. He has a single paragraph on his father's firm's website, where he's listed as a staff member with a degree from Cornell. But no picture of him either, only the briefest mention he's Mr. Bird's son. No Facebook or Twitter account for any of them.

What's up with these people?

I wonder about the age difference between Stephen and his sister. How strange it must be to have your father remarry so many years later and then have a sibling so much younger than yourself. Stephen would be more like an uncle than a brother to the girl. But they must be close if he's the one taking nanny candidate calls.

Finally the housekeeper comes back, beaming a huge smile in my direction, and calls my name.

But as I stand, I notice something strange in the corner. A pedestal table with something shoved in the back. It's covered in a blue cloth—a handkerchief?—but the cloth has slipped to one side, revealing a picture frame. A picture of a little girl. The photo is black and white but I can tell the girl has light-colored hair with a simple headband at her crown, her bangs cut neatly above her eyebrows. She's small, a toddler, maybe only two or three years old. It must be the daughter I'm here to nanny. But why cover the picture frame?

Maybe it's an accident. Another candidate placed their handkerchief on the table to get it out of the way and forgot. Or maybe it's the family's way of protecting the identity of the little girl.

Discretion is of the utmost importance, the ad emphasized.

I lock eyes with the housekeeper. If she noticed me checking out the photo, she doesn't let it register, only reaches out her hand and beckons me to follow.

CHAPTER FOUR

Collette Bird doesn't see me at first. She's seated and speaking softly to someone behind her chair. It must be her daughter, hiding. I can't hear what the little girl is saying, but she's certainly small and doing her best to stay out of sight.

I can't make out what her mother is saying to her either, so I try catching a glimpse of the girl instead. But the chair is one of those ornate, oversize settees where the upholstery stretches to the floor, and the way Mrs. Bird is sitting, she blocks most of the view.

I peer again at the bottom of the chair, excited about the chance to meet her daughter. I'm good with children—at least, I think I am. All she needs to do is come out and see me. We can play a game right here in front of her mom. I can tell her how pretty her dress is or I can ask to see her dolls.

But Collette Bird doesn't introduce me. In fact, she doesn't even look up. Nothing about her indicates she's noticed I've entered the room, she is that engrossed with speaking to her child. Collette takes her time speaking in a singsong voice and reaches down to hold the little girl's hand.

I break away my gaze and quickly check out the room. It's exquisite, a fireplace taking up one end, an enormous grate stretched across its opening, the walls on either side extending to ten-foot ceilings with oversize windows looking out to Roosevelt Park and what can only be the prestigious exterior of the American Museum of Natural History—my God, they're practically neighbors. The floor is wide-plank oak herringbone; antiques dot the mantel and line up along the glass table. Priceless works of art flank the door. On the opposite wall, a large European tapestry depicts ladies in waiting amid apple trees. The entire room is modeled after an art gallery.

I return my eyes to Mrs. Bird and shift my feet awkwardly, hoping to capture her attention. I think about clearing my throat, but I'm not sure if she would notice. She's lost in her own world, a private moment with her child.

After a few more moments, I try speaking. "Mrs. Bird?" But my voice comes out as a peep.

Collette Bird doesn't move. But then she says, "One second, darling," and I'm not sure if those words are directed at me or at her child on the floor.

I stand and wait, more seconds going by until Mrs. Bird finally looks up, the hand she's been using to caress her daughter slowly moving to her lap and covering her other hand, which is anchored by a large sapphire ring with a thick band of diamonds wrapped around it. The fingers of that hand are closed together. She's grasping something tightly. Whatever it is, she presses the item firmly against her belly.

Collette Bird raises her eyes, and I take a long look at the woman before me: the philanthropist who gives millions to children's hospitals.

Her legs are crossed. She's wearing a plum-colored sheath

dress, not tight but elegantly conformed to her body. Her face is heavily made up but not overdone, bearing the look of someone who can afford expensive makeup and has the leisure time to spend hours experimenting with it. Her hair is blond and pulled back, revealing dark golden highlights around her face. And on her feet, one-of-a-kind sequin-encrusted pumps—actual Manolo Blahniks, I've seen them featured in a magazine—deep purple to match her dress.

The awe hits me immediately. She's breathtaking, almost regal. An effortless beauty that I'm almost positive she has passed along to her daughter; the pair of them, I imagine, mirror each other perfectly. She looks kind too. She is everything you could wish for in a mother and I can't help wondering, with a pang of guilt toward Aunt Clara, what it would have been like having someone like Collette Bird raise me instead.

She's taking me in too. Nervously I smooth the bangs I've been trying to grow out the last six months and tuck them behind one ear. I'm grateful to be wearing my hoop earrings, a gift from Aunt Clara that I know are simple but elegant enough. She'd told me they'd be my good luck charm, and right now, I sure hope she's right.

My lips are dry but I resist licking them. I'm fidgeting endlessly. It's impossible not to feel self-conscious standing in front of someone like Collette Bird.

"Hello," she says, and her tone is warm and friendly, much like the housekeeper's.

I smile in return.

Mrs. Bird twists again in her seat and reaches for her daughter behind the chair.

I take my chance. "Is that your little one?" She halts, and I take a step back. "Is she shy? She doesn't have to be shy. Not around me, at least. She can come out whenever she wants."

At this, Mrs. Bird's hand relaxes, and a part of me relaxes too. Another stroke of her fingers, a gentle smile across her face as she murmurs something to the girl before turning around to face me.

At last, she points to a chair and motions for me to sit. I do so carefully, acutely aware of the one-of-a-kind Turkish rug beneath my feet, the three inches of plush padding, and the antique Baroque chair she is directing me toward. I place my purse on the floor and take another peek at the drapes, yards of embroidered French silk falling to the floor; the glass sculptures on the table clearly cost tens of thousands of dollars.

"I always marvel at people who want to be nannies," she begins. "So loving. So willing to take care of other people's children. Do you have any children of your own, Ms. . . . ?" She glances around as if looking for a sheet of paper.

"Sarah Larsen," I supply. And then, "No," I confess. "No children."

She glances at my empty hands, making a point of looking at my purse next. "Did you bring a résumé?"

I squirm and decide the best way to handle this is to come clean.

"I have to tell you something." I suck in my breath. "I've never been a nanny before." I wait for a reaction but there isn't one, only a serene smile. I keep going. "I wait tables in the East Village." She raises her eyebrows and I feel like a sham, wondering how much longer she'll let me sit before politely asking me to go, thanking me for my time, a gentle reminder that no family in their right mind would leave their child with someone who had no experience.

I wait, expecting her daughter to laugh out loud too, but neither of them makes a sound.

Instead, Mrs. Bird has the wide-open look of someone who wants me to keep speaking. She's waiting to hear what else I have to say.

Okay, she's giving me a chance.

"But I'd very much like to be a nanny," I add. "I'm good with children. I've dealt with hundreds of kids while working in restaurants. I cared for my aunt while she was sick. I'm young, have lots of energy, and I think that if you give me an opportunity, if you let me try, I could be of really good use to you and your family. I would be good to your daughter. She'd grow to love me, I know she would."

I pause, letting my gaze drop to my lap, knowing I've made the most pathetic case and I'm seconds away from finding myself back on the street.

She blinks. "I really like your honesty," she says, and the tightness in my chest starts to ease. "It's truly hard to find in people anymore. I believe you when you say you're good with children. It's funny how you can tell that about a person so quickly." She raises her eyes to meet mine. "Is your commute here very long?"

If she means the walk to the L train, a quick jaunt to Union Square, followed by the 1 train north and the walk from the subway—then no, not too long. Thirty to forty minutes tops.

What I want to tell her is I would walk miles to this place.

"Not far," I say.

"Sometimes, when it's urgent, I'll have the driver pick up the nanny. He's done it on a number of occasions. East Village, you said?" I nod. She does too. "That's something he could handle." I feel a pitter-patter in my chest; the tone in her voice sounds promising. She picks at an invisible piece of lint on her dress. "Tell me about yourself. What should I know about you?"

What could someone like Collette Bird possibly want to know about someone like me?

"I grew up in Virginia Beach," I tell her. "I went to college for a little while and waited tables until a year and a half ago, when I moved to New York."

"And what made you come here?"

"A new chance. Seemed exciting. The true melting pot of the world, right?" I offer another detail. "My dream has always been fashion design, that's what I used to study. New York has all of that, doesn't it?"

She smiles. "It certainly does." And she crosses her one-of-a-kind sequin pumps. "So Virginia Beach, you say?" She stares past my head. "I can't remember if I've ever been. I've traveled to so many places but that one . . ." She frowns. "It doesn't stand out."

"It wouldn't," I tell her. "Unless you really love crowded beaches and not-so-great seafood restaurants."

Another smile. "Again, more honesty."

I take a deep breath. I might be winning points here.

"Your family?" she asks. "Where are they?"

"My parents died when I was young." Her eyes pinch in the familiar look of sympathy I'm given whenever I share this detail about my life. But I'm used to it by now and don't let it get to me anymore. And besides, I was only five years old when they died. I don't remember them except for what Aunt Clara told me and a handful of pictures she kept in an album.

"My aunt raised me," I tell her. "I helped care for her before she passed away a few years ago." Another grimace, and now it's my turn to let my eyes drop. Three years since her death and it never gets easier. Unlike those of my parents, memories of Aunt Clara are always with me and it's hard to mention her, even now. She's the one who taught me everything, and it had been excruciating watching her get sick and being unable to make her better. With the limited resources we had, we did the best for each other.

"I'm so sorry," Mrs. Bird says.

I raise my eyes, not wanting her to think I'm an emotional basket case, that I won't be able to handle this job. I can't risk the chance of bursting into tears, not now.

"My aunt was very special, and when she died, I didn't feel the need to stay in Virginia anymore. She told me how much she loved New York and had always wanted to move back."

This earns a surprised look from Mrs. Bird. "She was from New York? Whereabouts?"

"Brooklyn. She took the train in every day while working at an insurance company."

"What brought her to Virginia Beach?"

"She wanted someplace to take care of me after my parents died. And she did everything she could. Taught me how to ride a bike. Volunteered at my school. Tutored me in math."

"She sounds like a wonderful person."

"Absolutely." I nod. "The best." The memories bring a warm rush of emotion. And now I regret wishing Aunt Clara had had money like Collette to show how much she loved me. She showed me in every way possible.

"And now you're following in her footsteps," Collette says, her eyes sparkling. "You're keeping her memory alive by bringing her spirit to New York."

I tilt my head—I'd never thought of it this way. Aunt Clara had made this city her stomping ground, and before she died, she told me where to find the best bagel shops and the farmers' market on Saturday mornings in Bryant Park, the best clubs for hearing jazz. She talked about taking free ferry rides to Staten Island so she could go out into the harbor and admire the Manhattan skyline.

I used to picture her—a younger, excited version of herself. Her brown hair in a ponytail as she often used to wear it, long before the cancer turned her hair into a shaggy bob and then took it away altogether. I'd listen to her stories and imagine her leaning against the ferry railing, her eyes looking out past the water, the large city before her with all its promise of a future, of the man she loved—the man and career she'd leave behind to raise me in a different state, alone.

Aunt Clara had dropped everything for me.

And when I stop to think about it, I guess I *have* been living my aunt's dream by moving to New York and bringing her home. All along, I've had a fairy godmother looking out for me at every turn.

Mrs. Bird has stopped asking questions. She's looking at me curiously, as if she'd give a million bucks to share the memories that are now running through my head. But she doesn't ask, doesn't pry, only lets me sit and enjoy them.

Five minutes in and this is the strangest interview I've ever had in my life.

"Yes, I suppose I have brought her spirit to New York City," I tell her, and she smiles.

I change position in my seat and try refocusing on the task at hand—this interview—and wonder if this is the right time for me to ask some questions of my own. After all, I still haven't met her daughter. I'd love to know more about her. Remarkably, the little girl remains quiet behind the chair.

"How old is your daughter?" I ask.

"She's nearly four. I also have a thirty-two-year-old step-son, my husband's son from a previous marriage. He lives with us sometimes." She tilts her chin. "I think you've already spoken to him on the phone?"

I nod, waiting for her to say more about her daughter, but she lets out a small laugh, realizing her goof. "I'm sorry, I'm acting like I've never done this before." Another giggle, one hand covering her mouth, red creamy lipstick revealing a row of perfectly white teeth. "You must think . . ." But she stops and takes a breath, steadies herself. She's almost as nervous as I am, which is bizarre since she's the one doing the hiring. "My little girl's name is Patty," she says, beaming a smile. "And she's my absolute most favorite, most important person in the whole wide world. Her fourth birthday is this July."

A girl named Patty who turns four this summer. I can handle that.

I take another look toward the chair. "Can I meet her?"

"Soon," she says, adding, "I typically like to meet with

the nanny candidates first and let Patty listen. Then whoever makes the cut can come back for a follow-up."

"Of course," I say. "What's she like—Patty?" My eyes dance toward the floor but the girl remains hidden.

Suddenly, I wonder if there's another reason this family wants to hide her identity. Besides absolute privacy, is something else at stake? Does she have an illness? Has she been in an accident and suffered a deformity? Though if that were the case, wouldn't they be hiring someone who can provide real medical care?

But Mrs. Bird doesn't reveal any such thing. "She's wonderful," she continues. "Petite, angelic. Blond like me. Well . . ." She touches her hair, another laugh. "She's a natural blonde whereas I'm still trying to be. She loves make-believe and fairy-tale princesses, the colors blush and bashful, which is a riot since she picked that up from some movie somewhere. She hates peanut butter. Doesn't like tube slides—I think the thought of getting stuck in one terrifies her. Doesn't like to fly, which is a shame because we used to travel so much, but we're hoping she'll grow out of it. She loves Disney movies and tea parties. Fairy tales and story time." There's a sharp intake of breath, her excitement building. "She's starting kindergarten next year, which is crazy—I can't believe it's already here." She shakes her head, amused. "It's remarkable how time flies."

"She sounds wonderful," I tell her, and mean it. If she's anything like Mrs. Bird is describing, taking care of this little girl should be a dream. Avoid peanut butter sandwiches and tube slides, I can do that. Should be easy enough.

I'm already picturing the places I can bring her: the shop off Columbus Circle where I've seen children's parties with cookies and teacups laid out on trays with teddy bears and slices of rainbow cake decorating the counter. A child's dream.

If Patty would come out, I could tell her all about it. We could make plans to go there together.

CHAPTER FIVE

===

"Larsen, you don't get to pick when you show up!" I'm late for my shift at Hearth and Paul is pissed.

I try coming up with excuses but then catch Jonathan's warning look from the other side of the restaurant—*Go easy,* he seems to be saying—and I look at his section, how it's already set up, tables wiped, and silverware rolled.

"I'm sorry." I rush to shove my purse in a locker.

Paul mimics me. "Sorry," he grumbles. "You're always saying you're sorry. That's your third sorry in a week."

I roll my eyes where he can't see me and hurry to tie the black apron around my waist. Back in the dining room, Jonathan points at my section, where he's already swept around the tables and I mouth, *Thank you.* Clipping a few pens to the front pocket of my apron, I flash him a grin to show him I'm okay, that I'm in good spirits and think the nanny interview went well.

Amelia swings by to check on me too. She hands me an order pad and says, "Chick, you've gotta start showing up on time."

I give her a little nod. We've become friends since about six months ago, when a group of us started going out together after work. I know she'd pick up my shifts if I was in a pinch, but like Jonathan, she also knows I can't afford to miss out on tips.

"I know," I tell her. "I got caught up."

She nudges her chin at Jonathan. "Your beloved set up your section for you." I follow her gaze. "That one's a keeper," she tells me with a wink and then pulls away, spotting a hostess leading a group to her table.

I spin away, too, thinking I'll tell her about the nanny interview later. She won't blame me for wanting an extra job. She knows how up to my eyeballs I am in debt and that I need desperately to find a way out. More than once she's picked up my bar tab when she knows it's gotten rough.

And even as I hurry to roll my silverware, there's a buzz in my back pocket. One look and I see a 1-800 number glaring at me. Another call—another demand for payment—and I swallow down the fear, the sickness in my stomach each time they ring, and slide the phone back into my pocket, hoping I can avoid them for another day.

When I check my phone later that night, I have a minute-long voicemail from Stephen Bird, not his stepmother, asking for a second visit. He tells me Mrs. Bird thinks I will be a good caregiver for her daughter but they still want to go over a few more things with me. He asks if I can return the following day at 3:00 P.M.

I can't believe it. I knew Mrs. Bird and I had a connection but assumed she'd want to talk to more qualified candidates, and now she's giving me a second opportunity. A thrill pulses its way across my chest. If I can start making more money, I can finally answer those debt collectors' calls. Finally, hope at the end of a long, dark tunnel.

But then I grimace. Three P.M. I'll miss the entire first part of my shift and Paul won't like it, not with me having been late today. He was shooting me disapproving looks when I passed him in the kitchen all night. I beg Jonathan to take my hours, his only day off, and he accepts, squeezing my hands as he tells me, "You can do this. They'd be crazy to want anyone else."

In the afternoon, the doorman greets me. "Hey, hey, you're back. Round two, huh?"

I smile eagerly with a bounce in my step, the excitement filling my chest. Not only do I have a chance at this job but there's a chance I'll see Mrs. Bird again. I'll get to meet Patty.

"You remember the drill? Elevator to the twelfth floor." He pulls open the door. As I pass, he sticks out a gloved hand. "Malcolm," he tells me.

I shake his hand. "Sarah."

"Nice to meet you, Sarah."

The elevator rushes me to the penthouse and I feel the rise and fall in my stomach that comes with the fast ride up.

To my surprise, the housekeeper doesn't answer the door this time. Instead, it's a man who looks to be in his early thirties. "I'm Stephen Bird," he says, ushering me in with a smile. "Welcome back." I've barely stepped into the apartment when he's asking if he can get me anything to drink. "Water? Coffee?"

"No, thank you," I say, looking around.

No signs of Mrs. Bird or the housekeeper. No Patty, either.

Stephen leads me away from the parlor toward another corridor. This one has a floor of black and white swirled marble, and my footsteps click noisily as we cross the surface.

Stephen brings me to a room that's his personal space by the looks of it—dark walnut paneling and mahogany furniture, a small collection of books I can only imagine are first editions stacked on a shelf, a flat-screen TV taking up half the wall. On the desk is a Mac laptop and one pen; he's tidy by nature. Beside the computer lies a single sheet of paper and I look closely—a copy of the nanny ad, perhaps? Next to that, a plate of sandwiches and pot of tea. Two ceramic cups.

"You sure you don't want anything?" he asks, acknowledging the refreshments.

The sandwiches are cut into small triangles with the crusts removed. One of them contains what looks like jam. I politely shake my head no.

"Tea?" Before I can say anything, Stephen is busying himself pouring tea and asking if I like sugar.

Well, if he insists. I tell him one cube, please.

He grins, appearing happy to play host for the moment, reveling in the opportunity to show his hospitality skills as he hands me a cup and asks me to sit down. The black leather sofa squeaks as I lower myself into the cushion.

Stephen is dressed for a day of leisure in his gray V-neck sweater, slacks, and brown loafers. His hair is a blondish red—the red possibly coming from his father, Mr. Bird, whom I hope to meet in time. Stephen is lean, and I imagine him running miles in Central Park or playing tennis for hours in the afternoon. Isn't that what rich people do? Or maybe he has a lifetime membership at the Health & Racquet Club. He's at least six feet tall with the smallest amount of stubble along his chin.

Stephen watches as I take a sip.

"Thank you for coming back," he says, sitting down. Again, the squeak and sigh of leather. "I appreciate you being so generous with your time."

"Absolutely," I tell him, trying to project what I imagine would be the practiced grace of a highly qualified au pair. "I'm sure you're looking to find a nanny as soon as possible."

"Yes, we are. My stepmother especially. It's comforting for her to have someone here with her and Patty."

I nod.

"Collette didn't seem too concerned with your lack of nannying experience," he says, and worry strikes my chest. "I think she sees potential in you, what you could be." And I feel the tension releasing. "She liked you right off the bat."

"I'm so happy to hear that," I say, easing my breath. "I felt like we connected too."

"She said time spent with you felt more like a conversation than an interview. Like two friends sitting together over coffee." He smiles. "That's important to her."

Another rush of relief.

"I know my stepmother would like you to come back for a follow-up conversation, but I also like to meet with each of the candidates who make the cut. You understand that, don't you? My father is a very busy man, you'll hardly cross paths, and while my stepmother is the one you'll be interacting with the most, I'm the one who takes care of most of the details, the payment schedule and such."

"Absolutely," I repeat.

"If you're hired, we'd need you to be here five days a week, Monday through Friday, from nine until about three or four." He waves his hand. "It depends on the day. Sometimes my stepmother lets the nanny go home early so she can spend quiet time with Patty.

"The pay is twelve hundred dollars a week." My heart somersaults—I'd have to work twelve-hour shifts at Hearth every day to make anywhere close to that much. "Patty doesn't attend preschool and my stepmother doesn't work except for her occasional board meeting at the hospital. Collette doesn't go out much. She gets tired easily, but she won't want you to see that, and she'll try to overexert herself. So we prefer she stays home and rests. She's also very protective of Patty so Patty doesn't go out much either, which means the nanny will stay here most of the time with Collette and the girl. You can have activities and play games in the apartment, whatever you like. There are plenty of toys and board games to keep everyone busy. Movies too." He leans forward, giving me a wink. "It's a pretty easy gig, to be honest."

So we hardly leave the apartment? We'll be mostly home-bound in this multimillion-dollar fortress of an apartment with an endless supply of board games and movies? No wonder no one is that concerned about my lack of nannying experience. This is going to be a piece of cake.

It feels too good to be true, and I think about my concerns from yesterday. Maybe the little girl did suffer an illness or was in an accident and there are all sorts of reasons for keeping her out of sight and indoors. Maybe she really does have a disability and I'll be expected to care for her in other ways.

As if reading my thoughts, Stephen says, "There's nothing wrong with Patty. She's very special to my stepmother. It took Collette a long time to conceive and she had multiple failed pregnancies, so she sees Patty as her miracle child. Collette is just very overprotective," he assures me.

He sits back. "You'll have help too. There's the housekeeper, Pauline, who is the most amazing human being in the world." He smiles fondly. "How she's managed to put up with my parents all this time, I have no idea. She'll occasionally take care of things for Collette too, appointments or ladies' luncheons, things for my stepmother to get dressed up for, but that's not often. And then there's Freddie, my favorite. Our personal chef. He makes breakfast, lunch, and dinner. Snacks for Patty, too, so you won't have to worry about preparing anything."

I try not to raise my eyebrows with glee. The full staff, the additional help—this job keeps getting better and better.

"Everyone *lives* here?" I ask.

"Oh, no." Stephen stifles a laugh. "Only the family and Pauline. She came to work for us when I was a kid. My dad asked her to move in and help out with everything and she never moved back out." He tilts his head and smiles. "Think of her as our right-hand lady. She knows everything, takes care of everything, and helps me keep my act together too." He laughs, and I settle in my seat, warming to this man.

"Pauline manages the household," he continues. "I live here but I also have an apartment in Greenwich. I escape there when I want to get away." He looks around the room, the man cave that's far nicer than any room I've ever lived in. "But I still like to come here. It's my home, where I grew up. Where Patty came home as a baby."

I look to the door leading to the rest of the apartment. "When do you think I'll be able to meet Patty?"

"Soon," he says. "Say"—and his voice rises—"would you like to take a look at her playroom?" I glance up, excitedly. "Come with me." He stands, taking my teacup and placing it on the desk behind him.

We head down another long corridor, and this time, I catch a glimpse of the kitchen: stainless-steel appliances and white marble, a large fruit bowl on the counter, dual ovens, and what looks to be a Sub-Zero fridge. Someone is working at the sink, rinsing scallions and placing them on a cutting board. He's wearing an apron and whistling to himself as he keeps his head down—this must be Freddie, the personal chef.

Stephen continues walking ahead of me at a fast clip. We pass one closed door after another until we're entering another wing. At the end of the hall, he thrusts open a door.

Pink carpet. Pink walls. Patty's playroom. An enormous wonderland for a child this age.

The playroom is more spectacular than any room I've ever seen. It's what you'd imagine a child's room might look like if they could ask for anything, and I mean anything. A crafts table in one corner with stacks of crayons and drawing paper. A wooden rocking horse, hand-painted, with its mane tied in pink ribbons and a step stool for reaching its leather saddle. An oversize rocking chair filled with plush animals. A nearly-six-foot-tall stuffed panda bear, the kind you'd find at

FAO Schwarz, sitting on the floor. The windows flanked by pink lace curtains. A dollhouse the size of an outdoor grill taking center stage with a colorful play mat spread beneath.

I spy a child's vanity: pink bubble gum nail polish, hairbrush, and lip gloss. A small mirror for peering at her reflection. A bay window with small round cushions and a view of the building next door, gray-washed walls and a balcony. Farther down, the green lushness of the park. On a child's table, a tea set midparty. Spoons and pretend cubes of sugar and cookies left on a plate. On the floor, a nursery rhyme book is lying open.

She's been in here today. She's been playing.

"It's wonderful," I say.

"Yes," Stephen agrees, stepping forward. "It really is."

I'm enraptured. If only every little girl in the world could grow up with a room like this.

Aunt Clara provided me with a loving home, there's no question about it. I had a bedroom filled with Little Golden Books, my own Barbie lampshade, and eventually my own stereo and desk, but nothing like this. This is straight out of a fantasy.

As a child, I always knew we had limitations. There were plenty of nights when she came home tired and sank wordlessly against the couch, giving me an appreciative smile as I microwaved our dinner. And despite her long hours, money was scarce, so I learned at an early age not to ask for too much. I was grateful for the time she could give me, and believe me, she gave every minute she could. But there were days, I admit, I wished for the commotion and laughter and extra attention I might have experienced if my parents were still alive, if there was more than just me and Aunt Clara living in the house. If I could remember what it was like to sit in my mother's lap while my father looked on.

Here, in this room, in this penthouse, I imagine an entire family doting on the little girl. Patty never wanting for anything; her parents only steps away, with a brother and household staff also looking out for her. Her experience, light-years from what I had. If she could know how lucky she is.

Stephen must see the wonderment on my face because he steps farther into the room and gestures for me to follow.

"My stepmother decorated and arranged everything herself. She has a flair for design; she's forever mixing up furniture and patterns. My baby sister loves anything pink as you can see." He laughs.

Transfixed, I move toward the dollhouse, wanting so much to kneel on the floor and peek into its rooms: the miniature toy furniture, the little doll family that Patty has carefully arranged on the couch, a wooden Dalmatian resting at their feet. The lights in the house are on, every room lit as if on permanent display.

Stephen says, "Go ahead, take a look. That's everyone's favorite thing."

I don't have to be told twice and drop to my knees. The dollhouse is a miniature mansion with a wide sweeping porch and staircase leading to the second floor, which boasts five bedrooms with little pillows placed on each bed. On the bottom floor, black-and-white checkered tiles for the ballroom. Tiny Tiffany lamps and crystal doorknobs. Little strips of flowered wallpaper. It's remarkable, and it must have cost a fortune.

"I always wanted a dollhouse like this," I tell him. "As a kid, I used to dream about having one."

Stephen smiles. "Well if you get this job, you'll be able to play with it whenever you want. You could come in here anytime."

CHAPTER SIX

═══

It's almost ten o'clock at night. Jonathan hasn't yet returned from covering my shift at the restaurant when my phone rings. It's Stephen Bird.

"Sarah?" he says, and my heart bangs a steady drumbeat. "I've spoken with my stepmother and there's no need for another interview. The job is yours if you'll take it."

I exhale.

If I'll take it? Is he crazy? This is amazing—a shot in the dark—and yet, somehow, I've managed to clinch it.

A weekly pay of twelve hundred dollars would do so much for me and Jonathan, it would change everything. The fear I've been living with—the tightened anxiety every time the phone rings or the wrench in my stomach when I see another Past Due envelope in the mail—would finally ease up. I'd be able to breathe easier. No more avoiding the apartment door and wondering who's hollering to collect. No more apologies to the neighbors about how I let the heavy banging on the door go on without answering. No more ignoring my neighbors' pitying, and often annoyed looks.

"Will you take the job?" I hear Stephen ask again.

The sound of a clattering cymbal goes off inside my head. My breath catches in my throat. "Yes! I'm thrilled to accept."

"Wonderful. We're excited too, my stepmother especially. Can you be here tomorrow morning at nine? I'd like to go over the contract."

Of course, a contract. I should have known they would have something that formal.

"Just a few things, nothing serious," he says. "We're excited to have you onboard."

Hanging up, I'm practically skipping where I stand, a tingling shooting to my fingertips and a light-headed glee sparking across my brain. Throwing out my arms, I jump up and down and do a little dance, realizing I must look ridiculous to anyone who is standing in their kitchenette and catching me through the window. But I don't care.

Let me shout my news from the rooftop! I beat out everyone else for the job and am about to work for one of the most glamorous families in this city. Five days a week, I'll peek inside their world—no, scratch that, not just peek—but *see*. Experience. Live. And all in the presence of the magnificent Collette and her little girl.

Jonathan is barely past the apartment door when I shriek, "I got the job!"

Astonished, he slides his backpack to the floor, watching as I bounce in place. His eyes light up.

I rush toward him, my arms circling his neck in a tight embrace, my mouth landing kisses on his cheeks and forehead. "I can't believe it! Isn't this great?" I pull back and proceed to move about in an animated jig. Amused, he laughs too.

"Tell me everything," he says.

"I start tomorrow. They're going to pay me twelve hundred a week. We basically don't have to go anywhere. The mother is some sort of intense helicopter mom who doesn't want her daughter out on the streets so all we do is stay home. My new boss is like a queen. And there's a housekeeper to help with everything. It's a dream!"

Jonathan rubs his head, his hand moving through brown waves that have dried with sweat after his being in the Hearth kitchen, his fingers catching in a tangle. "Twelve hundred a week," he breathes. "That's incredible. We'll finally be able to—"

"I know! It's amazing!"

He breaks into a huge grin.

He doesn't say it, but Jonathan is thinking about the bills as I am, the ones I can slowly start chipping away at, the ones that will finally feel less daunting. And I love him more at this moment, that despite the pressures of how much money I owe and how it's affecting the life we're planning together, he's never lost faith in me. He always figured we could work it out.

I've seen him go through the mail, his shoulders stiffening when he doesn't think I'm looking, the way he'll run his hand across his face, rubbing at the back of his neck, but stay quiet. He's never held the amount over my head or blamed me for how much has accumulated. We're in this together. He knew what he was getting into when he met me. It's a team effort, is what he says.

And now, a light at the end of the tunnel. I can finally tell the bill collectors I have some funds and that should hold them off for a little bit. I can push off the dreaded bankruptcy awhile longer.

I lunge toward Jonathan and grab his face with both hands, planting a kiss on his mouth. "This is huge," I tell him.

He wraps his arms around me. "Congratulations, sweetheart. Seriously."

"Congratulations to *us*."

He kisses me back. "Congratulations to us, indeed."

I'm back on West Seventy-eighth Street before 9:00 the next morning. Never have I been this excited to rush to work and be on time—correction, *early*—and I laugh. If only Paul knew I was capable of being this punctual.

Malcolm lets out a hoot. "Hey, hey, I hear congrats are in order." I cross the street, flashing him my brightest smile. "Welcome to the block. And welcome to the Bird family." He gives a playful bow.

Upstairs, Pauline is waiting for me at the door. She looks ready to give me a hug but stops short and pats me on the arm instead. Leading me to Stephen's study she says, "I'm so glad you took the job. You're going to love it here." I look over her clothes, once again casual for a New York City housekeeper: gray slacks, black sweater, and a single string of pearls at her neck.

But when we arrive outside Stephen's office, she pauses. The slightest halt. With one finger she pops an elastic band at her wrist—it's so quick I almost don't see it. Smoothing the elastic band she composes herself before pushing open the door, letting a smile return to her face.

It's an odd moment, but I brush it aside as she announces my arrival to Stephen Bird and he swoops his arm out for a handshake.

"Welcome!" he says. "We're thrilled to have you here." One nod to Pauline and she's quietly dismissed from the room.

He ushers me to the same chair as the day before, but this time, there is no offer of tea or sandwiches. We're down to business, and he's retrieving a stack of papers from a drawer and extending it toward me.

"Most of it is a formality. I'm sure you understand. My family insists on this sort of thing, particularly my father. He's intent on privacy. It's a big part of the deal. Everyone here has had to sign something like this at one time or another." I skim the first page, then the next, looking for anything out of the ordinary. The various clauses and sections appear straightforward enough.

I flip to another page.

Nanny services for the Bird family. Monday through Friday.

A block of text listing Collette Bird's name. My name. The word *Discretion* in italics.

I relax a little—it's all just over-the-top legalese. Five paragraphs when one would have done the trick.

Stephen sits back and watches me. "Like I said"—he gives another reassuring smile—"it's mostly a formality." He rests his elbows on the desk and taps his fingers against his chin. "All we ask, Sarah, is that you remain professional and responsible and courteous at all times while you're with us in our home, and discreet about our affairs when you're not."

"I can do that," I assure him calmly, while the whoop and holler of gratitude is filling my chest.

"Your weekly pay will be provided in cash. All you need to do is come here five days a week to this beautiful apartment." He spreads his arms wide as if even he knows how lucky we are to be in this place. "To that dollhouse I know you love so much."

I'm speechless, my heartbeat not having returned to its normal rhythm since his phone call the night before. Jonathan and I barely slept, staying up late and dreaming of what our life could be like once we've paid off my aunt's hospital bills. We'll build up our savings account. We even started talking about renting a small space for our wedding. Maybe he could pull some strings with Paul and see if Hearth could cater for a lower price.

And for the first time in a long time, after Jonathan curled to one side and fell asleep, I switched on a small reading light and pulled out my sketchbook, too excited to fall asleep myself. It felt good holding the drawing pencil against my hand again, the outline of the sketch coming to life on the paper. A faint outline formed and my pencil filled in the rest, darker shading, the swoop of a few more lines, before I realized what I was designing: a sheath dress similar to what Collette had been wearing, elegant and form-fitting, but my version was modified with cap sleeves. Her presence, her sense of fashion, was already inspiring me to draw.

Stephen pushes a pen across the desk. "Sign the last page, please. Date it, and we'll be good to go."

I flip through the document for a second time. Without further delay, I sign the last page as instructed and hand it back to Stephen.

He instantly drops it to his desk. "Wonderful. I'll make you a copy so you can take one home with you this afternoon." He jumps from his seat, saying, "Now let's go see what my stepmother is up to."

———

We find Mrs. Bird in the family room. It's as posh as the gallery where I had my first interview but not as formal. In here, the marble floor is covered with oversize dark blue rugs, conjuring up images of the ocean rolling out before us. The rugs have a luxurious shag quality, the material plush and textured beneath my feet.

Collette is no longer dressed to the nines and wearing designer pumps but remains impossibly chic in her stonewashed jeans and silk blouse. Gold espadrille sandals are strapped to her feet.

She rushes to hug me, the distinct scent of Chanel No. 5 spritzed through her hair and down her neck, and it envelops me as she wraps me in her arms.

"Oh, Sarah, I'm so glad it's you. I'm so glad you're the one we picked," she gushes.

My cheeks warm with pleasure. "I'm so happy to be here, Mrs. Bird. Thank you for hiring me."

She pulls back from her hug. "Please call me Collette."

"Okay." I grin. "Collette." My smile matches hers.

I look to the sofa, half-expecting to see a little girl about to jump into my arms too.

"Where's Patty?" I ask.

"Oh," Collette says with a pout. "She's not feeling well, the sweet angel. I think yesterday must have been too exhausting for her." She leads me to the sofa.

"I'm sorry to hear that." And I steal a quick glance at Stephen, wondering why he didn't mention this.

"Can she have visitors?" I ask.

She waves her hand. "It's best we not disturb her. I've instructed Pauline to let her sleep, get all the rest she wants, because tomorrow"—and she claps her hands like a child herself—"we will have lots of time to play."

I recline happily on the sofa. I'm over the moon at the realization I will be getting paid to just sit here with Collette. As much as I want to meet Patty, there are a million questions I'd love to ask this woman, such as where does she shop? Who's her favorite designer? Where did she buy those espadrille sandals, for example? The dress she wore during the interview? My eyes dart to the hall wondering when I'll be able to see her closet.

But I slow my breath—*take it easy*. I'm here to nanny, not to pester this woman about her fashion style. I'll get to know her over time.

She casts her eyes at Stephen. "Everything taken care of?"

"The contract is signed, yes."

"Good." And she gives him a long, drawn-out smile before turning to face me. "Oh, Sarah," she says again. "What a joy this will be. What fun. We haven't had a nanny here in quite some time . . . since . . ." She looks up at the ceiling before giving Stephen a puzzled look.

"Since last year," he says.

"That's right, since last year." She frowns. "I hated to see her go, she was so kind to Patty and me, young like you too. So much fun, but then she had to leave . . ." She waves her hand dismissively. "Something about another job. But then"—her frown turns right side up again—"if she hadn't left, we wouldn't have been able to find you, now would we?" She squeezes my arm. "And I just have a feeling"—she looks deep into my eyes—"this wonderfully profound feeling that we are going to get along so well. Like friends, like sisters."

Her smile is so big, her cheeks stretched so wide, her smile is scrunching the corners of her eyes. "I'll be the best boss ever, you'll see. You'll have never had another one like me."

Happiness radiates through my chest. I think about Paul as she clasps my hands tight in hers, the way he yells or is always scolding me for being late and how the money I make at Hearth, even if I worked there another decade, will never be enough to move ahead with my life—and I tell myself, no, I can't imagine having a boss like Collette Bird.

Jonathan enters the apartment with the distinct crinkling sound of plastic bags—takeaway from Hearth, the smell of tomatoes, white wine, and garlic making my stomach growl. He waves the bags, a large grin plastered to his face as if he's caught the biggest prize at work and places the bags on the small card table we salvaged from someone's castaway furniture left on the street. "You hungry?"

"Absolutely." I leap from the edge of the futon and fetch a set of knives and forks as he removes each to-go box and peels back the lids.

Scooping what looks like chicken parmesan and mushroom risotto onto the plates, pieces of focaccia bread too, he says, "Didn't have to pay for this one. Wrong order." He hands me a plate with a wink. "Our gain, huh?"

I'm so relieved to see food I sit down immediately, not realizing how famished I am, having spent the last few hours doing research on my phone and looking up nannying blogs and tips on how to be the best nanny, completely losing track of time. I hadn't paused long enough to think about food, let alone cook anything on our tiny stove, but thank goodness I have Jonathan. And my heart warms knowing how he's always like this, remembering to bring us dinner when I often get caught up in my own little world.

I'm on my third or fourth bite when I realize he's staring at me, expectantly. "Well?" he says. "Aren't you going to tell me how today went?"

I laugh, then cover my mouth with my hand to chew and swallow quickly. I say, "It was great. She's great."

He chuckles. "Let me guess, everything's great?" His eyebrows arch when he smiles, the dimple I love so much showing in his cheek.

Jonathan is as amazed as I am when I tell him how I spent the day sitting with Mrs. Bird and sipping coffee. We talked for hours—well, Collette did mainly. She prattled on about Patty and the fun she imagined we would have together: mornings in the playroom and afternoons putting together puzzles. I barely got a word in edgewise, which was fine since it was nice listening to her plans; she seemed to have so many of them.

She is so vibrant and enthusiastic about everything having to do with her daughter, that I would have sat hours longer listening to her. She's so loving, and takes so much interest in Patty's every move, how I dream my own mother would have been about me. She describes sitting and having tea parties with Patty like it's the most splendid, most wonderful thing in the world. I'm finding myself looking forward to the moment we can be together.

By noon, Collette had excused herself, telling me that as much as she loved the chat, there wasn't much reason for me to stay if Patty was going to remain in bed. I felt a tinge of disappointment, but then I remembered I would be here the next day, and the next.

Within the hour, I was home, loving the fact I had the rest of the afternoon to myself when I would have normally been on my way to Hearth getting ready for a long shift, hours of serving potato gnocchi and martinis to an endless stream of customers. I spent the afternoon researching nannying instead.

"You've got the sweetest gig," Jonathan says. "I'm almost jealous."

"Don't be," I tell him, but my heart swoons knowing how much it's true.

He grins. "Have you met the dad yet?"

I roll my eyes. "No, they said he's pretty busy all the time, so we won't cross paths much. But it's funny . . ." I tilt my head. "I expected they needed a nanny because neither of the parents would be around much, but the mom seems pretty homebound. I mean, don't get me wrong, she's wonderful and it will be nice to have her there. But it sounds like she'll be around a lot when I'm with the girl." I look at him. "What's the point of having a nanny then?"

"Maybe she has an office at home and needs quiet time?"

I consider this but find it highly unlikely, the way Collette has talked about tea parties and making brownies and the coloring books we will share with Patty on the living room floor. "I don't think so. I get the feeling she's going to stay in the same room."

"Must be nice," Jonathan says. "All that money to sit around, paying for someone to watch your kid with you." He takes another bite of his food. "Do you think she has visitors coming over a lot? Maybe she needs you to keep the girl occupied?"

I try envisioning lunching lady sessions with Collette in the role of the grand hostess. She fits the part perfectly.

But I shake my head. "I really don't know. Today was pretty formal. Signing the contract, going over stuff with the stepson. Then, with Patty in bed, we just talked. Collette told me about growing up in a small town in Connecticut. Both her parents were schoolteachers and she didn't have much money as a kid, which is amazing when you think about her life now. She was a beauty queen in high school and then moved to New York to model. She met Mr. Bird at some party and the rest, you can say, is history."

"She's his second wife though, right? His trophy wife."

I shoot him a look. "Don't be mean. They really love each other." I think about how her face lit up describing Alex Bird, how she thought he was the most handsome man she'd ever seen when he stepped into the room. *We weren't dating long when he asked me to marry him.* And the way she'd talked about Stephen: *Besides Pauline, he takes care of most everything.*

"So she's not a wicked stepmother?"

"No, the opposite. I think she gets along really well with Stephen. They're close. I'm not sure what the status is with his real mom but he and Collette seem pretty tight. Something tells me this isn't the first time he's done the interviewing for her either. There was a nanny last year too."

"Oh?" Jonathan stops. "Why'd she leave?"

"She took a different job or something."

"Must have been something fancy to walk away from the salary they're paying you."

I shrug. Collette didn't tell me the circumstances of the previous nanny and I hadn't wanted to pry.

"But didn't you say the stepson is in his thirties?" Jonathan asks, his eyebrows crinkling. "And he still lives with his parents?"

"He has his own apartment, but he keeps a room there. Trust me," I say, my eyes growing wide. "If you could see this place you'd want to stay there too."

CHAPTER SEVEN

===

It's Wednesday, officially my second day on the job, and I'm hoping to meet Patty. I've been hired to be a nanny and while I loved spending time with Collette, I'm ready to get to know the girl I'm in charge of. Since Patty is the one I'll be spending the most time with, I want to know we'll click.

"She's still feeling unwell, I'm afraid," Pauline says when I arrive at the apartment, and I feel my heart drop. Maybe there's something they're not telling me.

Seeing the look on my face, Pauline says, "I thought about asking Collette to call you and tell you not to come in, but before I knew it, it was almost nine and we knew you'd be on your way in so . . ." She doesn't finish her sentence, only turns on her heel, a quick smile over her shoulder to convey everything is going to be all right. She leads me to the kitchen and moves to the massive stainless-steel island at the center of the room. A French press has been left on the countertop filled to the brim with coffee, and Pauline lifts one of the three ceramic mugs set on the counter. "Cream or sugar?" she asks, and I nod to both as I watch her prepare my cup and hand it to me.

She leaves the other two coffees black, setting one of the mugs on the other side—for Collette?

But a man walks in, the chef wearing the same black apron and holding a bowl of grapefruit. He doesn't look up as he lifts his coffee and takes a big gulp.

"Freddie," Pauline says, scooting around the edge of the counter. "I want you to meet Sarah, the new nanny." She takes him by the arm and gestures for him to set down his mug so he can properly greet me.

I'm acutely aware of the disregard on his face. He could give two hoots about me being the new nanny. But despite his utter lack of friendliness, I have to admit Freddie the chef is remarkably good-looking. Suave and dapper, clad in a simple black T-shirt and jeans under his tidy apron. His silver-gray hair is cropped close to his head and he wears trendy black-rimmed glasses with rectangular frames. The tiniest hoop earring.

We shake hands and he doesn't make eye contact. As soon as he's able, he pulls away, his eyes dropping to the floor as he steps back and retrieves his coffee.

"Our new nanny," Pauline repeats, as if her first introduction didn't get through to him. "Isn't it wonderful to have a new one in the house again, Fred? Someone to keep Collette and Patty happy?"

He makes a sound, a grumble. An awkward moment follows as we sip in silence, but Pauline is intent on forging ahead.

"You come from the restaurant world too, am I right?" With the way she's set up the question, the arched eyebrows and optimistic look, I can tell how hard she's trying to bridge a connection. "Restaurants in Virginia Beach and the East Village, correct?"

At this, Freddie comes to life. He says, "Really? Which one?"

Eye contact. Finally. Plus, a triumphant smile from Pauline.

"Hearth," I tell him, doubting he's ever heard of it.

As I guessed, he says, "Nope, doesn't ring a bell." He twists his mouth, thinking and looking away again before asking, "East Village?"

"East Thirteenth Street."

Another blank stare. I'm not surprised, considering this chef must spend most of his days on the Upper West Side.

"Oh," Pauline says lightly, "there are thousands of restaurants in the city. How could you know every single one?" And she pats him on the arm, still looking for conversation topics. "Freddie here is a phenomenal chef." He doesn't acknowledge her, only takes another long swig until he's nearly drained his mug of coffee. Returning to the grapefruits, he proceeds to slice them in half on the cutting board.

Pauline plods along. "He makes the family breakfast, lunch, and dinner—although most days Mr. Bird eats at the office—and treats for Patty. Her favorites are strawberry waffles with whipped cream or blueberry muffins. Cups of hot chocolate too. Bowls of spaghetti. Eggs Benedict for Collette and those green smoothie things she likes so much. I can never get over how much spinach you put in them, or is it kale?" She pinches her face.

"Dinners that look more like an elaborate hotel buffet than a meal for three people," she continues, patting her waist. "Doesn't help me though, the temptation to sample everything right here in this kitchen. Freddie can make just about anything. He'll cook for you too if you'd like." And with this he pauses midslice, no attempt at disguising the blanched look on his face as Pauline says, "She'll be here most mornings, Fred. Lunches too. You can always make an extra plate for her just like you did the last nanny."

"I'm not getting paid for that," he says curtly.

She chuckles. "Oh, I'm pretty sure you are."

The exchange is made even more uncomfortable when he grunts. "You really don't have to," I say, trying to give him an out. I certainly didn't expect him to cook for me. "That's not part of the agreement." Or at least I don't think it is; neither Stephen nor Collette had mentioned it.

Freddie steps away. He keeps a computer on the far side of the kitchen, and with a click of the mouse, the screen lights up. He scrolls, checking on something, probably a food website or cooking blog.

He returns and says something about preparing chicken cordon bleu for dinner.

I try meeting Freddie's eyes again, not wanting him to be annoyed with me before we've had a chance to work together, but no dice. He refuses to look up.

Slicing the last grapefruit with the precise motion of an experienced chef, he takes two bowls and places a half in each one. He pushes the bowls toward Pauline.

"She's in the next room," he says solemnly.

I start to move, happily taking that as my cue to leave and follow Pauline. But she stops me in my tracks. Looking at my mug she says, "Oh, we always finish our coffee before we leave the kitchen."

I glance at her cup, it's empty. Peering at my own, I see that I still have some left.

I smile awkwardly and she continues smiling at me

sweetly. There's a flicker in her eyes. "Go on. We mustn't keep Collette waiting."

I down the rest and place my mug on the counter. "Nice to meet you," I tell Freddie, and at this, he gives the slightest nod, his attention fixed on the cutting board.

In the breakfast room, Collette is sitting at an oval glass table. The walls are covered in a playful flower print with a large fern propped against one window.

Collette doesn't jump up to hug me as she did the day before but she does give me an enormous smile as we enter the room, clearly delighted by both my arrival and the grapefruit Pauline places before her. She sprinkles them each with a teaspoon of sugar, scooping into the first half before saying, "Sit with me, please." And Pauline backs away, letting me slide into one of the extra seats.

I admire Collette, the linen pants and a relaxed white cotton blouse with its pointed collar and button cuffs. I've drawn something like this before, featuring a straight hem and front button fastening, but nothing like hers. Collette is wearing Chanel—the brand's highly recognizable interlocking Cs logo embroidered above the wrist.

On her lips, her signature red lipstick.

I watch as Collette eats before asking, "How is Patty?" I perk my ears for any sounds of her, perhaps a tiny cough from the next room.

"I'm afraid she's still under the weather today." And Collette looks at me. "She's very frail, you see. A fever or a small bug may not be that big a deal for other children, but it will sometimes take days for it to disappear in her."

Worry rattles my thoughts—I don't know much about children, but fevers lasting for days can't be good, right?

"Does she need to see a doctor?" I ask, spinning in my chair as if to consult Pauline, but the housekeeper doesn't look concerned. Perhaps they've already seen someone?

Collette says, "Oh, it's nothing serious. Just a low-grade fever. You'd be surprised at how children can be prone to these kinds of things when they're young." She picks up her spoon, her gaze returning to her breakfast. "And besides, I hate calling the doctor. He'll just want to put Patty on an antibiotic again, some pink syrupy stuff she'll be forced to slurp down, as if pumping her full of medicine will make it better—he's always doing that." She pinches her eyebrows together in a scowl. "I very much dislike bringing Dr. Edwards here, don't you agree, Pauline? He's a worm of a man." She makes another face. "Alex adores him. He's worked for us for years and been here for everything, every flu and illness, even Patty's birth, but I've never liked him. Not one bit."

"He's only trying to help," Pauline says gently.

But Collette gives her an exasperated look. "Well, Patty will be fine, she always is. She's just sleepy. Caught a bug." She turns to me again. "She'll be back to her old self in no time, you'll see. And I bet this time tomorrow you'll be able to sit down and play." She claps. "Oh, I can't wait for you to meet her. I know the two of you will get along splendidly, just like the last nanny. You really do remind me of her . . ." Her eyes drift away.

"Anna was all right," Pauline says.

Collette snaps to attention. "She was more than all right," she says, forcefully.

I give Pauline a funny look, surprised to hear her say anything to the contrary, especially when Collette sounds so smitten.

"What?" Pauline says, looking from me to Collette. "She was sweet, I'll give you that, but I'm not sure she enjoyed the job that much. Not in the end." She frowns. And then to clarify further, she says to me, "I'm not sure she really wanted to be a nanny. It was a means to an end for her. She just cared about the money. At the first opportunity she got, she found a different job, turned in her notice, and was out of here."

"To do what?" Collette asks. "Remind me . . ."

"She's a paralegal, I think." But Pauline looks stumped. "Actually, come to think of it, I can't remember." She shrugs. "Anyway, we liked her well enough. She just left so quickly, which left us high and dry for a while."

"Yes," Collette says. "That part was unfortunate."

"But she lasted a year so that's something." Pauline grins at me as if to say she hopes I last longer. And then to Collette, "Weren't you close to asking her to move in?"

My eyes bounce to Collette. Move in here? That's not something they expect me to do too, right? The apartment is amazing, but I already have my own place, plus Jonathan. That part was not included in the contract. Then I remember that Stephen forgot to give me a copy like he said he would.

"I don't think she was interested," Collette says. "She had her own apartment, her own life. But it would have been nice keeping her here with Patty. All of us together, never having to leave this place." She shares a smile with Pauline. "Wouldn't that have been wonderful? So convenient and safe."

"Very convenient," Pauline agrees.

I look around at the mirrored walls and one-of-a-kind paintings on either side of the kitchen hutch. The glass bowls and imperial Oriental vases with flowering pots. This apartment is spectacular but I don't want to live here. At the end of the workday, I want to go home to my fiancé and our life together.

I tell myself to chill out—no sense in letting my thoughts rush full steam ahead, worrying over something that won't happen. If living here was a condition of the job, Stephen would have told me so already. I settle back in my chair.

Collette, ever smiling, sets down her spoon and doesn't finish her grapefruit. With excitement she says, "I'm going to give my Patty girl a bath."

CHAPTER EIGHT

——

Collette gives no indication I should follow. She simply glides out of the room and I'm left sitting at the table. I turn to Pauline.

"You can hang out here, if you'd like," she says. "Shouldn't take long." And with that she heads for the kitchen. Down the hall, the sound of Collette's footsteps fades as she reaches the other side of the apartment and I stare after her. Why didn't she ask me to help her with Patty?

"Wait a minute," I call to Pauline, stopping her. "Should I go with you?"

"You'll be fine here," Pauline says and leaves the room.

I slouch in my seat.

From down the hall comes the sound of water gushing. Patty's bath.

I listen for a while to the clanking of dishes in the kitchen. Freddie and Pauline speaking. The thunderous rush of a bathtub filling with pipes groaning and letting forth water into what I assume is a large garden tub.

I rise slowly from my seat—I'll be proactive and offer to help.

I tiptoe down the hall, feeling my curiosity mount as I move quietly and quickly, past the family room, the one with the dark blue rugs, and past a corridor leading to what I think is Stephen's study, to a section of the apartment I'm almost positive Stephen showed me yesterday. If I'm right, the door at the end of the hall will lead to Patty's playroom.

But the gushing water isn't coming from the end of the hall. It's somewhere closer, only two doors away, and I'm thinking it's the little girl's bathroom. A small cluster of rainbow stickers and hearts are stuck to the doorframe about three feet above the floor, within child's reach. Like her mother, Patty must like to decorate.

The door isn't shut all the way and I hear Collette's sing-song voice, a cooing, adoring tone while she speaks to her daughter. And a giggle—the little girl's? More words from Collette, her animated conversation rising above the steady stream of water.

I step closer to the bathroom, but stop. Taking one look down the hall, I check for any signs of Stephen or Pauline, even Freddie, and the coast is clear.

But I feel a trickle of doubt. It's not my place to interfere—not yet at least. I haven't had a chance to establish myself with the girl as her nanny. This shouldn't be the way we first meet, me spying on her in the bath. I should head back to the breakfast room, where Collette asked me to stay, and demonstrate I can follow instructions at the very least.

But the sound of Collette's voice draws me closer to the door. What is she saying?

"The water's nice and warm, Patty Cakes. Climb on in."

I pause, the nickname making me smile as I picture the small blond girl from the photograph standing beside the tub.

"You'll love it." There's a tinkle in Collette's laugh. "This will make you feel better."

The faucet shuts off. The dripping of water followed by silence and then a gentle swish. Collette's hands running through bubbles. A quick pour followed by another splash, maybe the girl's toes or hands as she enters the tub.

"I'm so sorry you've been feeling sick," Collette says. "I'm sorry you haven't been feeling well."

More splashing. So far, Patty hasn't made a peep.

I'm starting to wonder if the girl can speak at all. Maybe she's hard of hearing. But isn't that something Stephen or someone would have mentioned?

I need to see.

I move closer. The gap in the door is about two inches wide. I'm confident that's enough room for me to see and I try not to make a sound. From the opening, I spot Collette, or at least the back of her head. She's on her knees next to— I was right—a garden tub, the sleeves of her white blouse rolled past her elbows. Her hands are immersed in water and her face is turned to one side but I can tell she's smiling, her lips curving up to her cheeks.

Bubbles rise above the water surface; there's the distinct smell of strawberry bodywash. Even at this distance I can tell she's poured in a hefty amount.

I watch as Collette fills a plastic cup with water, lifts it up, pours it down. Up and down it goes, the woman repeating the motion about a half dozen times.

And then she moves. Collette readjusts her position on her knees and turns to the other side. I now have a clear view of the tub.

But there's nothing.

She is pouring water *over nothing*.

There is *no one*.

Only repetitive motion. Up goes the cup, down comes the water. Another scoop of suds, the water cascading over air.

The hairs on the back of my neck do a slow march north. A rolling shiver races down my spine until I feel a cold lump forming at the center of my chest.

There has to be an explanation—it's not what I'm thinking. The little girl is hiding. I just can't see her right now.

In Collette's mind, she is bathing a child, there's no doubt about it.

Only there is no child.

CHAPTER NINE

The blood in my body runs cold, my heart banging against my ribs.

Collette is speaking to no one. She is washing an empty space in the tub.

I stare down the hall. If this is something wildly peculiar, something they wanted to keep hidden, they've done a terrible job guarding the secret.

I release the tension in my shoulders, telling myself there's no reason to panic, this is just a simple misunderstanding. But the shivering feeling returns.

Who has Collette been talking to?

I'm sorry you've been feeling sick.

This will make you feel better.

I'll find Pauline. She'll tell me everything I need to know. She's been here longer than anyone else on staff, since Stephen was a kid and since Patty was a newborn. She'll be able to explain this in two seconds flat.

I retreat from the bathroom, careful not to make a sound in case Collette looks up from the tub.

And then I bump into something—hard. Pauline is standing in the hallway. She's as rigid as a statue, her arms firmly by her sides. She sees my startled expression, and from behind me, I hear a splash of water and the sound of Collette's singsong voice. An eerie giggle. And Pauline's eyes widen. She lets out a discernible *oh* as she faces me.

I wait for Pauline to say something else, to give me the explanation I need, but she doesn't. Her silence is deafening.

"What's happening?" I ask.

But she still doesn't answer, only gives me a peculiar look.

"I'll head back," I stammer and turn, wishing I could erase the last five minutes.

But Pauline tugs my arm and my stomach twinges with panic. Is she going to tell me what's going on? Or does the look on her face mean she's going to march me straight into the bathroom and demand I explain myself to Collette?

But instead, her eyes soften. "It's all right," she says quietly. "You don't have to rush off. I know you must be curious."

I let my feet roll back on their heels—*curious* is an understatement.

I lower my voice, painfully aware Collette is on the other side of the doorway. "I heard the bathwater and thought maybe I could help. But I can go back . . ." I move again, and this time, Pauline releases me.

"Of course you did, dear," she says, smiling. "You aren't one to sit around and do nothing. I could tell that about you right away. I'm sure that's why Stephen and Collette picked you. I would have done the same."

"Yes." I appreciate the compliment but the unease is still worming its way through my chest.

The sound of splashing water stops. No more cups dunking.

Has Collette heard us? Does she know we're out here?

The door opens.

Collette steps from the bathroom; the lights from around the mirrors shine behind her head and glow through her hair, creating a golden halo. She takes one look at me and rolls down the sleeves of her blouse, a few splotches of water dotting the hemline. Another wet patch spreads across her linen pants where she knelt.

"Sarah?" she says, with faint surprise.

"I'm sorry to disturb you. I know Patty's not feeling well. I wanted to help."

She steps forward, surprising me. "Would you like to meet her?"

I feel a rush of emotions, confusion too. Patty *is* in there. I just didn't see her beneath the bubbles.

Collette pushes open the door and it creaks softly. I move forward, Collette shifting to one side as she gives me space to enter the bathroom.

I look ahead, ready to greet her.

CHAPTER TEN

———

But there's no Patty, only a tub filled to the brim with soapy water. No girl.

"Mrs. Bird . . ." I say. "I don't understand . . ." I peer at her, begging for an explanation. "Where is Patty?"

But Collette only laughs and gives me a look as if she's about to pinch my arm and yell, *Surprise! We've played a trick,* and the girl will come jumping out from behind the door. I'll feel like a fool but I won't be able to deny the relief.

Instead, she says, "What's the matter? Don't you see her?" And she broadens her smile. "She's right there."

I stare hard at the tub, a quiver in my stomach. But there's nothing but bubbles.

Collette touches my hand gently, making goosebumps spread across my skin. "She's right there," she repeats.

Stephen appears like lightning, as if Pauline has summoned him with an alert from across the apartment, and he's pulling me away, the worry unmistakable in his eyes, his face ashen as he motions for me to follow him down the hall.

When we arrive at his office, he sinks heavily in the chair behind his desk. "Patty doesn't exist," he says.

A thunderclap sounds in my ears—I'm sure I didn't hear him correctly.

"I'm sorry, what?"

"She doesn't exist—I mean, she did." He grimaces, his eyes dropping. "But she doesn't anymore. She died when she was young. She was only three." And I'm aware of my breath slowing. I'm hearing him, but not processing anything he's saying. "She died a long time ago. Collette has never been the same. My stepmother . . ." He glances at the door as if suddenly worried she's followed us. "She's been through a lot." His eyes slide back to me. "It's been difficult for everyone."

My mouth hangs open, as if I'm a fish that's been heaved out of the water and thrown on the deck, struggling to breathe, a panicked convulsion as I fight for each labored intake of air.

I don't understand.

What do you mean she doesn't exist? The words screech through my head but not a sound comes from my mouth.

"She was a toddler, she got really sick and the doctors said it was something contagious. We weren't allowed to say goodbye. After she died, her body had to be kept separate from everyone and Collette was devastated. Beside herself with grief. She didn't want to believe that Patty was gone— she outright refused to accept it. We all were in denial at first. She was here with us playing, and then, the grieving process set in. Losing my sister like that . . . she was so young, so tiny."

It's hard to keep up with everything he's saying. A pulsing rushes through my brain and clogs my head like cotton shoved inside my ears, muffling his voice. But then I hear him—and I can't stop hearing him—and now I wish he would stop. But it's too late. Too many outlandish words and revelations are coming from him now and he's looking at me and expecting me to understand.

So if she's dead . . . if she's not here . . . then who was Collette talking to?

Who was in the bathroom?

What am I doing here?

But what I ask instead is "When?" my voice coming out in a raspy croak.

"Almost twenty years ago. Before her fourth birthday."

Twenty years ago? Is that what he just said? She's been gone *twenty years*?

I lift my hands. "Wait a minute. Collette has spent twenty years pretending her daughter is still alive?"

"She's not pretending. She actually thinks she sees her. She saw her right there in that tub." He says this so calmly, so matter of fact, it takes a couple more beats for his words to sink in.

The girl died at the age of three, but Collette thinks she still sees her daughter. She believes in her head the girl is alive. She expected *me* to see Patty splashing in those bubbles just as she saw her.

The perfect image I've had of this woman comes crashing down. Her mesmerizing face, grace, and elegance. The way she floats in and out of every room. The magnetic smile and Chanel wardrobe; a life of luxury and carefree days playing with her daughter. But it's all a front. A mirage. Her mind is its own cage. Life with her daughter, a delusion.

And it hurts—I'm stunned—but most of all, my heart breaks for Collette.

She hires nannies because she thinks Patty needs one. Everyone in this house knows it's not true but goes along with it anyway.

No, everyone signed contracts and now they *have* to go along with it, bribed by a big salary—my cheeks flash hot at the thought of how eager I'd been to accept it myself, how few questions I'd asked—free gourmet meals and who knows what other perks they give the staff to keep them quiet.

"Oh my God," I whisper, dropping my hands into my lap. A loud rush of steam barrels through my head, my pulse quickening in my throat at every other realization hitting me too.

Patty doesn't need playtime or story hour or ice cream. She never has to eat peanut butter or be terrified of going down a slide again.

Because Patty is dead.

No wonder the ad emphasized *discretion is of the utmost importance*—no shit. You can't let something like this get out. And no wonder Collette, or Stephen, for that matter, wasn't concerned about me having zero nannying experience.

Because they don't need a real nanny.

Without Patty, there's no child to look after. No client.

And with no client, there shouldn't be a job.

Grief seizes my chest. Grief for someone I've never met. A little girl who, if she'd had a chance to grow up, would have been only a couple of years younger than I am today. She's missed out on so much. But Patty died twenty years ago and they've kept her enshrined as a forever three-year-old, going on four. I never stopped to question Collette's age either. She looks young, or I assumed she waited until later in life to have a child, as many in New York do. Not once did I think Patty was a child she gave birth to two decades ago.

So if there is no child, where does that leave me? What does the job entail? No lacing of shoes or brushing of pony-tails. No picking up after her or consoling her when she throws a temper tantrum. No calming her down to take a nap. No need for the dollhouse in the playroom or coloring books either. My visions of taking her to tea parties off Columbus Circle and slicing into pieces of rainbow cake vanish into thin air. There's no one to hold hands with as we cross the street, her tiny fingers laced with mine.

No need for anything at all.

CHAPTER ELEVEN

===

"I know this seems insane," Stephen says. And I swallow hard—*insane?* That's one word to describe it. "But it's the only way Collette can cope. It keeps her out of the hospital." His eyes squint painfully. "Patty's death nearly destroyed her and she was lost for a long time. It was awful, the trips in and out of the psych ward. Years where we didn't know if she would ever get any better." He flashes me a look. "I know what you must be thinking. That it's not right. How could we do something like this—the lies, the fantasies—how can any of this help her? But"—he stares achingly at me—"it does. It's better than the alternative."

His eyes blink fast to fight back the tears. "It's not right but it helps all of us," he continues. "Collette tried killing herself numerous times. If we lost her, my dad would never recover. After losing Patty, he can't lose Collette too. It's the only solution we've found that keeps her going."

He stops speaking. I wait for him to continue, but he doesn't. He's giving me a moment to recover from the bombshells he's just dropped—he's getting his bearings too. He seems shaken by what he's told me, the details he's shared. Things he would never tell anyone except for the few staff who work here.

When the silence lengthens, I tell him, "I don't know what to say," and it's the truth. What he's revealed is the wildest, most preposterous thing I've ever heard. Nothing could have prepared me for this, not the strange wording in the ad or the way Collette acted during my interview. Or the fact that my second day on the job, I still hadn't met the child.

And my mind halts again—the child behind that chair. There hadn't been anyone. Collette had been speaking to no one.

Did I get the job because I was the only dummy to fall for it? Was it because I connected so quickly to Collette or because I didn't question a thing they told me? Stephen must think I'm gullible and desperate, and I've done nothing but prove him right.

I fight the urge to stand up and run but force myself to stay in my seat, a tremble in my hands and legs. I'm shaking my head too, knowing this is beyond crazy. A dead girl . . .

I take a deep breath. "Everyone is in on this?"

He nods, confirming my earlier suspicions.

I think of Pauline, the way she'd nearly hugged me that first day, the warm pat on the arm, and I suddenly feel the first waves of betrayal, the first pangs of anger that everyone, including her, has been leading me on and lying to my face. How dare they—how dare *she*? She told me I was going to love it here. I trusted her.

The pop of the elastic band on her wrist.

Is that why she keeps it there? To keep her anxiety at bay dealing with Collette day after day?

And then Freddie. The perpetual scowl on his face, his indifference at meeting the new nanny. Because he knew they didn't need one. No wonder he's such an ass. Making hot chocolate and strawberry waffles for Patty is a waste of his damn time but he fakes it along with everyone else.

My chest hurts again, the reality sinking in. *There's no one to nanny.*

I cross my hands to Stephen in an X. Time-out. I need to understand a few more things.

"So all of you encourage this delusion?" I ask. "You let Collette think her kid is alive? You keep her in the dark with this charade and you bring in a nanny—you bring in *me*—and I'm supposed to do what? You expect me to just play along? Poor Collette." I wave my arm. "She has no idea."

Stephen tries to interrupt but I can't stop speaking, my anger and nerves taking over.

"You don't need a nanny—you don't need me. What you guys need is a doctor. *She* needs a doctor. Collette needs serious help. Someone to care for her and make her better." I feel a sob in my throat. "She deserves that." I feel my eyes grow big as I meet his face again. "And you've been doing this for twenty years? Are you crazy? Do you know how much worse you're making this for her?" I'm breathless. I've gone too far, said things I shouldn't have said to my boss.

I look at Stephen, feeling the flush in my cheeks. But can he blame me?

"How has no one stopped you?" I ask. "How has no one found out?"

"The contract," Stephen says, simply.

My heart stops cold.

I drop my eyes to his desk, seeking the contract he'd placed there, but I no longer see it. My signature, which had been nice and neat and looped in cursive with a ballpoint pen on the last page. Yesterday's date and my full consent to every single clause contained in that document.

"You never gave me a copy," I remind him.

To his credit, Stephen looks apologetic. "I'm sorry about that," he says. "I meant to." He glances at one of the desk drawers that's locked with a key. "I still will, of course."

"I didn't see anything in there about this."

"You didn't look close enough."

A warm flush rises in my neck. "Well you could have told me. You lied to me. You waited until it was too late, after I'd already signed the contract."

"I know this is highly unusual," Stephen says, and I look up in exasperation. "And I can't imagine what's running through your head." *Yes,* I nearly hiccup. *Like what other details have you buried inside that contract?* "But I assure you it's something you will learn to tolerate, to work with and respect. I'm sorry I misled you but there was no other way. Please give it some time. Give us a chance. You're not the first one to do this, the first nanny who's had to pretend. We're all here to help the best way we can. And since we've been doing this for a while, we have a system. Each of us has a role."

I think back to my first interview. He instructed Pauline to greet me. He made sure Collette never showed me a real girl. He's the one who encouraged me to sign the contract. He's been doing this for years.

There was the nanny last year.

And the one before that.

Exactly how many nannies have there been?

"I love her, you know. My stepmother," he says, his voice

turning soft. "My mom moved on a long time ago without us. She's in Europe, sometimes Hong Kong, wherever suits her fancy." He scowls. "But Collette . . ." He smiles again. "She changed our whole world around. Before her, I hadn't seen my dad that happy in a long time, and then to have a little girl come into our lives—a baby. She brightened up this place. They both did." His gaze drops to his lap. "Collette used to, at least. Before Patty died."

I'm heartbroken for him, I am, but the more I think about it, the angrier I am at how he duped me. What he's done. Anger flares beneath my ribs, but Stephen looks at me steadily.

"So you've never heard of us?" he asks.

A nervous flutter rises into my belly. What *should* I have heard? Are there monstrous tales about what happened to the nannies before me? Why did they really leave?

All that time I spent googling this family and barely found a thing, I should have been suspicious. No one's social media footprint is that small without effort, which means they've put a clamp on everything.

I return my attention to Stephen. Maybe I should have spent more time googling *this* man instead of his parents. I thought he seemed kind, the older brother vetting the candidates and being so involved in the process. No wonder he wanted to talk to each of us. Which makes me wonder, what else isn't he saying?

CHAPTER TWELVE

"I know this is unusual," Stephen says. "You can leave right now if you really want." His eyes flicker to the door. "But you'll lose the pay. *And* we can sue you." My eyes leap to his face, his tone suddenly drastic.

He cocks his head. "You agreed to a three-month stay. If you leave before then, we can take legal action."

Panic grips my throat, my mind flashing back to what was on those pages. *What the hell did I sign?*

I open my mouth to protest, but he cuts his eyes to his desk drawer. "That part was on page three." I sit back, wounded. "You signed a contract. You agreed to come here every day, Monday through Friday, except, of course, if Collette is unwell or you are unwell since you have sick days built into your salary. If you leave, we can file a complaint." He leans forward. "And there's more.

"You also signed a strict confidentiality clause—page four, section eight. The reason you've never heard of us is because we've done everything in our power to keep this family issue private. It is vitally important that it remains so. The previous nannies are under a gag order, as are you. One word to betray our trust and we will bring down the hammer on you. Your family too."

A clamor shakes the inside of my belly. He can't be serious.

"A conference room full of lawyers will descend on you before you know what's hit you." Jesus. He *is* serious. And my breath holds, my stomach churning in vicious flip-flops. "We go to these great lengths not to frighten you or be monsters, but to keep this private, not just for our family's reputation and the effect it would have on my father's business— a business I am very much involved with and stand to inherit one day—but for Collette's health. To keep her happy."

He stops, looking me square in the eye to make sure I'm paying attention, as if I haven't been frightened into hanging on every word. "If we even attempt to explain to Collette that Patty is gone, she threatens to take her own life. So we don't risk it. Because she's tried everything: razors, liquid bleach, pills, you name it. She walked out in front of a car once that left her with three cracked ribs and a broken arm." I suck in my breath. "Private institutions in Sweden. Hospital sanctuaries in Canada. A private island where she was flown by helicopter. We didn't see her for months." He sighs, a rattled breath that shakes his body.

No wonder Collette had spoken about the doctor that way. *He's a worm of a man.*

The doctor is here when Collette needs him, not Patty.

"So you keep her here instead?" I ask. "No more hospitals?" I think about the fact there is no nurse on-site, unless Pauline has been trained in first aid. But I suppose, along with Freddie and Stephen, there are enough of them here to care for her. And I guess that's my job now too. Keeping Collette calm.

"No hospitals," Stephen confirms. "Not if we can help it.

We keep her here, where her conditions can be controlled, where her setting is familiar and routine. And there's an entire household staff to make sure she's contained." He looks gravely at me and points a finger. "That means not leaving. I meant what I said to you earlier about keeping her inside, that all play activities should take place right here in this apartment. It's vitally important. She is not to leave ever. Leaving could risk her having another breakdown or exposing the truth." He shakes his head. "It would be a nightmare if it got out, and people would gossip. Under no circumstances can she leave the twelfth floor."

"So none of the neighbors know?" I ask.

"That's why we keep the penthouse with the entire top of the building to ourselves. Nobody to hear her or accidentally see her. If she has to make a public appearance for my father's business or if there's a company outing or a hospital board meeting—and fortunately, those occur rather infrequently these days—we allow Collette to attend but only to show her face. When she's out, she goes with a whole team of us surrounding her and providing extra control." He nods at me. "You'll be part of those efforts too, of course. But again, those outings will not occur often if I can help it."

"But people know about the death of her child, right?" I ask. "They remember her having Patty. They remember the girl dying, even if it was a long time ago. There was a funeral?"

"We kept it very private. Patty was so little, she stayed home and hadn't yet started school. And when she got sick, we treated her here. Nurses and the nanny staying around the clock to help Collette in every way they could. And when she died . . ." He coughs softly, turning his head so I won't see the tears. "We kept that private too. The funeral was swift and sparse. Closed casket."

He sinks back in his chair, looking exhausted and beaten down. While I'm still furious, it occurs to me the lengths this man has gone to to prevent his stepmother from killing herself. I don't like how he's doing it but he's trying to protect her. Helping his father. Bringing in nanny after nanny, possibly delivering this very sad speech over and over again. Not to mention dealing with his own grief at losing his sister.

I sit back. "Stephen—" I begin to protest.

But his voice rises suddenly. "We'll pay your rent."

My eyebrows shoot up.

"We'll pay your rent for as long as you're here. Even past the three-month mark if you agree to stay longer."

I'm speechless.

"Stay," he says. One part commanding, one part begging. "Stay and you'll earn more money than you ever have before. A break in rent too. How can you pass something like that up?"

CHAPTER THIRTEEN

"Look, Sarah," he says, clearing his throat. "My sister died. It was tragic, and we moved on—well, most of us, that is, except for Collette. And because of her we're stuck in this time warp, it's as simple as that. That's why you're here." He rests his forearms on the desk, looking at me head-on. "So here's the deal: this isn't easy on any of us but it's something we must do. We each have our jobs and yours includes being a nanny. You keep your mouth shut to family and friends. You don't ask neighbors or go nosing around for information. If you play by the rules, everything should be simple. Because I meant it when I said this would be a piece of cake. You only need to show up each day and twiddle your thumbs. There's no kid to chase after. No messes to clean up. You're here to keep Collette from second-guessing. You're taking on the job of—"

"Collette's caretaker," I interrupt.

Stephen's face blanches. But after a beat he says, slowly, "Yes, I suppose that's true."

I fold my arms, the unease growing in my chest even as everything I've just heard is slowly sinking in. The contract I've signed is binding. I'm trapped in this job for at least three months or they'll sue me . . . and how else had Stephen put it? *We'll bring down the hammer.*

My arms squeeze tighter.

"I'm here to make her think she needs a nanny," I say, surprised at how flat and even my voice has become. "I need to make sure she makes believe there is a child, that I also see Patty."

He nods. "Yes." And this time, he gives me a small smile, a look on his face that says he hopes I'm coming around to the idea.

"My real reason for being here is to watch over Collette. Make sure she doesn't stop believing and go off the deep end." I raise my eyebrows at him. "Help you maintain this façade you've expertly created. Prevent a family crisis while keeping her locked up in this penthouse."

Stephen raises his hands. "I wouldn't say locked up."

I shoot him a look. "Controlled. Maintained. Never to leave the twelfth floor, however you want to phrase it." I shrug. "But I get what's going on here. I've got it. No kid, no real job except to watch over Collette."

My heart aches again. Poor, poor Collette.

"It's just that . . ." I say, and stop.

I pause for a long time, not knowing how to form my next words. The excitement I'd once had about being a nanny, about watching over a young girl, is now dashed.

I whisper, "It's just that I thought I was going to be a nanny." And I blush, knowing how ridiculous I sound. I love sitting with Collette, but there is no child. And that was before—things have changed so drastically. "I don't know how I'm supposed to do this . . ."

And holy God, my voice is strained. I'm brokenhearted at what's really in store: long hours in the morning when Collette will expect me to stay in the breakfast room as I watch her eat, lunches with only the two of us while Pauline and Freddie pretend to ignore us in the kitchen. Day after day of oversize puzzle pieces and playdates in a girl's long-abandoned bedroom. The ghost of her in every corner. Collette at the center of it all, acting as if everything is normal and wonderful.

But Stephen only looks at me. "Does it matter?" he asks. And the sharpness in his voice stops me cold.

"The nannying part, I mean?" Stephen peers at my face until I'm squirming in my seat. "After all," he says, slowly, his mouth settling firmly, "how hard can it be?"

A crash. The sound of glass breaking followed by the hard tumble of what could be a chair—chair legs and a wooden seat wobbling and splintering against marble.

Stephen leaps up. "Collette." And he races from the room.

We find her in an area of the apartment I have not yet seen. It's a sort of lounge with a baby grand piano and floor-to-ceiling bookshelves, the books grouped together by color. A ridiculously large gold clock hammers away the seconds on a wall, the incessant ticking sound followed by Collette's wailing and broken glass that she's pushing aside with her feet.

She's swaying. The woman is wailing and rocking her arms.

I glance again at her feet—they're bare. She must have removed her sandals before kneeling beside the tub.

How long has she been in here? Where is Pauline?

And why isn't Collette still in the bathroom doing whatever it is she was doing—talking to Patty and running more bathwater?

Instead, she's alone and crying, her shirtsleeves wet and slipping from where they'd been rolled with half her blouse soaked up to her chest. My God, did she fall into the tub? Her face is streaked with tears, black mascara running down her cheeks in horrid thin stripes, her once beautiful face looking overrun with savage war paint. The woman before me is in so much pain.

Alarm bells clang loudly in my head telling me to get out of here, but I can't. I know I should leave this place, but I don't move. I stay put. Collette is so desperately in need of help that something inside my heart tears open.

Collette stares at Stephen, then at me. She cries and hiccups, her bare toes stepping in and around the mess she's made, at the shards of broken glass, as if trying to see how close she can step without cutting herself.

I look to see what she's broken and spot the chunks of a glass along with thicker pieces that have come from a tumbler. Next to that, a knocked-over chair with a clear liquid splashed across one side. The distinct smell of vodka. A bottle, I see, that is cracked in half with the bottom smashed to pieces.

I again look for Pauline. How could she have left? How is she not running in here right now, rushing to Collette's aid?

Is Collette wasted? She's upset, that much is clear, but is she also drunk—and before midday? What changed between the bathroom and here?

"I'm so sorry," Collette says, her voice shaking with tears.

She casts her eyes shyly at Stephen, then the floor, her hands twitching and fidgeting by her sides. "I didn't mean to . . . I'm so sorry . . ." she repeats.

Stephen moves to her, hushing, "Now, now," as he treads carefully around the broken glass. He kicks a larger piece away with his shoe.

I peer at her feet and look for blood, for a toe streaking crimson against the marble, but somehow, miraculously, she has avoided cutting herself.

She cries harder and clings to Stephen. She's barely able to look him in the eye, she's that overcome with shame. Stephen holds her too, but only formally. His shoulders are tight and pulled back as he pats his stepmother awkwardly on the back.

"Now, now," he repeats.

Collette is quieting, her cries evening out until she's sniffling. She sweeps her unkempt hair behind her ears, her gaze dropping to her shirt, at the skin she sees peeping through the wet material. "I'm sorry," she says again, and then her face jerks up, remembering that I'm standing there, and her eyes bulge at the realization I'm witnessing her in this state.

She gives out a yelp. "Oh!" she says and covers her face with both hands. "Oh, Sarah, I'm so sorry . . ." She glances again at her wet blouse, the trail of broken glass she's left on the floor. "I'm such a mess, such a fool. What you must think . . . I apologize."

What I must think? I'm still struggling with everything that is going on here.

Collette steps back and takes Stephen's hands in her grasp. "I got upset," she tells him. "You coming into the bathroom like that. I'd been running the bath for Patty, and then Sarah was there, and then she was gone. You took her and everything got topsy-turvy. I was confused—angry too—Patty getting out of the tub and running off the way she does. She hasn't been listening to me . . ." Collette pouts. "I tried to get her back into the tub and then look what happened." She holds out her arms. "I got soaked and Patty didn't care if Mommy ruined her shirt."

"I'm sorry that happened," Stephen tells her. He's quick to let go of her hands and gestures to the floor. "But you can't come in here and break everything. You can't cause a scene. Tell me you weren't drinking again. You promised."

Her shoulders shake. "I wasn't. I saw the bottle and wanted to get rid of it. Get it out of my sight before I could . . . you know . . ." Her eyes dash away. "Give in."

Stephen looks at the bookshelves. His eyes flick to the piano. "What's vodka doing in here anyway?" He turns furiously to the door as if wanting to interrogate someone, possibly Pauline or Freddie.

"I don't know how it got here," Collette continues. Stephen shoots her a look. "I promise. I got upset, but I didn't drink any of it." She's crying again, woeful tears running down her cheeks. The sway of her body is returning.

I can't tell if she's lying or not; can only watch, frozen to the spot. But now Stephen wants us to move.

"We need to get you in bed." He looks at me. "Will you help?" He holds out one arm, asking that I come to Collette's side and allow her to lean on me.

I'm jolted into motion. The nannying of Collette is officially beginning.

I stand beside Collette and she whimpers. The wet material of her blouse pushes against me as she holds my wrist for support. With her so close, I breathe in the woody jasmine scent of her perfume.

Her eyes shift to me. Her hair is a mess, mascara runs to her chin, but she's still trying to apologize. For a moment, she recovers, but only slightly.

Because she peers at me and says, "Don't forget to look after Patty."

CHAPTER FOURTEEN

Stephen checks on me twice before suggesting I cut out for the rest of the day. Collette is still sleeping and since she'll likely be out most of the day—I'm almost positive he's given her a sedative—he says there's nothing much for me to do. I don't have to sit with Patty. I want to remind him there is no Patty but decide against it and instead grab my jacket and head for the elevator.

It's a relief to push out of the apartment building, the glass door releasing me from the steady heat and heady scent of gardenias in the lobby to the colder air of the city street. I almost run smack into Malcolm. He's about to smile but takes one look at my face and stops. Something flickers in his eyes—camaraderie? An apology? Is he in on the secret too?

I don't ask. I just want to move away from here.

But half a block later I stop at the corner. Craning my neck, I look up and take in the apartment with a different pair of eyes this time, acute knowledge in my gaze. Staring at the twelfth floor, I take another good look at the penthouse that, as of three days ago, I couldn't wait to see.

The corniced roof carved from stone, resembling the looped swirled icing of a wedding cake topper. Decorative beams rising above each window. The drapes that are pulled to prevent people from looking in—who could *possibly* look in their windows that high up? And what I know the curtains are hiding inside: marble floors mopped to a shine, priceless décor, and gilded furniture. A covered-up framed picture of a little girl. A family who puts on the most epic of fronts with an unwell woman trapped inside. The dark façade of a building hiding decades of tragedy. A girl's playthings that someone should have packed away a long time ago.

I turn and walk at a steady pace, eager to put some distance between myself and that building.

Two blocks later I'm rounding the outer gates of the Museum of Natural History when my phone rings. I'm almost afraid to look—the same 1-800 number that keeps hounding me. Their calls, relentless and harassing. The fear lodges a stone at the back of my throat.

On top of everything, and after these last few hours, I still have this to contend with: a collections agency asking for the one hundredth time if I have the funds to pay my credit card—the one I maxed out when Aunt Clara was sick and I'd stayed multiple nights at a hotel closer to her treatment facility. We'd charged groceries and prescription medicine to that card too. And now, the credit agency is demanding what I owe.

I can almost time it by now. A week between calls from the hospital billing office. The credit card company, far more aggressive, with three to four calls a week. Sometimes every day.

With shaking hands, I shove my phone back inside my pocket and let the call go to voicemail.

A few more steps and I'm taking the first pathway into

Central Park. My head ducks under the shade of maple and elm until I'm joining joggers and dog owners out for a stroll. A young man hurls a tennis ball into the air for his cocker spaniel to retrieve. A throng of tourists walk together enjoying an audio tour, headphones hanging around their necks as they stop for a group photograph. The Manhattan skyline looms in the background.

If I keep walking, I'll eventually make it to the lake and I slow my pace. I'm not sure where I want to go, but I'm positive I'm not ready to go home yet. Jonathan will still be at work, which means the apartment will be empty, and I'm not ready to sit in a room by myself. But if he was home, I'm not sure what I would tell him. How to explain this?

And to think Jonathan's biggest worry had been a pervert dad who hits on nannies.

But then my heart stalls—I can't tell Jonathan. I signed a contract. I can't tell anyone. Jonathan can never know and I must keep this hidden.

We'll bring down the hammer . . .

Collapsing on a park bench, I close my eyes against the afternoon sun. A breeze ruffles my hair and the bench seat feels cold beneath my legs but that doesn't stop me from slouching down farther, my face turning toward the sun with a few rays breaking through the clouds to shine on my cheeks. Another couple of hours remain before my shift at Hearth.

My stomach turns. Why couldn't this have been a normal family? Why did I have to pick the one nanny posting that involved caring for a dead girl? If only I hadn't seen that listing. If only I hadn't made that phone call. I wouldn't know anything about this family.

But I wouldn't have met Collette—the pull I feel toward her, even now.

And I did make the call. I signed the contract. This is the deal I must contend with.

I think about Aunt Clara—what would she tell me to do? Would she worry over me? I wouldn't be able to tell her the details either, but would she sense my discomfort and tell me to push through?

I remember, when I was in high school, Aunt Clara coming home from work, exhausted, more so than usual. The deepening lines around her mouth, an increasing overwhelmedness in her eyes. Distressed and lost. She'd switched to a new job selling insurance for a much smaller agency, a single boss with Aunt Clara as the only other staff member in a one-room office. They were handling hundreds of claims with no signs of slowing down. While they worked to keep up, the boss was cracking under pressure.

At first I didn't know what was going on. But then Aunt Clara started bringing more work home. Piles of it. Errors she found in her boss's paperwork. Applications that hadn't been processed. She was working overtime to finish the work of both of them.

And then the screaming began. Instead of being thankful, her boss was furious about how she thought Aunt Clara was undermining her. But my aunt had only been trying to help. She didn't want the agency to go under since she needed to keep this job.

But the verbal abuse increased. At dinner, Aunt Clara would look crestfallen, overworked, but then she'd explain how she couldn't give up. Not only was she ensuring new policies were selling and higher commission rates would start rolling in, more money for us, but she'd also discovered some new things about her boss, Linda, explaining her rage.

Linda's husband had left her for a younger woman and was hardly seeing his kids. She was struggling to work while also raising three children. Without knowing a better way to cope, she was taking it out on Aunt Clara. My aunt's picking up her slack made Linda feel insufficient, and then resentful.

"Now that she's told me," Aunt Clara explained, "now that she's apologized, I understand where everything is coming from. I can't let this agency fall apart. We're going to find a way to make this work together."

"But she shouldn't be screaming at you," I said.

"No, but it's gotten better now that she knows I'm not the enemy." She made a face. "Is it perfect? No. But I can live with it for now."

Aunt Clara worked for that woman for two more years before finding a job at a much bigger agency. She'd put up with Linda and persevered for me. Above all, she'd given Linda empathy.

And I know I must do that for Collette—have empathy. And I must persevere for Jonathan. This nannying job is not even close to what I thought it would be. It's going to test my limits, but the money is worth it. The *rent money* is worth it—wait until I tell Jonathan about the added bonus.

I swallow the thought—*the bribe*.

I can do this for him. I can stick it out three months if that means Jonathan and I can get ahead of my debt. We can finally plan our wedding and set aside money for our future.

———

"You're late, Larsen!"

Once again, I'm sprinting into Hearth and rushing to tie my apron around my waist, swishing my hand in my front pocket looking for pens and doing my best not to show I've run the last ten blocks and am badly out of shape.

"I'm sorry!" I shout.

I'd lost track of time in the park, having finally called Jonathan during his break to tell him the only part I could— that our rent was taken care of.

Jonathan had stammered on the phone. "They're going to pay for *how long?*"

"For as long as I work there." My heart skipped a beat telling him the news. I could almost picture him standing at the back of the kitchen, wide-eyed and smiling in disbelief, the rush of color that fills his cheeks when he hears something good.

But Jonathan had also sounded perplexed. "Why? I mean, don't get me wrong, this is absolutely incredible. But why didn't they mention this when you interviewed?"

It hurt lying through my teeth. "I did so well they added this as a bonus."

Jonathan whistled. "Sarah, this is amazing."

And we'd gotten off the phone with Jonathan saying how proud he was.

A message had come in next, and right on cue, it was Stephen asking for my rent details and tenant information. It took several attempts to get ahold of Mr. Hadid, our landlord, before I had the correct documents emailed to the Birds.

I'd sat back on the bench, taking in what this meant. Rent paid in full for months.

I'd lost track of time. Some kid clattered by on a skateboard and I'd jumped from the bench as if I'd been electrocuted, realizing the hour, then running full speed out of the park to the nearest subway station, bobbing and weaving around people on the street before careening into Hearth's front doors and stumbling into the kitchen.

Paul sneers at his watch, then at me. "You're twenty minutes late, Larsen, and you've been late every day this week. Don't get me started on last month too."

"I'm here. It won't happen again, I'm sorry." I grab the closest order pad I can find and flash him my most apologetic smile. But it doesn't make the cut.

He shoots me an impatient look. "Last time, Larsen," he warns before turning on his heel.

I stare at my section. Once again, Jonathan has swept the floor, restocked the sugar caddies, and laid out my pieces of silverware, one by one. He gives me a thumbs-up, still grinning and cheesing over the rent announcement. I blow him a kiss.

Jonathan scoots toward me. Quickly—before Paul catches us—he squeezes me in for a hug. He's giddy with excitement, having let the news sink in for the last hour.

"I still can't believe it." His dimple highlights his cheek. "This is jackpot, baby."

I look into his face and can't stop grinning either.

"So what magical powers did you harness?" He pokes me playfully in the ribs. "What did you do today with the little girl that impressed them so much?"

I glance away, finding it much harder to lie than when I was on the phone.

"I still didn't meet her," I tell him. "It's how I interacted with Mrs. Bird."

He tilts his head. "Okay, so with Mrs. Bird. What happened? You must have done something right."

"Yes." I nod, although an image of Collette wailing and stepping around broken glass flashes across my mind. The way she'd run her hands through an empty bathtub. "We get along really well."

"Obviously," he says, giving me another playful squeeze of the elbow. But he tilts his head again. "So you still haven't met the girl?"

"No." And I avert my eyes a second time, feeling my pulse pounding in my neck. To busy myself, I rearrange the salt and pepper shakers even though he's already placed them in the correct spots.

Jonathan's smile falls short. He knows me well. "Hey, are you okay?"

I'm faltering. The worries are stacking inside my chest.

Maybe it's because I'm back in the restaurant. Maybe it's seeing Jonathan and his kind, eager face and hearing Stephen Bird's threats echoing in my ears. I have a strong feeling what I witnessed today is only a sign of more things to come and I won't be able to tell Jonathan about a single moment of it. I'll have to keep lying to him.

I move one more pair of salt and pepper shakers before pulling away.

He holds his stare. "What's up?"

"Nothing." I know I need to get my act together if I'm to keep my side of the contract, if I'm going to be able to barrel through this job and get the perks Jonathan and I so desperately need. I force a smile. "It's all good. She was still feeling sick so the mom gave her a bath. I stayed out of the way but then Collette and I had a wonderful chat together. It was nice." Another big smile, knowing I need to convince him that today was nothing out of the ordinary.

Maybe if I can convince him, I have a shot at convincing myself.

CHAPTER FIFTEEN

I can't go in. The alarm on my phone shrieks loudly and mercilessly. I smack my hand at my phone, fumbling around until I hit the stop button. The alarm cuts off.

I burrow deeper under the covers—I can't do it, can't make it to West Seventy-eighth. And to think, yesterday I'd been practically skipping my way to the Upper West Side. But now I'm struggling with how I can return; balancing my strong desire to keep this up for Jonathan's sake while dreading what will face me when I reenter that apartment.

But maybe I don't have to: Stephen promised sick leave. He owes me that much after everything he dumped on me yesterday. I'll tell Stephen I need some personal time to clear my head. Or, on second thought, I'll tell him I really am sick but should be better by tomorrow. I just need to hunker down for a day and take a breather.

I send Stephen Bird a text, leery that if I make a phone call he'll try to talk me out of it. I claim to be feeling under the weather, almost typing *food poisoning* but decide against it. The fewer details, the better.

It takes minutes for Stephen to respond and I wait, anxiously.

Eventually, he responds with *Ok. Get well soon.*

Fortunately, no questions asked. He must know yesterday spooked me but he isn't going to press.

I roll to the edge of the bed. Soon, Jonathan will be getting up and jumping in the shower, another shift awaits him at Hearth. I stare at our apartment walls: bare because we haven't had the time or the money to buy artwork or posters for display. I can't bring myself to go to West Seventy-eighth, but I sure as hell can't sit in our studio apartment all day. My thoughts alone will be enough to drive me crazy.

I stare out the window at the busy street below, which will only get busier as more people rush to their daily tasks. Oddly, I find myself wishing for the familiarity of Hearth, the servers I know so well, the routine order of things, where each table is laid out just so and the busy pace of serving customers keeps my mind off most everything else. I'm also wishing for Jonathan's company. I can't tell him what's going on but having him nearby will calm me.

I send a group text to the staff: *Anyone want to give up a shift?*

An immediate response arrives from Seth. He needs to help his girlfriend move into her new place and says the timing is perfect. *Thank you,* I type back. That settles it.

Jonathan is toweling off and looks surprised to see me pulling on my black pants and shirt, our restaurant attire. "So . . . you ran out of clothes?" he jokes.

"No," I tell him, moving to the wardrobe, where I'm almost positive I dropped my belt. "The little girl is still sick, and since it's been going on for a few days, they're taking her to a doctor." My cheeks burn and I bury my face in the closet, hoping he can't see the red splotches radiating down my neck.

"So you're going to Hearth?"

"I picked up Seth's shift."

At the bottom of the closet, my fingers wrap around a strip of leather, a metal buckle next. I pull out my belt and loop it around my waist.

"Cool. And you're still getting paid for this day, right? The nannying gig is salaried so . . ." He scrounges around for his uniform.

"Yes, I still get paid. We need the cash so I thought I'd go into the restaurant too. Extra money, you know?" I give him a faint smile. "Every bit helps."

He grins. "That's great. Plus . . ." He steps over and gives me a kiss. "We'll get to see each other today." Clasping my hands, he gives the familiar double squeeze.

She's sitting at my table—table eight.

Collette Bird. In my section.

At Hearth.

I feel the pitcher of water slipping dangerously in my grasp. Forcing my hand to cup the bottom, I keep the pitcher from falling and exploding across the floor. I take deep breaths. Don't freak out. Don't draw attention. What I need to do right now is steady myself and watch.

But she's busted me. I called in sick and she didn't believe me for one second.

She unwraps a silk scarf from her neck, the material so long and luxurious, it takes three full unwinds before she's successfully peeled it from her skin, her delicate white throat and sharp edge of collarbone revealed when she's done.

I'm startled.

Why is she here? Couldn't she have just called me and asked for an explanation instead? I could have made up something about the manager calling me in for the day.

More lies . . . and to Collette too.

My head whips across the length of the restaurant. Another question looms: How did she get out?

I'm not sure if she could have found her way to this place by herself. Stephen made it clear she was never to leave the apartment. But somehow, like a skilled escape artist, the woman has broken free. She dressed to the nines and snuck out of the penthouse on West Seventy-eighth Street.

But how? How could Pauline or Freddie, or even Malcolm at the front door, not know she left the apartment? Wouldn't they have seen? There must be a full-blown search going on for her right now.

Sometimes, when it's urgent, I'll have the driver . . .

Did she pay him? Slip the driver hundreds of dollars to bring her here? I think of how furious Stephen will be.

But I don't see anyone accompanying Collette. If the driver brought her, he's either parked outside or circling the streets.

Collette looks sorely out of place in the East Village, but there's no doubt about it: she made it out of the apartment. And for that, I give her credit. I didn't think she had it in her, especially after I saw how hysterical she was yesterday.

She's requested my section, which means I won't be able to avoid her. Maybe she felt the need to apologize some more. Maybe even explain, although the idea of her explaining anything to me seems far-fetched. She's the one, after all, who insists Patty is real.

I walk toward her, still clutching the pitcher of water.

Her blue eyes—with at least three coats of mascara on their lashes—light up when I approach. A steady gaze peers up at me, accompanied by a coy smile—similar to the look a child gives when they've been caught doing something naughty but think they can get away with it by being cute. If I had to guess, I'd say she wants to smooth things over, make everything that happened yesterday seem lighthearted and funny. As if, on a daily basis, it's perfectly normal for people to lose their minds at the drop of a hat and then sleep off the rest of the day, sedated.

She's here to make peace.

And wow, does she look better than she did yesterday. Color has returned to her face with rosy peach blush and dewy foundation applied to her cheeks. A sweep of taupe eyeshadow and her signature red lipstick. The familiar heavy spritz of Chanel No. 5. Her hair is freshly washed and pulled into a chignon, her honey-colored highlights blending in with the darker blond strands at her temples.

I suppose a night of medicated sleep and hundreds of dollars in makeup can totally transform a person. Remarkably, she is back to the woman I met on our first day.

And what she's wearing—a caped ensemble—dramatic and luxe as hell in a rich swirled caramel color and made from the finest wool. I find myself staring, wanting to reach out and touch the lines of her beautiful cape, to feel the fabric. I hold this moment in my mind for a design I want to sketch later.

On either side of her face, a pair of large ruby earrings swing back and forth as she bobs her head to me in greeting.

"Sarah," she says, her voice a gentle purr.

Once again, I am unnerved in her presence. I don't know what to say.

"Mrs. Bird," I say in return, and to my dismay, my voice sounds wobbly. I clear my throat. "Are you—" I look around. Still no sign of a driver or personal escort. No sign of Stephen barreling in to demand she come home.

My eyes drop to the shimmering crystal leopard-patterned pumps on her feet, Christian Louboutins this time, and decide she couldn't possibly have found her way to the subway and walked.

"Am I with someone?" she asks.

"Yes."

"No, just me." And she says this so quickly and with such giddiness, a woman enjoying her freedom, who knows she is getting away with it for now. "I hope you don't mind," she starts to say, then looks around the restaurant with slight alarm, as if considering for the first time that I might not want her here.

If she'd wanted this to be a private conversation, picking a restaurant at peak lunch hour in the middle of the East Village wasn't the brightest choice. If she wanted to be inconspicuous, she's failing at that too. Nearly everyone in the restaurant has noticed her. As she sits at my table, people are taking the time to stare.

New York City may be a constant spectacle of the rich and the glamorous, the eccentric and fashionably flamboyant, but right now, Collette takes the cake. No one steps into

Hearth wearing a caramel-colored cape and crystal shoes and sits alone. Everything about her reeks of money.

I pour a glass of water as she studies the menu. She flips to the back. "What's good here?"

"Are you planning to eat?"

She lets out a laugh, one hand lifting to the side of her throat. Slender white fingers trace the length of her neck.

"Of course." She lets her eyes cross the room. But her smile is soon followed by a look that borders on scolding. "This *is* a restaurant, isn't it?"

I bite my lip.

Jonathan hovers nearby. I see him at the coffee station. He's glancing at the woman at my table, then back at me, and I know there's no reason for him to think this is Collette or to suspect something is amiss. I've described her, yes, but he can't think my new boss would visit Hearth.

"I don't have the biggest appetite," Collette says. "But I would like to eat something small, so anything on the light side you could recommend would be just fine." She gives me an expectant look. "Maybe a soup or salad?"

I shift my weight to one hip and think of what won't take too long to prepare. "Do you like tomatoes and mozzarella? The caprese salad might be a nice choice."

She smiles, snapping the menu shut. "Sounds lovely."

I'm stepping away when I look back. "Anything to drink?" I glance at the wineglass that I desperately prefer remain empty. "Besides water?"

Collette checks the water glass on the table before dismissing the empty goblet. Another classic Stepford wife smile as she beams at me. "I'm fine with water, thank you."

The occupants of table nine wave their hands. A father

and his two daughters, who've spent most of their time over plates of ravioli and osso buco bickering about what the daughters deem to be their father's strict rules. At one point during lunch, one of the girls, about twelve or thirteen and wearing a jean jacket with colorful patches on the sleeves, crossed her arms and refused to eat the rest of her meal, sulking, while the other sister argued with Dad.

When I approach, the father looks to me for help as if he can't get the check fast enough.

I run his credit card, quickly dropping it on the table and trying my best to give him a sympathy smile that says, *Hang in there*. I feel the words resonating with me too as I return to Collette.

She's arranging the silverware, carefully placing her knife, fork, and spoon equal distances from one another. The knife handle is lined up with the base of the spoon.

"Can I help you with something, Mrs. Bird?" I finally ask.

She looks up, rattled by my question, lost in thought. Blinking once, then twice, as if she's trying to remember who I am or figure out what she's doing here. Is she on something? But to my relief, her confusion—if that's what it was—promptly disappears. She's smiling again, her eyes clearing.

"I asked you to call me Collette," she says. Then more quietly, "And I want to apologize. For my behavior yesterday, for how I acted." Her mouth twists at the word *acted*. "I lost control." She waves her hands, a little too flippantly. "I do that sometimes. I've always been an emotional person. I hope you can forgive me?"

A huge part of me wants to believe her, but another part

isn't so sure. I'm worried that what I saw in that apartment is common—that's what kept me up so late last night. The fear that Collette is prone to these erratic mood swings and Stephen has been downplaying her condition for my sake.

She fiddles with one of the napkins. "When Stephen told me you weren't coming in today, I got nervous. He said you were sick"—she gives me a knowing smile—"but I had a feeling that wasn't the case." She looks around the restaurant. "You must have wanted a break from me. To come back here where no one's going to yell."

"I'm sorry, Mrs. Bird. It's just—"

"Collette," she again corrects me.

"Collette, I shouldn't have bailed on you like this. It's just, yesterday was intense . . ." I scrunch my eyes. "And I thought maybe you weren't feeling well today either so maybe you could use an extra day of rest."

She cocks her chin. She's not buying it.

"I'm sorry it got intense," she says, but sounds frustrated. "I didn't want it to end up that way." She drums her fingers on the table. "How can I make it up to you? How can I get you to come back?" The sincerity in her voice is fading. She's too loud. I look around, aware that Jonathan has returned to his section while other servers are circling their tables and tending to customers. Paul will be coming out to check the front of the restaurant at some point too.

"I'll be there tomorrow," I say quietly.

"Are you sure?"

"Yes." I'm hoping she'll mimic my voice at a near whisper.

But Collette doesn't want to be quiet anymore. Earlier,

when it had been about her, her apology for her own unattractive behavior, she had been careful to lower her voice. But now, when it's about me and my intentions, her discretion is out the window.

"I need to know you'll come back," she says. "Tell me there's no chance of you skipping out on me and Patty tomorrow."

Tomorrow is Friday. And then it's the weekend. I can handle one day.

"Yes, I can be there tomorrow," I tell Collette, hoping she'll drop it and wait for her salad instead.

But she only glares.

"You'll come back to work for me tomorrow? I have your word?"

I shift my feet. "Yes."

"I'll see you Monday through Friday, no matter what." She's not letting up. "You agreed to work for us, Sarah. I expect you to show up."

My eyes cut left, then right, scanning the tables. "Mrs. Bird, we can't talk about that right now."

"I need you to commit."

"I *work* here, Collette," I say. "This is *my job*. No one knows I'm splitting my time at another place. I haven't told my boss yet."

And with that, she instantly flushes. She doesn't like being defied, and certainly not by me.

But she has to know this is the wrong time and place, that you can't go into another person's place of employment and make a scene.

But that doesn't stop her. She thinks all she needs to do is show up at the restaurant and apologize and everything's fixed.

She gazes at me as if to say, *See? I can do this on my own. I don't need Stephen or Pauline.*

For the first time, I'm starting to think Collette is more capable than she lets on.

CHAPTER SIXTEEN

Just like that, her mood changes. Collette's emotions shift with the wind until we find ourselves approaching a category three storm.

"You're upset with me, aren't you?" she says, her hands fluttering to her face. My insides squeeze. Oh no, here she goes—tears are welling in her eyes and the sides of her cheeks are caving.

"I'm so sorry . . . I'm not sure what's wrong with me . . ." She rocks to one side of her seat as if preparing to leave, a hand dropping below the table in search of something, and I look down, seeing what she's looking for, her monstrous Louis Vuitton handbag, which appears to weigh about fifteen pounds. She's lifting it to her lap—struggling, really—the handbag making it as high as her knees before she drops it again, then heaves it up. I stop myself from helping her. What is she looking for? Tissues? Pills? A hidden flask?

But she's reaching for a wallet, fishing out a crisp fifty-dollar bill that she places on the table, whispering something through her tears about "For the salad," before standing up. She's stumbling from the table and knocks into the back of someone's chair nearby.

Shit.

"Wait," I say. "I didn't mean . . ." I reach out my arms as if to steady her, catch her if I have to, and look around again, nervous about Paul suddenly appearing.

But Collette is stepping away, bustling from the table, the Louis Vuitton weighing down her stick-thin arm and threatening to snap it like a twig. She turns, as if wanting to say one more thing, but her handbag knocks into a chair, causing it to rattle and thump on its legs, and soon every single customer is looking her way.

"Collette," I call for her.

She digs in her bag for something else and finds a pair of sunglasses, the oversize shades covering the top half of her face. "I didn't mean to . . . I shouldn't have . . ." And she moves away quickly. She's on the run.

I look to the window—still no sign of the driver. Collette will be wandering the sidewalk aimlessly, lost and alone in this great big city.

And just as I'm about to call for a cab or order an Uber, she shrieks, "I'm your boss, Sarah!" Her voice cuts through the air like a battle-ax. She spins around to face me. "*I'm* the one who calls the shots, don't forget that!"

I'm staring at her, my heart falling to somewhere close to my waist.

She's at the front of the restaurant. The audible gasps from customers, coupled with their blatant stares, make my face burn with an intensity bordering on nuclear.

Jonathan is frozen midstep by the ordering station, not knowing whether to put himself between me and the wailing Collette or let me handle the situation. I can see it in his eyes—he wants to help. Amelia is beside him too, the pair of them watching openmouthed, not knowing what to do.

Paul comes running out of the kitchen, making my heart rocket from my stomach to my throat. I'm screwed.

"Ma'am," Paul says, and he's holding his hands out to Collette as if meaning to corner a wild animal.

But Collette doesn't move, and he swings his head at me. "Larsen, is everything all right?" But the way he says it is more like *Take care of this.*

I shuffle where I stand. "Everything is fine, sir."

But Collette is crying again and Paul looks at me with disgust. Everything is *not* fine, and he knows it.

"Ma'am," he says. "Would you and Ms. Larsen like to go outside and talk for a moment? I can bring you some water." He looks around as I did earlier, hoping—praying—that someone has come to fetch her and can whisk her far away from here.

But Collette shrinks back and then her eyes turn cold. "I need Sarah to come with me right now."

Paul swings his head back to me, as does everyone else in the restaurant. "Right now?"

I give him a small shake of my head, my eyes drifting to two other tables in my section, knowing they haven't cashed out yet. I can't walk out of the restaurant until closing time.

But Collette won't hear no, and as I hesitate, she adds, "Come here *now*, Sarah." Her voice escalates. "I mean it. Come with me right now or you're fired."

"Fired?" Paul asks, and he stares at me. "Fired from what?"

"Working for me," Collette answers him, and I want to disintegrate right there on the spot.

On the other side of the restaurant, Jonathan closes his eyes as he finally understands who this woman is. Amelia's mouth drops open.

I don't move, but I know what I need to do next. I should beg Paul's forgiveness and ask him to join me in the back office, where I can explain—I'll explain everything. I'll still stay at Hearth but—

Paul doesn't give me a chance. "You have another job with this woman?" His mind slowly connects the dots. "Is that why you've been late this week, and all the other times before?" He makes a face. "I knew it." He points a finger at me.

I should say something. *I've been meaning to tell you, was going to tell you tonight. Can I still stay on for weekends?* But Paul shuts that down.

"I'm firing you first." His voice drops, as if he's suddenly aware of everyone watching and listening. "Grab your stuff," he orders.

I squeeze my eyes shut. Collette stands by the door, showing no sign of sympathy. No apology for her outburst or remorse for costing me my job. She's completely unconcerned that she has humiliated me in front of my manager and coworkers. In front of every single one of these strangers.

I want to crawl into a hole and hide. Better yet, I want to kick over the nearest table.

Collette is getting what she wants, and what she wants is me.

I walk quietly to the back of the restaurant, grabbing my purse from my locker before reappearing at the front door. I give Jonathan a reassuring look, but I can tell he's furious. In the time I've been gone, he's been arguing with Paul, trying to defend me.

I meet Jonathan's eyes and try telling him it's not worth it, that we don't need to cause a bigger scene right now. But he's not backing down.

"Sarah didn't do anything wrong," Jonathan says.

Paul's eyes flash with the look of someone who's about to lose his shit. His jaw tightens. "Cool it, Romero," he warns.

"You shouldn't fire her," he insists.

Paul is glaring at Jonathan, then turns his fury toward me, shooting us both a look as if to say he knew this was coming, it had been only a matter of time before we caused drama at his restaurant.

"You want to make this worse for you and Larsen?" Paul asks, sweeping his hard stare at both of us.

I shoot a pleading look to my fiancé. "It's okay, Jonathan. I'll go."

"But this isn't Sarah's fault," Jonathan says. "She's got to make more money. She can work this other job and still stay here, okay? Please?"

"No, *not* okay," Paul hisses. "And who do you think you are, telling me how to run my business?" He waves his hands, wanting nothing more to do with this—with us. "Get your stuff. You're out of here too!"

My jaw drops.

Jonathan reels. *"What?"*

"You can't be serious," I tell Paul.

"Oh, I'm absolutely serious," Paul tells me. "I've had enough. Out. The pair of you. *Now.*" He raises an arm toward the door, dismissing us both.

Jonathan and I stand outside. We didn't even get to collect our tips; that's all gone now. Neither of us has a job—at least not at Hearth. I may or may not still have a job with the Birds.

Jonathan paces in front of the restaurant, stunned, while I face the street, arms by my sides, not knowing what to think.

I'm waiting for him to start yelling. Cursing. But all I hear him say is "Go after her."

I spin around.

"That woman," he says, pointing at the back of Collette, who is now walking calmly from the restaurant. "Go after her," he repeats. "Get your job back."

My eyes bulge.

But I see the look on his face, the panicked expression. If I've lost the nannying job too, then we have nothing. It would be the end of our paid rent, along with any shot at paying off Aunt Clara's medical bills or plans for us to get married soon. I'd have to file for bankruptcy. Our dreams, dissolving and falling apart.

I chase after Collette.

CHAPTER SEVENTEEN

===

Collette clearly has no idea where she's going. She's bumbling along like a lost puppy by the time I reach her. I tug at her arm. "Collette."

Her eyes meet mine. She's pleased I've caught up so quickly. The anger from earlier has been replaced with a satisfied smile. But she doesn't say a word.

"I'm sorry," I tell her, motioning in the direction of the restaurant. "For back there, how I handled myself. Please don't fire me. I need this job. I want nothing more than to be your nanny. I'll make up for it, I promise." I clasp her arms, knowing that I'm begging. "I don't have my job at Hearth anymore so that shouldn't be a problem. I can be with you every day, no matter what. I'm all yours." I add, "Yours and Patty's."

At this, Collette's smile grows wide. "I'm glad you're coming to your senses," she says, then bobs her head at the restaurant. "I'm assuming that was your boyfriend?"

"My fiancé."

"Oh, you're getting married?" I don't like how she's said it. She eyes me. "So let me get this straight: You've got no more restaurant job. Your fiancé is out on the street too." She presses her hands together, giving me one blink, then two. "You need me."

The manipulation.

I'm torn between my instinct to run as far away from Collette as possible while terrified I'll never find another job that pays as well as the Birds do. Certainly not one with paid rent.

I'd actually answered one of the bill collector calls this morning and for the first time ever talked to them about setting up a payment plan. I don't want that feeling to disappear.

I look at Collette. She's right, I do need her.

"From now on," she says, "you never let me or Patty down again."

I nod, almost imperceptibly.

"We're walking," she instructs me.

I glance to Jonathan, still lingering outside Hearth. He lifts his head, watching.

"Where?"

"Seeing as you're too sick to care for Patty"—she says this with her fingers in air quotes—"and you no longer have a job at the restaurant, I would say you're free for the rest of the afternoon." She nudges her chin forward. "We're going."

I glance at Jonathan again and wave, indicating I'll catch up with him later. He observes us carefully, lifting one of his hands in a cautious send-off that causes another tremor through my chest.

We travel a couple more blocks before turning on East Tenth Street. Collette is heading to Tompkins Square Park.

She enters through the first gate, and as we walk along the path toward the playground, sounds of children's laughter come at us from all directions. The swings are filled with younger ones while preschool-age tots shoot down the slide for kids their size. Parents and nannies stand around parked strollers. An elderly couple sit beside each other sharing a newspaper.

Collette motions to an empty bench and we sit. We haven't spoken since we entered the park, and she doesn't seem in a rush to do so, only holds out her cape so as not to wrinkle it against the seat. We watch the children for a while, the way they hop from one piece of playground equipment to the next, their squeals reverberating from metal slides, little voices shouting, "Catch me!" as their laughter mixes with barks from a nearby dog park, the squeaky opening of the gate.

Collette says, "Patty loves playgrounds too."

Present tense.

I stay silent.

"She's always trying to make new friends. Asking if they'll play chase or hopscotch," she goes on, crossing her legs, her three-inch heels glittering beneath the sun. "Lately, she's taken to the monkey bars and it's quite impressive to watch. Those tiny arms swinging from one bar to the next. I was never good at that when I was a kid. Were you?" She doesn't wait for me to answer, only laughs. "I never had the strength. But my Patty"—another giggle—"she's a strong one, that girl. Much stronger than me."

I shift uncomfortably in my seat and keep my eyes forward.

With or without a nanny, this woman is hanging by a thread.

CHAPTER EIGHTEEN

══

"Want to do something fun?"

I nearly whimper. I just want this day over with so I can return to Jonathan and reassure him I got my job back. I need to tell him it's going to be okay.

"I can't," I tell her.

"What?" She shoots me a punishing look. "You have more tables to wait on?" She stands abruptly and clasps my hand. "Sarah, whatever it is you're about to say, whatever you think you had planned is canceled. Your fiancé will be all right for a short time without you. You're coming with me and I'm taking you someplace special."

My gut squeezes. "Mrs. Bird, I don't think that's a good idea."

She won't hear it. "The driver will take us. It will be a nice surprise." She crosses her heart, her lips curling. "Trust me."

As we return to the entrance of the park, a black Cadillac pulls up and a driver wearing a crisp black suit jumps out to open the door—so she really did convince someone to take her out.

But I don't move.

"Sarah?" Collette says, pulling on my arm. She digs in her

wallet, a one-hundred-dollar bill showing up in her hand. "Three more of these when you go home."

I stare. "You're going to pay me four hundred dollars to go somewhere with you?"

"Pretty fantastic, yes? Bet you wouldn't have made close to that working at your restaurant job." She shoves the money in my pocket.

I wince. "Collette, you don't have to keep handing out money—"

"No," she says, her eyes softening. "But it would be nice to spend some time with you. I've been so lonely . . ." She hiccups a breath, and dammit if my heart doesn't pull. "Please, Sarah." She holds my hand and begs.

I can't abandon her. I can't let her go off in this car alone.

"Please," she says and leads me to the car.

Once we're inside, she calls out an address on Broadway to the driver.

We're weaving through traffic before chugging slowly north up Sixth Avenue. Collette stares straight ahead, the same mysterious smile on her face; the throngs of people on the sidewalk are of no interest to her.

I'm tempted to look at my phone, pull it from my pocket and search for what's located on Broadway.

At least we're staying in the city, I tell myself. We're not leaving Manhattan. We're not crossing state lines.

I think of Jonathan. What's he doing right now? Is he worried sick? Is he pacing the apartment and wondering what in the hell happened to us at Hearth? He must be freaking out—he's worked at that restaurant since long before he met me and will be stressing about where he can find his next job.

I shoot him a text. *I'm so sorry. I can't believe Paul did that to you.*

A quick response back. *We'll figure something out.*

He texts me again: *What about you? Is everything okay?*

I glance quickly at Collette. If she's noticed I'm texting, she doesn't register.

She's keeping me as her nanny.

Another glance out the window. We're turning at Bryant Park.

I'll be back in a couple of hours. I love you.

We travel a short distance farther on Broadway until the driver pulls over. Collette looks up at the building we've stopped in front of, pure excitement lighting her face. "I'll call you," she tells the driver as we step from the car.

"Do you see the rooftop?" She points to the balcony. Chiseled concrete blocks and an elaborate railing. "That's where we're heading."

She takes my arm and the pair of us sweep through the lobby to a bank of elevators at the back, gold-colored art deco doors that open slowly with a ding. She pushes the button for the twenty-fifth floor, the rooftop.

A strange feeling flutters inside my stomach. I'm still leery of this woman but can't help feeling intrigued about where we're heading. When someone like Collette Bird says we're going somewhere special, what exactly does that mean?

We emerge on the top floor to a high-ceilinged lounge burnished with gold mirrors and a marble bar along the back wall that has high-backed stools and clusters of seating on either side, lounge chairs covered in blue velvet, and vignettes of tubular brass. A gorgeous parquet floor is at our feet. Wrought-iron light fixtures hang above our heads.

Bartenders look to us from their stations, their vests a deep red color with white collared shirts rolled at the sleeves. A woman glides out to us from behind the hostess stand wearing long, flowing pants and a striped blouse, chandelier earrings dangling from her ears. She motions to the roof terrace and we follow, finding the balcony, where a long stretch of tables and bench seats are decorated with yellow pillows and small votive candles ready to be lit as soon as the sun goes down.

Collette has brought me to some swanky bar.

The hostess hands us a pair of menus and tells us to enjoy our visit.

Nearby, small plates of food are scattered across tables as guests sample appetizers, and bask in the sunshine, most of them wearing oversize sunglasses similar to Collette's, and drape their arms lazily over the backs of their friends' chairs, wrists weighted down with Rolex and Cartier timepieces.

"What is this place?" I ask, squinting into the sun.

"Greta's on the Roof," she answers, looking around. "Isn't it fabulous?"

I stare at the crowd, seemingly cut straight from a *Vogue* spread, the gorgeous people holding aloft martini glasses and highball whiskeys. "They're all fake, every single one of them," Collette says.

I give her a funny look. "How do you know?"

"Oh, I know."

"Then why are we here?"

"It's fun. I thought you'd like it, you being young and hip and all." She winks at me before staring across the balcony. "My God, it's been ages since I got out, it feels so good," she says. And she stretches her arms above her head as if relishing her newfound freedom. "Alex is always telling me to stay home and rest, but how much rest does a girl need?" She pouts. "I get so bored, and today, I needed a day out." She smiles conspiratorially. "If it weren't for you and your little fib about being sick, I wouldn't have left. It feels great to take a day trip."

Even though it's a jab at me, I still can't believe it. This woman, with all her money and perfectionist makeup and hair and elaborate wardrobe, has nowhere to go. Her own family keeps her in a gilded cage.

When was the last time she *did* go out? I wonder.

Collette says, "This is only my second time to Greta's. The first was their VIP opening reception, and I've meant to come back ever since." Her eyes flit away. "Oh . . . but that was so long ago . . ." She pauses, her voice drifting, but then her eyes wander to the arched doorway at the bar, her excitement bubbling. "I love the story behind this place: former penthouse in the twenties that once belonged to a woman named Greta Van Berg. She was widely known as a socialite and loved to throw parties." A faraway glint floats across her face. "Can you imagine what it must have been like? Living up here, far above the city. The drama and magic of this place, looking out twenty-five floors above everyone else. I bet they thought they could conquer the world back then. New York City coming into its own." She laughs. "What I wouldn't give to have been a fly on the wall."

I look around and for the briefest of moments, let my imagination run wild with what she's described, envisioning glorious parties with women in opulent gowns and men in dapper suits smoking from long cigarette holders. A far cry from what I've ever known, but a time, I believe, where Collette would have fit in perfectly.

Collette scans the menu. She never did have her caprese salad at Hearth and I'm wondering if she's hungry. I slide the drinks menu away from her carefully.

A waitress appears. Her green designer wrap dress flows to her ankles with strappy gold heels on her feet and bangles sliding up one arm—nothing like my Hearth uniform.

"Today, we're offering a special on magnums of champagne," the waitress suggests. "May I bring one to you?"

"Sounds lovely," Collette says. "And something to nibble on too. Whatever you think is best. A sampling of treats."

When the waitress disappears, I shoot Collette a look. "Are you sure we should be drinking?" I ask pointedly.

But she ignores me. Instead, she tilts her face to the sunshine and presses together her lips.

Moments later, the waitress returns carrying an ice bucket and a bottle. She pops the cork with a flourish and pours the pale, sparkling liquid into our glasses. Collette pushes both glasses toward me. "It's all yours."

An entire magnum to myself? At least that means Collette won't be drinking.

Several more minutes go by, the silence sitting awkwardly between us. I take a sip, and then another, my nerves calming as a buzz slowly warms my body.

"I want to show you something. Something special," Collette says and pulls an item from her handbag. She clutches it in her hand. "I hold this very dear."

I lean forward but can't tell what it is, she's got it covered with her palm. Ever so slowly, she releases her fingers one by one.

Blond hair.

A pink ribbon tied at the end.

"I carry it with me everywhere I go."

I take a closer look—a lock of hair.

And just as I realize who it must belong to, she confirms my fears, "It's Patty's." And the champagne rises from my stomach.

CHAPTER NINETEEN

===

Collette strokes the hair. "It's beautiful, isn't it? So silky. She has the most shining head of blond hair you've ever seen on a child. So exquisite." She's trancelike again. "I love my Patty so much, I keep this with me always. I never want her far."

I try looking away but can't. She continues petting the hair as if it were a live creature, as if she is stroking the head of her own child in her lap.

"Whenever I'm away from Patty, this brings me comfort," Collette says. "Thank goodness Pauline was happy to stay home with her today; she's still feeling so poorly, the sweet girl. So if I get a chance to leave the house, go for a drive—find you"—she shoots me a look—"I always have a piece of Patty with me." She cocks her head as if willing me to understand. "And if I'm feeling the slightest bit nervous or unsure about what I'm doing, holding this in my hand calms me. A lock of hair can do wonders, did you know that? I feel her with me. She is," she repeats, "my absolute most favorite, most important person in the whole wide world. She'll be turning four this July."

A chill in the air hits me suddenly. I can no longer feel the sun shining on this rooftop. She's repeating herself, totally unaware that she's uttering the same sentiments she shared during my interview. And I now understand—this is what Collette does. Her life is lived in a loop, her minutes and days resetting until the next morning, when she can repeat it all over again.

Something occurs to me—the object I'd seen Collette holding during my interview. She'd been clutching it in her lap and keeping it close.

That same lock of hair. Her talisman.

"Would you like to hold it?" She grabs my hand and forces it to my fingertips.

I recoil, but Collette doesn't seem the least bit bothered. "It's okay," she says. "Take it. It's so soft, you'll see." She presses the lock, her most sacred item, farther into my hands.

Part of me wants to scream.

Has she been carrying this thing around for twenty years?

Horror grips my body, my hands trembling at the touch, and I want to drop it like a hot potato. I can't give it back to her fast enough; I shove the lock across the table and push it into her hand.

The waitress appears, her green dress fluttering, and my eyes leap at her presence. She's setting down a tray of small plates: avocado toast with smoked salmon, poke-style tuna lettuce wraps, and flatbread with melon and prosciutto sprinkled with mint leaves.

Collette claps her hands. "Perfect." The waitress pours me another glass of champagne.

"Please," Collette says, motioning to the food. "Help yourself."

My stomach rolls in defeat. My appetite is shot—I feel sick, and honestly don't know if I can bring myself to touch the food.

But Collette insists. "Don't let it go to waste."

Gingerly, I sample the avocado toast, then the lettuce wrap, the concoction nearly falling apart in my hands. Collette looks relieved to see I'm eating, and she smiles, reaching for one of the flatbreads and taking the tiniest bite of crust. "Good?" she asks.

I nod, swallowing. I take another sip of champagne, then a bigger gulp, enjoying the bubbly sensation against my tongue as it starts to numb the thoughts racing through my head.

"I like spending time with you," Collette tells me.

I set aside my plate. She does the same, although she's hardly touched a thing. I take another sip. She takes a sip of her water—to my relief, so far, no champagne. But we're mirroring each other and it's so weird, I stop moving just so she will stop copying me too.

"It feels natural with you." Collette grins. "Like we're friends."

I swallow anxiously.

"With the other nannies, it was always forced. Or they would quit, like the last one."

"How many nannies have you had?" I ask.

"Three." Her answer surprises me. I thought they would have had a string of them by now. "We had one when Patty was born, and she was fantastic. The best. And then another, Therese. She stayed with us for a while but . . ." She winces, unable to finish her sentence. "And we had the young lady last year. We already told you about her. And now you.

"I want this to work," Collette says, getting down to business. "I'll do what it takes and pay you more than what Stephen offered you. Eighteen hundred a week." I almost choke on my champagne. "A real salary, so you don't need a second job. And even though he told you to come at nine A.M., let's change it to ten. No need for you to rush. Ten A.M. until four, that's all I ask, Mondays through Fridays, including paid holidays and sick leave, days I have to cancel or am not feeling well, or don't need you to show up. Sometimes, I just like spending the day home alone with Patty. We'll sit together in the playroom."

I shift uneasily in my chair and think of Collette alone in that playroom . . .

She prattles on. "But no matter what, you'll be paid, even if you don't have to come." She removes her sunglasses and raises an eyebrow as she looks at me. "I'm sure that's more than any restaurant can offer and much more than what you're receiving now. You'll never get another job like this and you know it." She smiles. "You'd be a fool not to stick with me."

I don't know what to say, and in that moment, her eyes meet mine and her smile wavers, her emotions quickly swinging around as if battered by a storm. "Don't you want to be with me, Sarah?" she asks. "You and me and Patty?" A sadness fills her face. "Say you'll stay. Say you'll stick with me. Okay, Sarah? Please?"

My mind struggles to keep up with her ever-changing moods. Although Collette has been abstaining from champagne, I've continued to drink, and now I feel tipsy. Over the last twenty minutes, the champagne has gone straight to my head, my once steadfast, defensive boundaries softening and turning fuzzy.

I reach for water instead, needing to clear my head and focus.

I know this is crazy. *She's crazy.*

They're *all* crazy.

And yet . . . there's something about Collette. Something that draws me to her. I can't explain it. Underneath the manipulation and erratic moods, this is a deeply lonely woman. A woman in pain.

Even though my heart aches for her, I can't help imagining the agonizing moments I'd be spending with her in the apartment if I stay. The hours spent reading out loud to a girl who isn't there. Bathtubs with bubbles filled to the brim but no child inside. Afternoon snacks where the plates will go untouched. Crafts tables and art projects where I'll be the only one swirling the paintbrush. The beautifully delusional Collette watching over me in a daze.

The champagne buzz still swirls in my head, my resistance diminished, along with the afternoon warmth. I watch the sun finish its slow descent below the skyline, a few rays peeking from either side of the glass buildings and shining onto the street.

And that's when I realize—she may have done this on purpose: gotten me drunk to whittle me down and encourage me to say yes.

For the second time, I realize no one in the Bird household may be giving her enough credit.

Collette is studying my expression, her face angled to one side in wonder, long, mascaraed eyelashes blinking. A smile is forming again, a bright lipstick grin, no teeth show-ing.

She's hopeful. She'd give anything to know what I'm thinking.

Then she asks, "You want to go somewhere else?"

And to my surprise, I don't say no. I'm curious to see what else Collette has up her sleeve.

CHAPTER TWENTY

The driver takes us to Fifth Avenue, to the luxury department store Bergdorf Goodman. And I'm bursting with giddiness—half champagne buzz, half genuine excitement—at being dropped off by a chauffeur at the front door of this iconic store.

Dazzling bright lights beckon to us from inside, shelves and racks filled with gorgeous fabrics, divine to the touch. Gucci. Dolce & Gabbana. Tom Ford. New arrivals placed center stage and showcasing Saint Sarah and Givenchy. Valentino Garavani shoes and Balenciaga handbags.

A woman in a Prada coat walks nearby, allowing a saleswoman to spritz her with perfume. My head is dizzy with fascination as I marvel at the hundreds of thousands of dollars in price tags around me, fashions that have been highlighted on the runway.

This is a dream—somewhere I've never imagined setting foot inside, let alone shopping. Fashions that I've clipped out from magazines are hanging *right there* on that rack. I've seen those designs on clothing blogs too. On impulse, my hands reach out to touch. On another rack, the very Givenchy silk scarf blouse that inspired several of my sketches is displayed in all its grandeur. I pause at the table, letting my hands runs across the silk bow at the neck.

But Collette is cruising ahead, zigzagging through the crowd and maneuvering around display counters like she knows exactly where she's going, knows exactly what she's looking for, and I race to keep up. But then she stops. She's confused. Lost. Her last visit to this store may have been months or years ago, and the counters and displays are turned around.

She looks up before taking off again, and I follow her to the elevators. At the fourth floor, a sign reads Couture Evening Collections. A sea of glittering gowns lies ahead and my head swivels, taking it all in, my feet stepping double-time to keep up with Collette. We pass blank-faced mannequins in Marchesa Notte dresses, sequin threads in bright red, and a new designer's wares from a successful run at Fashion Week on center display. I just saw this dress online.

I want to start at one end of the store and touch every item, feeling the satin and beaded material between my fingers. I want to try something on. I want so much to have my sketchbook. Maybe I can return here—maybe with Collette—

A dress stops me in my tracks. An Oscar de la Renta gown.

A gorgeous black and white V-neck number, tea length with a tulle A-line skirt and mesh bodice and unlike anything I've ever seen: ballerina-inspired with the most intricate threadwork—and did I mention it's an Oscar de la Renta? Not a print ad I've torn from a magazine or an Instagram post, but the real thing. *The* actual gown.

My hand reaches out to the dress, the black tulle swishing

against my arms as I trace my fingers along the seamed waist.
The price tag: $5,990.

"You can have it," Collette says.

An electric jolt strikes through my chest.

She touches the gown. "It's yours."

I step away. "No, I can't."

"Yes, you can." And she eyes me up and down. "What size
are you? A six or eight?" Collette waves at a salesgirl, who
rushes over. "A six, please," she decides for me. When the
salesgirl reemerges, the dress she carries is even more divine.
She holds it against me.

"Stunning," Collette says, the look on her face approving.
"You have great taste."

My heart skips a beat.

Collette's eyes are sparkling, and there's a sudden flush to
her cheeks that resembles something akin to pride. She looks,
all at once, more vibrant and alive than I've ever seen her. A
woman who enjoys lavishing gifts on people. A woman who
wants to buy a girl a dress.

And I get it now. She's still trying to win me over.

But I'm also touched. She remembers what we talked
about in my interview, my love for fashion. How I studied
design in school.

I shouldn't take it, it's a bribe. *But it's working.*

"Do you want it?" Collette asks. I still haven't taken hold
of the dress, too afraid to touch it as the salesgirl holds it
aloft. "Shall we find a dressing room for you?"

Once I put this on, I'm a goner. No way will I want to put
the dress back. One look in the mirror and I'll want to keep
it forever. You can't decline something like this.

I think about Aunt Clara, and my memory flashes back to

Homecoming, my senior year. We hadn't gone dress shopping because we couldn't afford it. I planned on borrowing my friend's dress from the year before, but Aunt Clara surprised me, saying she'd saved up enough money to buy several yards of fabric she thought would work perfectly for a design I'd been sketching. Over the next two weeks, I made my own dress.

When Aunt Clara saw me leaving the night of Homecoming, she'd touched the jade-green fabric and told me I was the most beautiful girl at school. She had never looked happier. Prouder.

And now here's Collette, with no need to buy me a dress at all, whipping out her credit card and charging six thousand dollars as if it's nothing.

"Where the hell have you been?"

Stephen thrusts the apartment door open as soon we arrive on the twelfth floor. His face is red, his eyes wild, bright crimson streaks on his neck.

"What in the hell, Collette?" he seethes, yanking her by the arm.

She whimpers as his fingers press tight against her skin until white splotches appear. "I went out," she tells him.

He hauls her to one side and channels his anger at me next. "I see you're not sick," he says, his words cutting and sarcastic. "But somehow you managed to meet up with Collette."

I look to her for an explanation, the story we'll give him. But when it's clear there isn't one coming, I say, "She came looking for me."

Stephen whirls on Collette. "You can't go out. Not without telling us first. Remember what happened last time?"

Collette shrinks away.

He swings his attention back to me and takes one look at what's in my hands, the heavy garment bag I carried in from the car. "What's that?"

"A gift," Collette tells him. "I didn't want her to leave us, not like the last nanny." She gives Stephen a begging look. "We can't go back to square one, not again." She tugs his arm, then turns to me. "This one is so kind, so easy to talk to." Her eyes grow teary. "I don't want to lose her." She cries for me. "Sarah, please say you'll stay. Please promise."

"Well, she has to stay," Stephen informs her. "The contract required her to commit to at least three months." He shoots me a look. "She won't want to give up her rent money."

I squirm in my shoes, even more wary of the man I once thought was so caring and kind.

Pauline rushes toward us, her arms extended as if she can't reach Collette fast enough. She wraps the woman in an embrace before fawning all over her. "Oh, Collette, don't do that to us again. You gave us such a fright." She's patting Collette now, touching and reviewing every inch of her body as if she might be hurt. As if she'd been to a war zone and not another neighborhood of New York.

She sets her eyes on me next. "What were you thinking? Keeping her out like that?"

"It wasn't her," Collette says. "I went on my own and Sarah took care of me."

But Pauline flaps her arms about like a concerned mother hen, murmuring in Collette's ear and whispering to her that everything is going to be fine. No wonder the woman feels like an invalid at home—they treat her like one.

Pauline whisks Collette away as if she were a wounded animal, talking about running a bath before returning her safely to her bed. They leave me stuck with Stephen.

"Follow me," he says, and I do so, reluctantly, draping the garment bag over my shoulder.

We return to the family room, where the lush blue rugs blanket the floor and he tells me to sit. It takes him a few seconds to gather his thoughts. He's looking not at me but down, the red of his face having faded and his cheeks returned to a normal color.

"How did she find you?" he asks.

I set the garment bag across my lap. "Somehow she figured out I was at the restaurant. I have no idea how she knew."

"Did she try going to your apartment first?"

"I don't think so. I was at work and she showed up wanting to order lunch." I look at him quizzically. "How would she know where I work?"

"Pauline said you told her about Hearth. She must have mentioned it to Collette. She must have assumed you were there." He pauses. "How did she get to you?"

"The driver."

He makes a face. "Not our driver. He knows better than that."

"Well someone drove her there because the same man drove us to some bar and then out shopping."

A panicked look crosses his face. "Did she drink?"

I shake my head.

He releases his breath, but it's not enough to calm him.

"She must have called for one of those driver services. Henry would have never let her leave this place. He's under strict orders." He thinks some more before asking, "How was she?"

I hesitate. How much should I tell him—that she was fine until a mood swing came from out of nowhere and she freaked in front of the entire restaurant, managing to get both Jonathan and me fired? That I'm not sure who all was there, I don't *think* anyone knew her, but I'm not positive none of the customers took her picture or recorded a video of her outburst?

I decide not to tell Stephen any of this. He's got enough to consider and has spent the last three to four hours worrying himself sick. The less he knows, the better.

"She was okay. She ate, we talked. She wanted to shop." I point to the dress. "I think she had an okay time."

"Did she talk about Patty?"

"Of course."

"Did she act like Patty was there?"

"No. She said Pauline stayed home with her while she was out with me." I leave out the part where she'd shoved his dead sister's hair into my hands. "She was fine, really."

Stephen holds my stare. He wants to believe me, he desperately *needs* to believe me. The alternative—public outburst, pictures, neighbors talking, another breakdown—would be too much to bear.

He steals a glance at his watch. "My father will be coming home soon and he already knows what happened." He frowns. "It could get ugly. You should probably go before he gets here."

But it's too late. From down the corridor comes the sound

of a door opening, then slamming. Keys thrown onto a side table. Heavy footsteps I assume belong to a man march steadily down the hall, shoes pounding against marble until at the far end the sound comes to a stop.

Another door opens, then slams with a boom.

The cries of a woman—Collette. Shrieks from Pauline as she rallies to her employer's defense.

A loud baritone voice. A deluge of words, anger and outrage and something about his wife disobeying him. Something falling to the floor.

That is how I first come to know Alex Bird.

CHAPTER TWENTY-ONE

It's just after 9:00 A.M. and I'm preparing to leave for West Seventy-eighth Street. "Are you sure you're going to be okay?" Jonathan asks, his brows pinched.

"I'll be fine," I tell him, zipping the sides of my ankle boots and trying my best to act nonchalant. That's all I seem to be doing in front of everyone these days. Making them think I'm calm. Lying.

"That woman," Jonathan says. "The lady you're working for. She seems . . ."

"High-strung?"

"You could say that."

"Overdramatic?"

"Crazy." He utters the word firmly.

"You're the one who told me to go after her, remember? You know we need the money."

"I know, and we do." He drops his back against the wall. "But I panicked, both of us kicked out on the street like that."

I don't answer, and instead rub my sweaty palms against my pants. I can still hear Collette crying.

"Sarah, she doesn't seem well. She flipped out in front of *everyone*."

"She was overwhelmed."

"That's a lot more than overwhelmed. It was a complete meltdown." He slows his words. "I'm not so sure you should be working for her."

I brush my hair as a distraction, pulling the bristles through to the ends and trying my best to keep my emotions in check. Tucking my bangs behind my ear, I glance at the time: only a few minutes left before I need to get going.

But Jonathan doesn't let up. "Does she always act that way?"

"No," I lie. *Sadly, she can get much worse.* "She was worried about me not coming back to nanny. She didn't like me waiting tables at Hearth."

"Well she took care of that problem, didn't she? And my job too." He folds his arms tight. "What am I going to do?"

I pause as a wave of guilt rolls over me. I've been so wrapped up in myself I haven't truly considered what this is doing to him too. We spent a couple of hours looking at job postings, other restaurant gigs, but there've been no callbacks yet. I'm hoping something comes through soon.

I move toward him for a hug. "I'm so sorry about that. I really am. I had no idea she'd do that."

But he rolls his head to one side to avoid my embrace and my arms fall short, dropping at my hips.

"Jonathan, I'm sorry," I say again, but he doesn't meet my eyes. "Any leads from Carl?" I ask.

Our friend Carl has worked for years in various restaurants around the city, including his most recent stint at an Italian wine bar in SoHo. I'm hoping he'll be able to hook Jonathan up.

"He's putting in a good word for me," he says, and finally meets my look. "What about you? Should we submit your name also?"

I grab my purse. "No, I'll be fine with the Birds. Remember the raise?"

"You mean the bribe?"

"Eighteen hundred a week, Jonathan . . ."

He knocks his back against the wall. "I just don't like it, the more I think about it. This woman. The rest of that family. I don't have a good feeling about them."

He turns away and the tightness spreads across my chest. I hate lying to him. He's looking out the window, his back facing me, and for the first time in our relationship, he's not angling for a goodbye kiss. He's letting me go without so much as a hug. No double squeeze of the hands to let me know he'll be thinking of me.

And with that, I leave the apartment and tread heavily down the steps, my heart sagging, guilt twisting in my gut.

I'm barely through my first week of this job and it's already causing our first argument.

Pauline and Freddie are in the kitchen when I arrive. They tell me Collette is sleeping in so I have time to relax, although I'm not sure relaxing is anything anyone in this apartment can do just yet.

The mood is somber, the air thick with what took place yesterday, the fight no one seems willing to acknowledge. Before Stephen had hastily shown me to the door, I'd heard glass breaking.

What happened after I left?

Poor Collette, punished for going out into the real world. Trapped in here, in her prison.

No wonder she's crazy.

I watch Pauline and Freddie for a while. No chatting over coffee today. Pauline pops the elastic band at her wrist as I slide in next to her stool. Her mouth is pulled tight.

It's not my fault, I want to tell them. I didn't mean for this to happen. *She's* the one who came looking for *me*, remember?

Although I'm sure they think there's more I could have done to stop it. I could have said no to that rooftop bar and insisted the driver return us swiftly to West Seventy-eighth Street.

Remember what happened last time? Stephen had said.

I can't stand the silence. I have so many questions for the rest of the staff. For starters, why didn't they warn me?

I try a different approach with Pauline.

"I'm sorry," I say. "I had no idea she would come find me." Her shoulders tighten.

She keeps her head down. As for Freddie, he's still acting as if I'm not there and pulls a pork loin from the freezer, swinging the door shut.

"Pauline, you know everything," I tell her. "You've been here the longest but I'm still learning." She faces me finally, her eyes blinking, registering her agreement. "I'm looking to you to help me do the best I can for Collette and for everyone else." I swallow my pride. "Make sure what happened yesterday doesn't happen again."

Pauline looks me over before crossing her arms.

I decide to lay it on thick.

"It's a beautiful home," I say. "You must work very hard to keep it this way." No response so I add, "The kitchen is lovely too. Everything so spic-and-span. You must be at it constantly."

Another cool gaze from Pauline before she eventually cracks a smile. "It takes a lot of work. A place this big requires continuous care."

"I can tell."

I glance again around the kitchen, and it is indeed spotless, just like every room.

"What was Collette like?" I ask, and her chin jerks up. "Before Patty died? Did she used to be okay?"

"She was more than okay," Pauline answers. But then she pauses, as if reconsidering her tone. The redness in her cheeks begins to fade. "She was—still is—one of the most beautiful people I've ever known. She's lovely."

I nod, remembering the pure joy in Collette's face when she bought me that gown. The dazzle in her eyes as she picked out dresses for Patty too. She clearly thrives on being able to do nice things for others. "She is lovely. I bet she was a great mother too."

"Absolutely," Pauline says, and I feel the knot in my stomach releasing, relieved to hear her finally talking. "She was completely dedicated to that child. You would have never known a more devoted mother. Patty was all that mattered to her."

She takes another long look at my face. "Look," she says. "What happened yesterday—Collette is going to try to leave again."

"I know."

"She'll promise you things, bribe you, manipulate you. She'll find a way to make it happen."

"But what if I'm with her every step?" I offer. "I can make sure she—"

"What?" One of her eyebrows raises. "Behaves?"

"Yes," I say, thinking it over. "Yes, that's exactly right."

"How did that work out yesterday?"

I take her point and change the subject. "So you were here when Patty was born, right?"

She nods. "I was only twenty-eight when I started working for the Birds." She reaches to fill her mug of coffee, and in a moment of solidarity pours one for me too. "In the beginning, they were all wonderful. So much fun and full of energy. Collette was only a few years younger than me but a real beauty." She touches her short, drab hair. "Quite the hostess too. Lots of evening parties and gatherings. But that all stopped when she had Patty. Caring for a baby caused her to slow down and settle into family life and she stopped partying so much. Motherhood suited her. She was an adoring wife to Alex and developed a close bond with Stephen. An even closer bond with her own child, of course." She smiles, the memories stirring her emotions. "I've never seen her so happy as she was back then."

She looks away. "Stephen didn't always have the best relationship with his father." She hesitates at first, wondering how much to share with me. She blinks steadily before proceeding. "Alex can be somewhat of a workaholic, you see. Very formal, not the friendliest of men when you first meet him. But I suppose that's how he's gotten as far as he has with his career.

"His first wife left him after only a few years and left Stephen behind—he was only a kid. Alex didn't have the time to care for him, but truth be told, he didn't make the time. He didn't know how to be a dad or pay attention to his son, and Stephen languished . . ." She shakes her head. "But that all changed when Alex married Collette. She brought sunshine back into this house and that baby girl was an extra bonus. Soon Alex was spending more time with the family, including his son. He was cutting down on his travel and choosing to be home, which was a real first. It was as if, with Patty's birth, he also remembered he had a nine-year-old son. And Stephen began to flourish under the attention. It was wonderful to see."

Her eyes cloud over and she wraps her hands tight around her mug.

"But then Patty got sick. She had always been small and a little bit frail, a premature baby. But at age three, her immune system took a real dive and she had to spend her last few months in bed. Collette was racked with fear and all the anxiety that comes with caring for a sick child." Pauline draws a heavy sigh. "She returned to drinking, and it incensed Alex, as you can imagine. Her drinking all the time prevented her from taking care of Patty properly, and it only got worse when the doctors said there was nothing more they could do." Pauline wipes the tears on her cheeks. "That beautiful baby girl. It was awful. The doctor said no parent should ever see their child that way. They refused to let anyone into the room, and that made Collette go crazy." She hiccups a sob. "I never got to say goodbye either."

"Holy shit," I breathe, and Pauline's eyes flinch, making me cover my mouth. "I'm sorry."

"I know Stephen told you some of this already, but not everything. I apologize for the extra details."

"No, it's okay," I assure her. "I want to know everything."

She takes a deep breath. "I'm sure Stephen told you the funeral was closed casket. We weren't allowed to see Patty one last time, and I think that's what really put Collette over the edge. She became convinced that everyone was lying, especially the doctor, and that Patty wasn't dead. She accused us of hiding her. And then there was that horrible incident when one of the doctors accused Collette of harming her own daughter, implying she caused the girl to die."

She takes another sip of her coffee. "The family fired that man immediately. It was an insane idea. Everyone knew Collette would never harm her own child. Alex felt it necessary to have the funeral as soon as possible and it was too fast for Collette, in my opinion. It was too much for her to process in such a short period of time, and I was worried about how she'd react to that too. Her whole world came crashing down, and she was denied the closure of seeing her little girl one last time. She began to drink heavily, and I mean heavily." She looks me in the eye. "Have you heard of someone drinking themselves to insanity?"

I nod. If this is what happened to Collette, if she really did drink herself to insanity, that would explain so many things.

"Well that's what happened to Collette. She drank herself into a state we've never been able to repair. No number of doctors or amount of counseling could do the trick, and everyone panicked. The first nanny—Ms. Fontaine, the one who was with us when Patty came home from the hospital—

left. She'd grown so attached to the girl, and when Patty died, she was heartbroken, just like the rest of us. But she left with no goodbyes, only a note, packed her bags in the middle of the night. Collette felt abandoned all over again, and she went into a tailspin, spending hours in the girl's playroom wishing that both her daughter and the nanny were by her side. Imagining the girl was still with her." Pauline drops her eyes to her lap. "The second nanny helped for a bit." But then she backtracks. "Well, she helped her, but also dragged her into a deeper mess."

One hand drops to her wrist. Pauline tugs once again at the elastic band there, making it snap. Catching my gaze, she quickly lays her hand flat.

"What happened?" I ask.

"Therese thought it would be good for Collette to talk about Patty out loud."

Therese . . . I remember the name. "The second nanny."

"Yes," Pauline says. "She lasted fifteen years."

My breath catches. *"Fifteen years?"*

"She stayed with us a long time." Pauline's mouth presses together. "But to Collette, time makes no sense. Patty remains a three-year-old while Therese's fifteen years seemed like only a short while."

I wait for her to continue, my mind struggling to understand how this nanny lasted as long as she did.

"Collette was in and out of hospitals for years and nothing worked," Pauline continues. "And as you've already been told, suicide attempts came next, many of them. Alex hired Therese as a personal aide, someone who could monitor Collette while also keeping her company. Someone she could talk to. Slowly but surely, Collette began to improve, and with each day, she got stronger and was capable of having conversations again."

Pauline's face shines with admiration at this point. "Therese did wonders for that woman, I'll admit that. She coaxed her through some of her most difficult days and got her up and able to participate in outings once again. But soon, something changed. Collette insisted Therese was the nanny. I don't know where she got that idea from, but she insisted Therese was there to care for Patty and not her. She claimed she could see Patty everywhere. The little girl was in the apartment with us. And strangely, Therese went along with these thoughts, almost encouraged her like it was some form of therapy. They pretended Patty was right there with them. They held her hand. They laid out her dresses, took her to the park, spent hours in the playroom. I was never comfortable with it, but it worked.

"Collette got better," Pauline continues. "She was delusional, yes, but at least she was back in the land of the living. What Therese was able to do was nothing short of a miracle and Collette stopped drinking. They dusted Patty's playroom furniture, folded her bedspread. They brought the girl cookies and pretended to show her how to paint. But then it went overboard. Collette would stay up until three or four in the morning talking to her daughter. She'd go shopping and bring home bags filled with new dolls when there was no one to play with them. I admit, it got creepy. Therese said at least it was keeping the woman alive; she was finally going out in public and seemed happy again. No more suicide attempts. That's what we had hired her for, wasn't it? But Collette was believing it more and more and getting extreme. It was like she could reach out and touch Patty—as if she could see her, just as clear as she was seeing me and Therese. She'd spend hours holding a pretend Patty in her arms."

Pauline's eyes flash angrily now. "That should have been the first sign the plan was backfiring. But despite my protests, Therese encouraged Collette to speak to her daughter. Tell her the many ways she loved her, her favorite things about the little girl. Her wishes for Patty when she grew up. And it's like Collette got stuck. Frozen in denial."

Pauline shrugs, but the shrug is so heavy, her shoulders sag. "Something changed with Therese too. Maybe she started falling for it also, spending so much time pretending a woman's daughter was still alive."

I look at Pauline and remember how she'd stood transfixed in the bathroom, staring at the tub. She'd almost appeared ready to see Patty pop out from beneath those bubbles.

I suppose it could happen to anyone—if you let it. Spend enough time around someone saying certain things, believing certain things, and you could lose your grip on reality.

"But the worst part," Pauline says, straightening her back, "was when Therese came up with the idea of throwing Patty a birthday party. She must have thought it would be a nice gesture, seeing as Patty didn't make it to her fourth year. But Collette clung to the idea like a maniac. She loved it, thinking it was exactly what Patty needed, and unfortunately, it's something she has done ever since."

She'll be turning four this July . . .

She's starting kindergarten . . .

The continuous loop. The never-ending story.

The child who is always about to turn four.

The birthday party Patty missed.

My heart lurches—my contract with the Bird family will cover July. Am I going to have to plan a party for a dead girl?

CHAPTER TWENTY-TWO

A buzz from the wall in the kitchen. I whip my head around—it's coming from an intercom system.

Pauline looks at me. "That will be Collette. She's up and waiting for us in the breakfast room."

I slide from the stool, readying myself to see her. Will her eyes be puffy from crying?

But just as before, Pauline says, "Finish your coffee." And she drinks hers down, motioning for me to do the same. It's an odd habit, but I comply anyway—anything to keep this woman on my good side. I don't want to appear wasteful, but it's odd, the way she watches me take every gulp. She doesn't move until I finish.

We find Collette sitting at the same glass breakfast table. Pauline places the grapefruit halves before her with a spoon and sprinkle of sugar.

Every day, repeating itself.

"Please sit," Collette says to me.

I watch her carefully. If she's at all upset about how yesterday ended, about much trouble she'd gotten into last night with her husband or if she's still dopey from whatever medication they gave to sedate her, she doesn't show it. She's all smiles. She's hit the reset button.

And she's dressed in a gray cardigan and slacks. No formal getup like what she wore yesterday. Her hair is pulled into a ponytail as well, with minimal makeup; she's forgone her usual ornate jewelry and perfume. We look like two friends sitting together for breakfast.

"I'm so glad you're here," she says, but then lowers her voice. "I got scolded for being out."

Pauline shoots me a warning look before stepping out of the room.

"We shouldn't do that again," I tell Collette.

She drops her chin and whispers, "They can't tell me what to do. I am so sick of being in this apartment all the time. Plus, it's not good for Patty either. She can't stay indoors all the time."

"But, Collette—"

"Don't worry. It's not like I plan on going out today. No," she says, scooping a section of grapefruit and putting it in her mouth. "We'll hunker down since I'm sure"—and she cuts her eyes left and right—"we're on lockdown. Stephen was so upset with me. And Alex . . ." She doesn't finish her sentence.

I watch her pick at the fruit.

"You being here," Collette says, "with me and Patty is a wonderful way to spend the day." An eerie, radiant smile returns to her face and she clasps her hands. "It'll be perfect." She rises from the table. "Patty's in her bedroom. Let's go see her since you haven't seen the castle bed yet." Her eyes glitter with excitement as she grabs hold of my arm. "Patty can't wait to show you."

We return to the hall with the playroom, and next to that door is another, painted with pink and white flowers and pink trim. Collette places her hand on the doorknob and gives a gentle knock. "Patty?" she calls. "It's Mommy." She smiles. "I've brought you the new nanny . . ."

The door swings open—and for a split second my heart freezes with terror, thinking we'll find a small child standing there, rumpled nightgown hanging past her knees, a sleepy look in her eyes from having just woken up—

Of course, there is no girl. The room is empty.

But if I was impressed with the playroom and its glorious dollhouse, it's nothing compared to this space. Patty's bedroom is spectacular.

The walls, just like next door, are painted in her favorite colors, blush and bashful. Pink lace curtains adorn a bay window with a single seat cushion covered in pink stripes. At the center of the room sits the main attraction: an oversize canopy bed designed like a castle. It's amazing, with its white wooden columns and turrets capped in white. And stairs—*actual stairs*—leading to the girl's mattress, which must be at least five feet off the floor. Pink bedsheets and a white comforter. The bed is surrounded by a railing: one part for safety, I'm sure, to keep Patty from falling, and the other part for decoration, similar to a castle's fortress wall.

Pink fabric matches the curtains and drapes from all four posts of the bed with large sash ribbons tied at each corner. Above the bed, a chandelier—the child went to sleep with her own honest-to-God chandelier sparkling above her. What magical dreams she must have had sleeping beneath her own crystal light piece.

I feel as if I've stepped into my own dream, the bedroom from a childhood that, until now, I didn't know I was missing.

What had Patty's early childhood been like? Did she know how lucky she was? Did she know that not every child has a room like this? Bedtime must have been a dream—her whole life must have been a dream. While I lay awake trying to remember what my parents looked like or spent years desperately clinging to the sound of my mother's voice, which faded more with every passing birthday, Patty slept like a princess. But she couldn't have known—she was too little. It's not her fault she was privileged and born lucky. She was a Bird.

Collette stands next to the bed, the castle turrets towering above her.

"Patty," she says, turning to face me. "Meet your new nanny."

And I squirm. I'm not sure where I should look—down? Next to Collette? In front of Collette? I follow her eyes to where she must think she sees the little girl.

"Hi," I say faintly.

Collette breaks into a smile. "So many toys," she says, and picks up a doll propped on a pillow. "Patty, would you like to show Sarah what you have?"

I don't move from my spot by the door, but I see what she's holding up. An American Girl doll that I recognize immediately.

As a girl, I had begged Aunt Clara for one, had written a dozen letters to Santa but never received the gift. The doll I coveted, the Samantha Parkington, was an orphan just like me, except raised by her grandmother. I remember asking my aunt how Santa could have messed this up. Why didn't he bring me a doll like he did the rest of the girls in my class? But Aunt Clara reminded me there were other things to be

happy for. I tried so hard to be happy when I opened paja-
mas instead.

I watch Collette brushing the American Girl doll's hair
with her fingers. She's whispering something and talking to
Patty, asking about the doll. She moves in front of a stack of
toys next, a Polly Pocket and a set of My Little Ponies. She
opens the door to an Easy-Bake oven, peeks inside.

Besides the castle bed, which would make a child happy
no matter which generation she's part of, the rest of the toys
are outdated. This room is a time capsule. Little Mermaid
Ariel. Beanie Babies. A Little Tikes vanity table. A set of glitter magic wand pens scattered on the desk. A handful of
Troll dolls, their neon-colored hair spiked high above their
heads, swinging in a banana hammock. I used to have the
same Troll dolls. I used to covet my friends' Beanie Baby collections too.

All around us are remnants of the time when Patty was
growing up. She had her own Furby, a Bop It, and the once-
popular Barney doll, everyone's favorite purple dinosaur.
The same stuff I had wanted to play with and couldn't have,
although I do remember Aunt Clara bringing home a couple
of Barney books from a consignment store.

Next to the older toys is evidence of Collette's shopping
splurges over the years: the newest American Girl dolls, those
Bratz dolls that became so popular, and already assembled
Lego sets.

But the vintage toys remain supreme.

Collette motions beside her. "Patty," she says. "Why don't
you show Sarah your new Game Boy?" She points at the device.

I stop dead in my tracks, unsure what I'm supposed to do. How does this work? The Game Boy isn't going to magically teleport its way to me, I know that much. Is Collette going to reach for it instead or am I expected to pick it up first?

Collette doesn't move.

I close the gap between myself and the dresser until I'm lifting the device. Collette smiles.

"She's always trying to figure that thing out, but it's too complicated for her, I'm afraid." She motions at an empty space next to her as if meaning to shush her child. "Now, now, Patty, you're so young. Not many three-year-olds have videogames, let alone know how to play them."

Collette spins around. "Do you like it?" she asks, gesturing to the rest of the room, and it takes a second before I realize she's talking to me and not Patty. I set down the Game Boy as she moves on. "We spend so much time in here, don't we, Patty? Tell Sarah."

She caresses the bed comforter, and I have a feeling Collette sleeps in here quite often. An ache in my heart consumes me, imagining her telling everyone Patty wants her to stay, that she wants another bedtime story, and falling asleep next to what she thinks is her daughter, but is only a pillow.

"It took a team of workers to assemble this thing," she says, admiring the bed. "It's one of a kind, custom made. Not another one like it in the world. Alex made sure of that."

"It's beautiful. She's so lucky."

"Yes," she says, a shine returning to her eyes. "So lucky . . ."

———

Collette is asking for hot chocolate. It's Patty who wants it, she adds with a wink.

"You haven't had breakfast yet, Patty Cakes, and you already want a treat."

But what Patty wants, Patty gets, and for the first time, I see Freddie in action.

He's moving about the kitchen and commencing what appears to be lunch prep, the pork loin I saw him pulling from the freezer now thawing in a pan.

"Patty just showed Sarah her bedroom," Collette announces to them.

Only Pauline nods her acknowledgment.

Collette continues, "Now she's asking for a cup of hot chocolate. Oh, Freddie," she says. "Will you make her some?"

The man doesn't make eye contact, but says, "Yes, no problem."

He pulls a small mug from a cabinet, a mug that's been hand painted with a rainbow, the name "Patty" drawn across the design in puffy letters.

"Patty drinks everything from that mug," Collette says. "Doesn't she, Freddie? Juice, milk, water."

He doesn't answer, only heats up some milk in a pot. From another cabinet, he pulls a container filled with chocolate shavings.

"Would you like one too?" Collette asks, and I shake my head no.

Within minutes, the hot chocolate is ready, and Freddie is taking great care in carrying the rainbow mug on a glass tray toward the girl's mother. Two large marshmallows rest on the surface with rich chocolate underneath. I eye the mug anxiously.

What are we supposed to do now? Wait for Patty to drink it? Make pleasant conversation while pretending she's sitting on the kitchen stool enjoying her hot chocolate?

Collette positions the mug on the counter. She looks to the unoccupied space beside her and says, "Now be sure to blow on it, Patty. It will be too hot." She lowers her face. "Just like this." And she's blowing across the surface, letting out small puffs of air.

I look away.

Collette touches the mug. Is *she* going to drink it?

But she doesn't. Freddie turns his back and proceeds to wash the milk pot at the sink.

I wait for any cues, hints as to what I'm supposed to do next. Do I sit or stand? Wait for Collette to say what we'll do next, or will she carry on a conversation with her daughter? Or will she make conversation with us instead while the mug of hot chocolate remains on the counter?

As the minutes pass, I watch it growing cold.

Collette removes her slippers and drops them to the floor, tucking her bare feet under her on the stool. Finally, she asks, "What do you think of the dress?"

I jump to attention. "I love it. It's gorgeous."

I made a place for it in a corner of the apartment as soon as I returned home last night. The dress and its garment bag were heavy as I carted it through the subway station and then along East Ninth Street, but I'd made it. The closet was far too cramped to risk shoving a designer gown among the rest of our clothes, so I'd hung it from a spare hook on the wall. Jonathan had only raised his eyebrows at me when he spotted the Bergdorf Goodman label on the bag.

"Alex is hosting a small party tomorrow night," Collette

says. "We haven't had people here in ages, certainly not the kinds of dinner parties we used to throw back in the day. Don't you remember, Pauline?" She doesn't wait for the woman to answer. "After yesterday, Alex threatened to cancel the party. He said he didn't think I could handle it, whatever that means." She scoffs.

"I'd like you to join us," Collette says. Out of the corner of my eye, Pauline's mouth opens in protest. "You can be our guest. A chance to wear your new gown—I mean, where else are you going to go dressed like that? You can stay by my side and Alex won't mind. It will be so fun to have you."

I'm torn. Yes, I'd love the opportunity to wear the dress and already I'm imagining the kinds of gowns the other guests will be wearing, a Valentino or an Elie Saab, Collette's gown too—I wonder what fabulous garment she'll be wearing—and I would love to see this place all decked out for a party, but tomorrow is Saturday and Stephen never said anything about me working on weekends. Furthermore, what will the guests think? Who will they think I am? There's no possible way Collette can tell them I'm the nanny.

Alex and Stephen won't go for it. But Collette seems to think this is the grandest of plans. In her mind, it's a done deal.

"Tomorrow night," she says, clutching my hands. "Oh, please say you'll come. You can arrive in your dress just in time for the party." Her voice ramps up in speed. "Or better yet, come early. We'll get ready together. I'll fix your hair. We can do our makeup and you can help me pick out my dress." She's on a roll now, her eyes shimmering.

I hesitate. What will her husband say? Have other nannies attended private events?

I look to Pauline for guidance, for the woman to interject and wave off this crazy proposal. We can't have Collette getting carried away if the answer is going to be no. But Pauline doesn't say a word, and after a beat, she gives me the faintest of nods.

Collette sees the blink in my eyes. "So is that a yes?"

"I don't know. I think so . . . ?"

Collette slips off the stool to hug me. She wraps her arms around my neck and is giggling, kissing me on the cheek.

"This makes me so happy," she says, clutching my hands once again and stroking them with her perfectly manicured fingernails. "I knew it." The moment is so intimate, with our faces only inches apart. "When we met, I knew there was something special about you. I could feel it in my bones. I knew we were going to get along, that we had a connection. A chance for us to become good friends."

And I'm once again struck by her use of the word *friends*. She sees me as so much more than the nanny. The two of us worlds apart, and yet she doesn't see it that way. Lunches and tea parties, and under different circumstances, the two of us going to barre class or on additional shopping excursions. And not just to Bergdorf Goodman. We could stroll arm in arm through the exclusive shops of SoHo.

But then I glance again at the hot chocolate, where the marshmallows are now melting and collapsing toward the bottom.

Collette smiles as if she sees her daughter, Patty, taking another sip.

CHAPTER TWENTY-THREE

To my surprise, Stephen doesn't call and tell me not to come in the next day. Instead, he sends a text with two simple lines: *Wear the dress she bought. We're telling everyone you're the niece.*

So that's how this will play out.

But I'm too distracted to give it any more thought because I'm buzzing with excitement at the chance to wear a six-thousand-dollar gown to a fancy party on West Seventy-eighth Street.

Even Jonathan registers the thrill on my face. We're on better ground today after having talked things over late last night, especially when, to make it up to him, I ran out this morning and bought bagels from our favorite shop.

Extra cheese, I ordered at the counter, knowing how much Jonathan loves when the cheese melts against the bread. As an extra treat, a blueberry muffin that he unwraps, a smile returning to his face.

"I know you're a strong person," he says as I fluff out my dress. "You've got this. But it's my job to worry over you, okay?"

I smooth the skirt of my gown one more time before moving closer to him. "I know. And I'm sorry about you losing Hearth—"

He waves his hand. "Paul's an ass. I should have left a long time ago." He sets down his bagel. "Besides, I got another gig."

My heart leaps.

"I picked up a catering event tonight. I'm hoping they'll call me back many more times too."

"That's wonderful, Jonathan."

He takes both my hands and gives them the familiar double squeeze, and my chest quiets. We're going to be okay.

As if reading my mind, he says, "It's all going to work out for us both, you'll see."

That afternoon, I call for a cab, Collette having slipped me the cash to pay for a taxi since she doesn't want me dragging the gown back through the subway.

The street outside the Birds' apartment is abuzz when I arrive—two catering vans and a florist, with Malcolm pointing this way and that and asking someone on the street to move their car so the caterer can park. He's directing another group to the service elevator at the back of the building. He's so busy he barely tips his head in my direction as I push through the lobby door.

Upstairs, the commotion is building. Pauline greets me, but she's distracted, saying something about Collette being in a tizzy. Another snap of her elastic band.

In the dining room, the event planner is setting out plates. A line of champagne flutes crosses the table already laid out with black tablecloths and tall white candles placed in glass holders. In the kitchen, Freddie is barking orders at the catering staff. Delicious smells of sweet potato and a butternut squash purée waft from the oven. Another heavenly smell, and I'm thinking it's marinated crab claws cooking in a pot. In the hallway, a woman passes by with a vase filled with peonies and white roses.

I stare in wonder. The Birds must be dropping a small fortune on this party.

But nothing I see prepares me for what's waiting in the bedroom. And no wonder Pauline makes a point of closing the door behind us and locking it as soon as we enter.

Bedsheets are pulled to the floor. Collette has spilled something on the carpet: beige powder, liquid makeup, a rubbed-in stain. Dresses worth tens of thousands of dollars have been thrown to the floor in a disarray of colors and fabrics. One of the gowns looks like it's been stepped on repeatedly, a strand of beads pulled off and scattered every which way.

And in the bathroom, sitting before an immense vanity, is Collette, wearing a silk floral robe. A woman is tending her hair, teasing at the roots and systematically spraying it with something meant to cover any signs of gray—and presto. Collette is returning to her blond and vibrant self again.

"Sarah," Collette says enthusiastically as soon as she sees me. "What do you think, hair up or down?" If she threw a fit earlier, the presence of the hairdresser seems to be calming her. She breaks free from the stylist and brushes strands from her eyes. "Pauline says down, but Bridget says up."

My eyes slide to the prescription bottle next to the sink, the lid open.

"What do you think?" she asks again.

"Down," I say, but only to side with Pauline.

Collette chews her lower lip carefully, her blue eyes widening. "Down," she announces, tilting her chin at me. "You're right, Sarah. It's time I try something different."

I spot something far more dangerous than the Xanax on the counter: a bottle of champagne with several glasses filled. Has she been drinking? Why hasn't Pauline stopped her? I can't tell if any of the glasses have been touched. They don't appear to have lipstick stains around the rims—yet.

Bridget finishes teasing her hair and is smoothing it gently with a round brush. Generous spritzes of hairspray follow, with touch-ups using her fingers.

"How's Patty?" the stylist asks.

I try not to flinch.

Pauline's shoulders square up, but Collette can only smile at how kind it is of Bridget to think of her daughter.

"She's doing well," Collette answers. "We're already making plans for her next birthday."

"Fun!" the hairdresser exclaims and adds more hairspray. "You're always going on about Patty. I was hoping I'd get to see her today."

"I know, sorry about that. We sent her to a friend's."

"I've been doing your hair for how long—three or four years?—and still haven't met your daughter." Bridget shakes her head. "How old is she now?" But Collette doesn't answer. "You really should bring her to the salon and let me do her hair. Or I could come here and let her play with my makeup."

Collette nods. "She'd love that."

"So," Bridget continues. "What are you planning for her birthday?"

This gets a huge smile from Collette. "I'm thinking of having a party here. A circus theme or maybe a toy train. A big birthday cake."

Bridget pauses with her comb. "A toy train? Like one the kids can ride or just for decoration?"

"I was thinking of renting one, the kind that's on tracks. They can ride in the train cars as it plays music."

Bridget laughs. "That would be wild. I think all I had for my birthday when I was a kid was a sleepover and pizza." She continues working on Collette's hair. "Where would you put it? You'd have to clear out a bunch of furniture."

"The dining room."

"Wild," Bridget says, and she stands back, assessing Collette's hair before applying a few more doses of hairspray. "You know," she says, "I heard about this carousel you can rent if you want. It comes with lights and carnival music and kids can ride on the bears and horses."

Collette's eyes light up. "How many children does it seat?"

"I think four. But I'm sure you could shop around and see what else is out there."

Collette's face brightens with the possibility. "I want this," she says decisively. "Where can I find it?"

Bridget sets down her brush. "One of my clients told me. I'll ask her about it and get back to you."

"Yes, that sounds wonderful. A carousel . . ." A dreamlike expression drifts into Collette's eyes. "Patty would love it. What a marvelous idea for a party."

"She'd be the most popular girl on the block."

"Oh, she already is."

The woman uses her hands to bounce the edges of Collette's hair into perfection. "I think you're ready."

Collette stares at her reflection for a long, steady moment.

"Bridget," she says, to emphasize how important this is, "when you find out more about that carousel, please let me know. I may just buy one and keep it for Patty."

CHAPTER TWENTY-FOUR

Holy shit, I breathe an hour later. *I'm about to go to my first party in an Oscar de la Renta gown. Somebody pinch me.*

"Ready?" Collette asks.

Pauline and I had convinced Collette that the floor-length royal blue gown with feathers on one shoulder—a purchase from a trip to Paris that she had yet to wear, judging by the tags still hanging on it—was the perfect dress for the evening. She'd paired it with Giuseppe Zanotti rose-gold three-inch stiletto sandals with the most delicate crystal-embellished appliqué wings. I was treated to a hairdo of my own from Bridget, a bun to complement the ballerina tulle of my skirt, and my pick of makeup from what surely equaled thousands of dollars in cosmetics from Collette's stash.

She turns to me, her eyes filled with Xanax and happiness, and tells me I look gorgeous. And I *do* feel gorgeous. Looking in the mirror, I almost don't recognize myself and blink away a tear.

Never once did I think while flipping through fashion magazines or after moving to New York, the months when my sketchbook fell to the wayside, my inspiration dimming with no money to buy anything and no time off from the restaurant, that I'd have a chance to go to an event like this.

To stand proudly in a gown that I would have only gawked at online. To have someone sweep my hair into a bun and tell me I'm pretty.

If only Aunt Clara could see me now.

The music guides us to the dining hall, where we find guests mingling with drinks. A trio of violinists performs in the corner.

A woman in a black strapless number immediately approaches Collette. They exchange air-kisses, their eyes roaming up and down each other as the woman talks loudly to Collette, exclaiming repeatedly how well she looks. "It's been so long," she says again and again.

Collette is all smiles, but I can see she's forcing her enjoyment. Something in her face tells me this is a woman she doesn't care for.

"And who is this lovely lady?" The woman faces me. She is all orange-red lipstick and emerald jewelry.

I feel instantly exposed. How am I supposed to respond again?

"My niece," Collette says. "Visiting from Virginia Beach."

Oh good. I breathe a sigh of relief.

"She's staying with us for a little while," Collette tells the woman robotically.

"Oh, how wonderful," the woman remarks, and I stand awkwardly.

The woman swings her attention back to Collette. "How on earth have you been? It's been such a long time. You've been hiding away. We missed seeing you at Friday's lunch." She prattles on.

"Lots of activities," Collette tells her. A nod to me. "And spending time with my niece."

The woman smiles. "Family is oh so important." Her voice drips with charm.

"It is."

The woman looks across the room. "And Stephen is here too, I see."

"Oh, yes. He's always with us. Alex wouldn't have it any other way. Me either."

"He's grown into such a wonderful young man." The woman faces me again and assesses my gown, her smile and nod meaning she approves. "You have such a beautiful family. So good to have young people around, don't you think?"

"Yes, it's wonderful."

On cue, Stephen appears and gently pulls at Collette's elbow, asking if we'd like a drink. He leads us away while nodding at me.

"You look beautiful," he says. He plucks two glasses of champagne from a server holding a tray and places one in my hand as he keeps one for himself, Collette's hands remaining empty.

"You'll need to meet the Batemans," Stephen tells her. "The whole reason my father is hosting this little gathering."

Like Collette, I glance around the room at the large catering spread, the violinists, and sprays of blooms set about in glass vases. There's nothing "little" about this gathering.

He nudges Collette gently in the direction of a man and woman who look to be in their late sixties and who are walking toward someone else—a tall gentleman wearing a black tuxedo with reddish brown hair and only a flash of silver.

He is jaw-droppingly handsome and possesses the most

elegant disposition. He turns, motioning to Collette to join him, and I can only ascertain that this is, at long last, the elusive Mr. Bird. Tonight, he's beaming. Seeing him like this, it's hard to imagine he's the same man I heard yelling furious threats at his wife.

Collette leaves me without pause. With every step, she propels herself across the room toward him like a magnet, nothing but beautiful smiles for her glowing husband. Their explosive argument from the other night forgotten.

I stand and watch with Stephen.

He clears his throat. "Welcome to the family," he says, smiling at his own joke. "If you're their niece, that makes you my cousin, right?"

I give him a strange look. He'd been so outraged before and now he's teasing me?

"Did you guys call the other nannies nieces too?"

"Never." He leans in. "This is a first."

I make a confession. "I'm sorry for calling in sick. I should have told you I was working at the restaurant instead."

"Well, Collette told me what happened. Seems she got you and your boyfriend both fired." He casts me a sympathetic look. "Sorry about that. But she also said she upped your pay so . . ." He rises on his toes before rocking back on his heels again. "Hopefully that means you're staying."

"Yes," I tell him.

"How is everything going? I hope you're handling everything all right?"

I think again about the hot chocolate turning cold. The multiple games of Chutes and Ladders where Collette pretended Patty was the champion every single time.

"It's been okay," I tell him. "We get along well."

"So I see." He waves his glass at the room. "Inviting you here tonight, buying that dress—like I said, it's certainly a first."

We sip the rest of our champagne in silence, watching his father and stepmother. Alex's hand is resting at the small of Collette's back. It's a loving touch, not possessive. He looks like a man who very much wants for this evening to go off without a hitch, for everyone to see his beautiful wife and be assured that everything in their world is perfect.

Alex says something to the other couple and they share a laugh, Collette too. Their glasses tinkle as they raise them in a toast.

Stephen interrupts my thoughts. "Take it one step at a time," he advises, "and watch her carefully. As you've witnessed, her moods can swing at the drop of a hat." He steps away and gives me an awkward wink. "See you around, *cousin.*"

I'm left trying not to fiddle with my dress. But with no one to talk to, no clue as to what I should do, or who most of the people here are, I back away to a table, deciding I should help myself to the hors d'oeuvres, charcuterie platters with figs and warmed Brie, and pots of what looks like raspberry jam mixed with tiny slivers of peppers.

From my corner, I eat slowly, taking small bites and trying to blend in at the fanciest party I've ever attended. But the truth is, I'm nervous, I'm lonely, and I'm starving. I knew I should have eaten before I left the apartment, but I'd been too excited.

I'm biting into a crostini when I sense someone coming up by my side, someone in a crisp black tuxedo. And it's not Stephen.

"So . . ." he says slowly. "You're my niece."

I nearly drop the crostini.

I look up, desperately wishing I had a napkin to wipe my fingers, but there isn't one handy so I rub them together instead, knowing I have no choice but to lock eyes with the intense stare of Alex Bird.

"It's Sarah, isn't it?" he asks.

I swallow and nod. He is even more handsome close-up.

"How are you, Sarah?" It's odd, the way he keeps repeating my name.

"I'm okay," I reply meekly.

He chuckles. "Alex Bird," he says, as if for clarification. "And as you can expect, we're happy to have you. Collette is . . . well . . ." He gazes in the direction of his wife. "She's happier than I've seen her in a long time. It can only be because of you."

"I'm not sure I've done anything . . ."

"Of course you have."

My eyes dart away, an immediate blush warming my cheeks.

"Now the other evening," Mr. Bird says, and his voice quiets. "That was unfortunate." I shift uncomfortably in my heels. "We were scared to death wondering where she was. I only wish she'd told someone and then we could have known she was okay." He lingers on the word *okay*, and I wince, not knowing how to explain the situation.

"I'm sorry it's taken so long for us to meet," he continues. "I meant to visit sooner but Stephen has been taking care of everything, as he always does. He's so good about managing things for me."

"Yes, he is," I admit.

"And how are you?" Just like his son, he asks, "How are you coping with all this?"

"I'm learning." It's about as honest an answer as I can give.

He steps closer and looks deep into my eyes. I can scarcely breathe, he is standing so close. "I know Stephen has explained how delicate our situation is."

"Stephen has told me everything," I assure him. "You don't need to worry about me."

But Mr. Bird holds my look for several more seconds, as if trying to figure out if he can trust me, if I've truly grasped the gravity of their family secret. After the last few days, how could I not?

"I hope that's the case. Collette can be hard to handle and it's difficult for people to understand. They don't know what it's like to lose a child—it's horrific." He looks again to Collette, my eyes following. "This is all I can do to keep her happy." Fortunately, her back is turned and she doesn't see us speaking. A trio of women keep her engaged in conversation. "I need you to understand that I will do everything in my power to protect this family." His mouth turns into a hard line. "And I do mean everything."

"Of course," I say, but find my voice is shaking. "I promise you have nothing to worry about."

"Promise . . ." he says, repeating what I've said, and a smile appears on his lips as if mocking me. He looks away again.

CHAPTER TWENTY-FIVE

═══

Collette makes it through most of the party on her best behavior, but what she doesn't do is eat. And to make it worse, in the last twenty minutes, she's been sneaking glasses of champagne.

At first, I'm not sure what I'm seeing is right. But there she is, taking a champagne glass with her to the bathroom and then knocking back another one in the hall. She claims she needs to disappear to her bedroom for some alone time too, but I'm almost positive she's taking another pill.

I announce this to Pauline and she quickly tells me to handle it since Freddie is calling for her in the kitchen. I try easing the champagne glass out of Collette's hand, but she snatches it back from me.

Another wobbly smile. "I'm fine, thank you," she says curtly.

Soon, Stephen is catching my eye, his jaw clenching. It's time to wrap up the party, he knows it, and he works with his dad to escort the last remaining guests to the elevator.

They're just in time, because the pitch of Collette's voice rises steeply, her speech beginning to slur. She's stumbled upon another serving tray filled with champagne flutes and gulps them down, one by one. Stephen throws me a look as if to say, *Get ahold of her,* as I scramble to her side.

Collette teeters in the center of the room. All the guests are gone. The violinists are packing up their cases too, and Stephen hands each of them a wad of cash as they move to the door. Without the music, all that's left is the clinking of plates and glasses as they are stacked and whisked away. More clanking is heard in the kitchen; Freddie is telling someone to toss out the extra food. Collette's strange little laugh sounds.

She swirls into view, her eyes shining with a daring playfulness and champagne bravado. "The music," she says. "Oh, it was lovely." She dances in place, sashaying from side to side, her arms extended in front to mimic a partner.

Stephen tries to ignore her, but his cheeks are reddening. Mr. Bird is already loosening his tie, and Stephen does the same.

Collette dances close to her husband. "I did well tonight, didn't I?"

He smiles, but only for show. A member of the catering staff is still clearing a table.

"I can do this now," she tells him and stops swinging. "I can go to parties, no need to hide me away. I can drink too . . ." she adds, gleefully. "You don't need to worry. I have Sarah to help me now."

Stephen whispers something to Pauline, who turns and directs the last of the servers to leave, her arms rounding their backs as they head for the kitchen.

I'm left watching, not knowing what to do.

"You looked stunning tonight, Collette," Stephen tells her.

She faces him and blinks her eyes slowly.

It's a compliment, but something happens in that instant. A cloud falling over her face. Collette raises her hand, a trembling finger, and points in Stephen's direction, her mouth opening as if about to shout something—but why? If she screams, everyone in the apartment will hear.

Stephen's face blanches.

I hurry into action. "Collette," I implore. "Let's go to your room, shall we? Put away our dresses?" My eyes are wide, eyebrows arched. I'm praying to God she listens, that she'll turn and leave and not create a scene. I can save this night and keep Collette in a happier mood. I can prevent her from suddenly falling into pieces.

Collette looks at me and drops her finger. She runs her hands through the feathers of her dress instead. "Sarah . . ." she says, a smile returning to her face. "Of course." Whatever she'd been about to get so angry over is now forgotten.

I hold her arm and coax her to follow, and she does, practically turning into putty at my touch. No more dancing feet. No more imaginary music in her head. She's compliant, and more important, she's leaving. I can take her to the bedroom and glide her peacefully into bed.

Over my shoulder, both men are nodding, relief written across their faces. "Another scotch?" Mr. Bird asks his son, and they disappear down the hall.

Outside Collette's bedroom, she stops short. "I'm not ready for bed yet." She looks toward the playroom. "Please." My plan to get Collette undressed and settled dissipates.

She opens the playroom door and it creaks gently on its hinges. Two lamps light the corners of the room with a soft glow. Each room of the magical dollhouse is lit up too with its own miniature candelabra.

Collette carefully removes her shoes and leaves them on the floor. She kneels in front of the dollhouse, her hand reaching for one of the dolls, and I notice immediately it's a little blond girl wearing a pink dress.

"Join me?" Collette asks.

I remove my shoes too. Padding across the carpet, I kneel beside her, my hands remaining in my lap since I'm not sure what to do, not sure if she'll want me to touch anything.

Collette smooths the doll's dress. The blond hair is tied with a ribbon, and she strokes the end of the ponytail too.

"Would you like to hold her? Here you go." Her eyes are wobbly as she thrusts the doll in my direction. "Take it."

I don't move.

"Sarah," she says and places the doll directly into the palm of my hand. She squeezes my fingers until I have a better grip. "It's Patty's favorite. The most important."

Two inches in height, the doll weighs a few ounces, nothing more, and I'm holding it between my thumb and forefinger, lifting it until it's eye level so I can inspect its small features: the carefully painted face with blue eyes and pink lips, the A-line dress, the tiny white bobby socks and buckled shoes. The doll is stiff but can bend at the waist, allowing it to sit at the miniature dining room table. The arms and legs extend.

I gaze at the dollhouse and wonder which bedroom is hers.

"Top right," Collette says, following my gaze. "To the right of the stairs."

I should have guessed this room belongs to the girl doll. It's covered in pink wallpaper with a pink bedspread too. Teeny tiny teddy bears and a toy train. The room a child like Patty would have picked for her most favorite doll.

"There's a whole family," Collette says, and she points out the dolls in the other rooms. One of them has short brown hair and is wearing a suit. Another doll wears an apron and a blue dress, two brothers, a baby sister in a crib, a dog, a parrot in a cage, and two cats. "We used to have a pony," Collette says. "But we can't find it anymore." Her eyes swirl, speech still slurring. "Silly Patty . . . she lost it . . ." And then she says, suddenly, "The doll's hair is Patty's."

Instantly, I drop the doll to my lap.

It lands with the tiniest of thuds at my knees before rolling to the floor.

Collette scoops it up. "Please don't do that," she scolds. "You must be gentle."

My hands shake. "I'm sorry."

Collette checks the doll's face. "This was given to her on her birthday, it's very important." She gives me a warning look. "Please don't drop her again."

My breathing has grown shallow. What is it with Collette insisting on keeping her daughter's hair? The lock of it in her purse. The hair on this doll's head.

I stare at it again—the *dead girl's* hair. Blond and tied with a pink ribbon. A shiver reaches down to my toes.

"Patty didn't like it at first when I asked to cut her hair," Collette explains. "But when I told her it was for the new doll she was so excited. A toy to match her in every single way." Collette clutches it tight to her bosom, blue couture dress, feathers, and all.

I swallow the knot in my throat as she continues to stroke the doll's face with her finger. She smooths the pink fabric at the knees.

"We must keep it safe," Collette says again, and she sets it on its bed. "Patty will come looking for it when she returns in the morning. She'll want to play with it first thing."

And with that, she tugs a string for one of the miniature Tiffany lamps, switching it off, pulling at it and turning it on again. She does this repeatedly, both of us staring at the blinks of light coming from the lamp. My teeth grit at the repetitive clicking.

Collette yawns. Leaving the Tiffany lamp on, she pats the Patty doll on the head.

"I think I will go to bed, after all," she says, yawning again, and rises to her feet, not asking me to go with her. I think she intends on sleeping in that dress.

She steps away, abandoning her stiletto heels on the carpet.

"Will you clean up this mess?" she asks.

Perplexed, I look at the dollhouse. Everything is where it needs to be. My eyes sweep the rest of the room. Besides the storybook that remains open and the tea party still in progress on the table, glittery cubes of sugar resting in teacups, nothing is amiss. The room is spotless.

Collette stops at the door before saying, "Good night, Sarah."

She is suddenly sad. Pale and lost, and I can't imagine why. She'd been so excited to show me the Patty doll, but now it's over. Her moods, ever-shifting.

She leaves and I stare at the dollhouse for a little while longer. The last few moments have been downright eerie. My boss, an emotional roller coaster.

Behind me, someone clears their throat.

I whirl around—it's Stephen—and my hands clamp to my chest.

"I'm sorry, I didn't mean to frighten you. Has my step-mother gone to bed?"

"Yes, a few minutes ago."

He glances at the hall before returning his eyes to me. "I wanted to check on you, make sure everything was okay."

My voice turns somber. "Collette told me about Patty's hair. On the doll."

He nods. "She insisted on cutting it from her head before she got too sick."

"Is there anything else I should know? Anything else that's connected to Patty?"

"What do you mean?"

"Anything else in this house made from Patty's hair or clothes or belongings? Things I should never touch?" My eyes race across the room. "Things like that creepy lock of hair she carries around with her?"

His eyes dart open with surprise. "I didn't realize she was still doing that."

"You haven't seen her carrying around your sister's hair? She was gripping it when I came for my interview. She made me hold it the other day at the bar."

Stephen looks away for a moment. "She's had a tough time."

"She's delusional."

"I know."

"She really needs help."

"We've tried."

"I'm really worried about her."

Down the hall, we hear a scream.

CHAPTER TWENTY-SIX

——

Collette is cutting the designer gown from her body. Slashing at the material—making sporadic crisscross patterns across her belly, jagged lines at her thighs until tufts of feathers fly everywhere and blue silk lies in ribbons on the floor.

She is wearing nothing but a strapless bra and panties and Stephen catches himself at the door, averting his eyes until I'm pushing against his back, squirming to get by him. I stammer at the sight of Collette Bird wielding a pair of scissors.

Faint lines appear along her arms, stomach, and legs. In seconds, they grow darker, a bold red—the first trickles of blood against her skin.

Oh, my God, she's slashing at her body to get rid of the dress.

I rush toward her.

"Stand back!" she shrieks, waving the scissors. "Don't come close!"

What the hell is happening? She'd been showing me the Patty doll and the dollhouse. What changed during those few short steps down the hall? What enraged her to the point she would slice off her own dress? From one shoulder, more blood, a slow but steady streak, runs past her elbow.

"Don't come near me," she breathes.

She looks sickly, her blue veins pressing hard against the paleness of her skin.

Stephen takes a small step. "Collette," he says. "Let go of the scissors. Please. Everything will be okay. We can help." He's trying to preserve her modesty, glancing toward her then averting his eyes quickly from the spectacle of his half-naked stepmother. "Please calm down and put the scissors away."

She jabs the points toward his head and screams. "Stand back! Don't come close!"

Stephen flinches. I rear back too, a cold fear spreading the length of my body.

Collette teeters, the top half of her body swaying as her feet wobble unsteadily against the floor. She fights to hold herself upright, her mouth is a warped *O*, lipstick smudged at one corner, her hair a stringy mess as wet tears seep against the strands. But she's raging. Her eyes are lit with hatred—Collette, a wild and uncaged animal; a scene straight out of a horror film.

"Collette . . ." Stephen tries again. He holds up one hand, either in a sign of peace or because he's planning to grab the scissors and use his other arm to shield himself if she attacks.

She lunges forward anyway, the shiny gleam of the scissor points stabbing dangerously close.

Both of us gasp, and I duck behind Stephen. Swinging my eyes toward the open door I'm thinking, *Where in the hell is Mr. Bird? Why isn't he dealing with this? This would be a great time to drop your scotch and help. Your beloved wife has turned on a dime again.*

But he doesn't appear.

No one is coming to help. This is up to Stephen and me to deal with.

Collette is sobbing, her shoulders shaking as she mumbles and sputters with every word. "No one . . ." she says, "un-der-stands me . . ." She straightens her arm again, veering close, the scissors held out like a weapon to keep us back.

"We're trying," Stephen says. "We're really trying."

"Shut up! You don't have a clue, you can't possibly know. You never have. You never will."

I cower, my eyes peeping around Stephen's shoulder.

She glowers at me. "Don't go near him!" she says. "Don't trust him. You think he's so good . . ." She shakes the blades, a frightening curl at her lips. "But he's not." My heart drops to my stomach and her voice lowers to a peculiar whisper. "Don't trust him, Sarah . . ." she repeats. "Don't believe a word he says." I take a step toward the door.

"That's enough," Stephen tells her.

"Get away from him," she says again, her eyes hardening. "Get away from Alex too. From me—from all of us. You shouldn't be here!"

She lunges once more, screaming, *"Leave, Sarah!"* And that's all I need to hear.

I bolt down the hall and run as fast as I can from West Seventy-eighth Street.

By midafternoon Sunday, I've received three bouquets of flowers, one cookie cake, a box of chocolate-covered strawberries, an Uber Eats delivery of surf and turf from one of the more expensive steakhouses in town, a certificate for a full-day spa treatment, and my own bottle of Chanel No. 5—the full ounce size. The onslaught of gifts is maniacal.

I know I shouldn't accept them. But the gifts keep coming, deliveries arriving each hour until it's nearly predictable. Another sharp buzz punctuates the quiet as another delivery worker presses our downstairs call button, and my stomach fills with half dread, half curiosity to see what's arrived next.

I picture Collette sitting at the computer, gripping the mouse, clicking on one order after another, every charge sent to her credit card, hoping her gifts will make up for what she's done.

But *she's* the one who told me to get out.

I hailed a cab last night in my Oscar de la Renta gown and didn't take a full breath until I knew we'd safely rounded the corner and were barreling down Columbus. I pretended to be asleep when Jonathan arrived home, but now my fiancé is staring at me as our apartment fills with deliveries.

"Does she think it's your birthday or something?" he asks jokingly. But there's a seriousness in his eyes too. The stockpile of gifts is over-the-top and I'm worrying about how much longer I can keep hiding the truth.

What could I possibly tell him that would make him understand? My new boss lost her shit again but this time she lunged at me with scissors?

Jonathan is picking at another cookie, the floral arrangements crowding our one and only table. "It's a little much, don't you think? I mean, I know you're good. Her daughter must be in love with you, but all this too?" He lifts the box of chocolate-covered strawberries.

Jonathan pops one of the strawberries in his mouth as my phone pings. My eyes shoot to the screen.

Please forgive me, the message reads.

It's Collette.

The phone dings again. *I was out of my mind. I won't do that again, I promise.*

I don't answer, only stare blankly at the screen.

Please come back.

Please, Sarah. Please.

The messages keep coming. Ten in all.

I drop my phone.

An hour later, Jonathan and I are consuming the surf and turf—damned if we're going to let good food go to waste—when the door buzzer sounds once more.

Jonathan starts to get up, but I stop him. "It's my turn." And I leave the door open a crack as I take the stairs.

Blond hair through the window. Oversize shades. This is no delivery person but the woman herself. Collette is cupping her hands against the window and she smiles the moment she spots me taking the final stair. A knot forms in my stomach.

She's wearing a gorgeous Easter egg blue trench coat with a matching hat and standing on the pavement in long sleeves and pants—the outfit chosen, I'm sure, to cover the slash marks I know are hidden underneath.

I halt. The only thing separating us is the glass door of my apartment lobby. I'm not sure I'm ready to face what waits for me on the other side of that glass.

I look to see what she's carrying, paranoid she's still brandishing a pair of scissors and could slice at the air as soon as I open the door. But there is nothing in her hands.

Against all instincts, I open the door. She's whimpering. But it's time to tell her I'm quitting. I'll hate to leave her alone in that apartment at the mercy of her controlling family, but I can't do this anymore. I need to find a way out of that contract and she'll need to understand.

I study Collette. Behind her, a driver, not the one she hired earlier in the week, is sitting behind the steering wheel, the engine left running. She's bribed someone else this time.

I keep my foot barricaded against the door.

"You shouldn't be here," I tell her.

Her eyes round. "I'm so afraid you're going to quit."

"I need to, Collette."

"Please, you can't!" Her voice rises. "Let me apologize. What I did last night, that wasn't me—it's this new medication they put me on." I let out my breath—so many excuses. "I shouldn't have been drinking. The doctor, these new meds. They made me crazy." She pulls the sunglasses from her face, her eyes searching mine and threatening to spill fresh tears. "You have to believe me. I'm so sorry." She reaches for my hand, but I instinctively pull back. She lets her hand fall to her waist, her face crumpling.

"Please forgive me," she cries.

I have to be firm. "This isn't working, Mrs. Bird. I'm so sorry. I'm turning in my notice—"

"No! Please don't do that!"

"I can't do this. I tried, but I can't. Last night was—"

"I'm switching to a new prescription. I won't drink again. Alex says he'll never host another dinner party. I can be better, Sarah, I know I can. Last night was rock-bottom and it really woke me up, the thought of losing you. I hate that you had to see it, you and Stephen both. No one should have to go through something like that. Alex hasn't stopped yelling at me."

I'm wondering if Stephen has been hollering at her too—
he'd been inches from the end of pointed scissors, just like I
had.

"It scared me and I know it scared you too. For that, I'm
sorry."

I hear a shake in my voice. "You could have hurt one of
us. You were hurting yourself. You need help, more than I
can give you."

She looks down and rubs her arms self-consciously. I can
only imagine what she looks like underneath. Under that
gorgeous trench coat must be strips of bandages.

"You've already been helping me so much. The thought
of what I did, how much that impacted you, I'm more re-
solved than ever." She stands taller. "I'm changing my ways
and getting healthy again. I can get better. But I can't lose
you, I just can't." She lifts her hands again, but this time lets
them drop. "Please don't quit, Sarah. Please give me—us—
another chance. We can make this right again. Patty needs
you after all. She'll be devastated."

Patty.

I can already imagine the torture Collette's putting herself through thinking of how she's going to tell Patty another
nanny has left them.

I move to shut the door. "I have to go."

But her arm shoots out and she braces herself against the
metal frame. *"Please, Sarah!"* Her desperation increases.
"They'll send me away if I don't get better. They'll get rid of
me, I know they will."

"They only want to help."

"It's *not* help," she shrieks. "It's another prison. A horrible, cold prison. I don't want to go there anymore."

"The hospital—"

"It's not a hospital. That's what they call it but it's not. It's a horrible place. So cruel." This time, she grabs my arm and I freeze, my feet locked to the ground.

Stephen told me psychiatric wards. Private clinics. There should be a trained medical staff. A supportive environment. With their kind of money, only the best facilities and state-of-the-art care for Collette Bird. Not some run-down institution. Not a place Collette would describe as a prison.

"I heard them today," she wails. "Stephen talking to Alex. Alex was consulting with someone on the phone." Her eyes fill with tears. "It's coming, I know it is." She swivels her head as if at any moment someone is going to sneak up on the sidewalk and grab her by the arms. With her kicking and screaming, they'll haul her away.

An image pops into my mind of two rough orderlies strapping Collette to a chair. Her head hanging limp, lips and chin trembling, bare legs freezing beneath a paper-thin gown. Left alone in a room where no one is caring for her. Freezing temperature. The wonderful facilities the Birds say they're placing her in nothing but holding cells.

Is *that* why she hasn't gotten any better?

Collette's fingers hold tight to my arm. And I can't stop staring—the look of terror on her face. Pure fear.

"Please don't let them do this to me, Sarah," she pleads. "Don't let them take me there."

CHAPTER TWENTY-SEVEN

—

I show up to the Birds' the next day at 10:00 A.M., the nerves in my stomach unrelenting, as Collette's face bursts into a smile the moment she sees me. Her elation is palpable. But so is her relief. Whatever fate I've saved her from, Collette was genuinely terrified of it.

"I'm so glad you're here." Her cheeks blush red, there's a sob she tries to swallow away.

She sneaks a glance behind her as if frightened by something, or someone, lurking in the corner; she doesn't feel safe and in the clear just yet. And I can't help but look too, my own fears ticking up a notch.

But there's no one in the corner. No orderlies. No Stephen or Alex Bird.

I follow her to the family room, and she presents a tray of croissants, sliced melon, and two mugs, and without asking, pours me a cup of coffee. Her hands tremble, but she adds the cream and sugar anyway as if wanting so much for everything to return to normal.

What I notice first: She's already breaking her habit. No grapefruit halves at the breakfast table.

I wait for Collette to speak first. But before she gets a chance, she's interrupted by Stephen entering the room.

"Hello, Sarah," he says, an apologetic tone in his voice. "Thank you for being so"—he struggles to find his next word—"understanding."

I hold his look.

"Saturday night was quite a shock. For all of us." He stares steadily. "Are you all right?"

"Yes," I tell him, but find that I'm leaning away when he sits beside me on the couch.

"Collette has made several promises," he informs me. "We had the doctor return and switch out her medication. She is *not* to drink again." He shoots her a look. "And she promises to never act that way again—my father won't stand for it. Me either." I see Collette running her hand along one arm, the bandages that are poking out beneath her sleeve.

"We won't be sending her away either," he adds, and Collette sucks in her breath. He registers the sound with a tightening of his lips. "We're hoping we can move forward with your help."

Glancing at Collette, I suggest, "What if we relaxed some of the rules a bit?"

His mouth twitches.

"Hear me out," I add, revealing the plan that's been circling in my head since last night. "What if we ease Collette out of the apartment some more? Small trips. Little excursions. She enjoys it so much and I think it would do her some good." Beside me, Collette's chin lifts. She is stirring in her seat, her hands clasping together as she listens.

But Stephen appears alarmed. "More outings?"

"Yes." I choose my words carefully, finding it odd to be talking about my boss when she is sitting inches away. "She needs more normalcy. More human interaction—more fun. So she doesn't feel trapped here."

"She's *not* trapped."

"Confined to the twelfth floor," I remind him.

He returns my stare coolly.

"I think it would help a lot," Collette speaks up. Her voice is throaty but she's hopeful. "You can trust me not to drink in public, Stephen. Sarah and I have so much fun together and it would be nice to get out more." She presses one of her fingers hard on top of her hand. "I won't feel like I'm sneaking out either. You would know where I am at all times."

"And Patty?" Stephen asks, his gaze focusing solely on me.

I return his look. "I'll be there every step of the way. Patty will remain by my side."

He studies Collette, studies me. A bob rises and falls in his throat as he contemplates our suggestion. The possible pitfalls too. My ability to contain her. Collette's ability to contain herself. Her last few public outings have been rocky at best.

But with the two of us staring, pleading, he is willing to try something new.

Finally, he says two words, "All right." But he doesn't look happy.

The exhale from Collette's mouth releases as she stands and claps happily. She swings her arms as she scurries down the hall. "Wait until I tell Patty."

Stephen gives me a stern look of warning. He locks in on my face. "Don't mess this up."

———

We take it slow. Our first outing that afternoon is to a bakery called Delish within walking distance of the apartment. Stephen begrudgingly gives his approval.

Collette is giddy, her hand scooping into the crook of my elbow as she propels us along. She's changed into a new outfit, as if the relaxed pantsuit she'd been wearing earlier was unworthy of such an occasion, and is now sporting satin high-waisted trousers and a long-sleeved eyelet blouse; a glamorous black-on-black ensemble. I don't have the heart to point out we're simply going to a café.

But I also know what else the high-necked blouse is affording her—complete coverage of the cuts she's made to herself.

Dozens of people fill the café and Collette appears unfazed by the noise. In fact, she's downright elated, attracted by the commotion of people around her. She's already pointing out desserts Patty will enjoy.

We find a table in the corner and I order a blueberry scone while Collette asks the server for a Danish and a pot of English tea. She is sure to include a jam tart and chocolate éclair for Patty.

"Your favorites, aren't they, sweetheart?" She motions to the empty chair beside her. The server gives her an odd look before glancing over at me, and I tense for a moment, but then he only shrugs and turns away, marking our order on his pad.

Minutes later, he brings a pot of tea and three cups, not asking who the extra one is for and I breathe another sigh of relief. Collette reaches to pour the tea. She hands me the blueberry scone and, on the extra plate, places the chocolate éclair for Patty. "Don't make a mess," she tells her before eating her Danish with a fork.

Collette looks around the café, delighted at the hubbub of customers and the tinkling of the bell above the door every time someone new walks in. The excitement of this approved outing shines in her eyes. This is something she knows she won't get into trouble for later, and I sit back, marveling at her transformation. In my hand, my phone in case Stephen calls.

Collette says, "I'm so glad you were able to meet Alex. It was wonderful of you to join us at the party." She takes another bite of her Danish and implores me with a look. "I love him. I know he can seem tough, controlling even. But he's a good man. He wants what's best for our family."

I pick gently at my scone.

"Four years, can you believe it?" she says. "He made me wait four years before we got married." She laughs. "Silly man. And now we're coming up on our ninth wedding anniversary. I wonder what we'll do to celebrate . . ." She takes a sip of her tea.

And I catch her words—ninth anniversary. But the Birds have been married much longer than that. The time loop is still there.

"His mother is the one who pushed us to get married. She wanted a huge, over-the-top event even though my family could hardly pay a thing. But that didn't stop her. She took care of every expense." She shakes her head. "But it made me a guest at my own wedding. She took over everything. But after the wedding, we were happy. Really happy. Alex and I, together in our beautiful apartment and traveling to Venice and Paris, wherever we wanted to go. And we were always on the go. Go, go, go . . ." she repeats, a faraway look taking shape in her eyes. She gazes steadily out the window as her teacup rests in her hand. The extra cup for Patty is cooling too.

"We always wanted a big family. Lots of kids to chase after because lots of kids would mean plenty of grandkids too." She gives a faint smile. "When Patty came into our lives, it was the most wonderful day." She reaches over to pinch the imaginary girl. "I've never seen Alex so happy. He admits he wasn't around much for Stephen, but with Patty, he's very hands-on, isn't he?" Another smile at her daughter. "He loves his Patty Cakes. You've got him wrapped around your finger, don't you, sweetie?" She giggles. "Our baby girl . . ."

Moving the tea to one side, Collette pulls something from her purse and slips it into my hand. The softness of the item presses against my skin, the braided softness. Human hair.

I stare for the longest time.

Blond hair tied with a pink ribbon. Patty's hair.

My heart seizes.

We're in public, so even though she's once again produced something from her dead child's body and placed it in my hands, I can't react. I can't freak out, even though what I want to do is drop it fast, like I did when she showed me the Patty doll. Or push away from the table and run screaming, but I can't do that here, not when we're in a public setting. Not when we just convinced Stephen to let Collette venture out more.

This is part of the deal. She's going to be like this, I must expect it. I must learn how to work with her.

My eyes dart from side to side, but of course no one is

looking; they're too engrossed in their own conversations. And if they were to notice, how would they understand the significance? It's only a lock of hair.

"Patty insisted you have one of your own," Collette says. "She let me cut off a piece just this morning. What a sweet girl."

I can't seem to keep my fingers folded around it.

"It's a gift," she says when she notes my hesitation. She flashes a quick grin at her daughter. "A gift from Patty and me. She's so happy to give this to you. You don't want to upset her." Another gentle nudge. "Take it."

My stomach rolls. *Take the damn hair, Sarah.*

"It was always Therese's idea," Collette adds. "She says keeping a lock of Patty's hair is a good luck charm." She looks at me sweetly. "I want you to have good luck too."

CHAPTER TWENTY-EIGHT

===

"What happened to Therese?" I ask Pauline.

We've returned from the bakery. After a quick check-in with Stephen to say everything went well, Collette excused herself to take Patty to the playroom. "I'd like some alone time," she tells me, padding down the hall.

Pauline is wiping a table in the living room, a blue piece of terry cloth and bottle of cleaner clutched in her hands.

When I ask, she straightens her back but doesn't answer.

"Therese?" I say again. "What happened?"

"I don't know."

"You don't know?" I narrow my eyes slightly. "She worked here fifteen years and then she decided to quit? What happened?"

"It was a long time ago. Therese isn't here anymore."

I dig into my pocket and hold up the lock of hair. "Do you have one too?"

She startles. "Is that hers?"

"No, she gave me one for myself."

"Today?"

"Yes, today. She said it was Therese's idea for us all to have one, but why? Therese hasn't been here in years. It . . ." I dangle the hair again. "It doesn't make sense."

Pauline resumes her cleaning. "Collette listened to a lot of what Therese told her. Just put it away and don't worry about it."

"I need to understand why the woman left. Why would she ditch this job and the Birds after so long?"

Pauline sets down the bottle of cleaner with a thud. "She didn't ditch the job."

"So where did she go?"

Pauline raises her eyes. "She died."

There's a thud in my chest. "What happened?"

"Therese was a great person, she really was. But she was getting too clingy with Collette. Too dependent. Like her job here was everything she had in this world." She gestures at the room and I nod, encouraging her to keep going. "I felt like it was getting to be a bit too much and Collette agreed. She needed some personal space. After all, fifteen years together is a long time."

I think about Pauline, how she's been here longer than that—more than twenty years, she'd told me proudly—and how she lives here too, hasn't known another home since she was in her twenties. She's become just like Therese without knowing it.

"We talked several times about Therese making her own friends and spending time in the city. Collette told her it wasn't necessary to be by her side all the time, that she could care for Patty sometimes on her own. We tried to be encouraging. We thought it would be good for her to expand her circle. And that's when it happened."

My heart races.

"She didn't know her way around without Collette or the driver. She was like a child herself, not knowing which direction was north or south, which way to turn if she wanted to go to Chinatown or Battery Park. God forbid she try figuring out the subway, so she walked everywhere. But then *bam*—" Pauline punches a fist into her other hand and I flinch. What an odd and impersonal way to describe the death of someone she knows.

"She was hit by a cab. The driver had been speeding, but Therese wasn't paying attention. She didn't look where she was going and she stepped right out in front."

The look on Pauline's face. What she's just told me troubles me, but the look on her face is more eerie. It's as if she thinks it was the woman's fault.

CHAPTER TWENTY-NINE

The following morning, a text message arrives from an unknown number.

Can you come in at 12 pm instead of 10?

It's not Stephen, and it's not Collette. I've programmed both their numbers. Alex?

Who is this?

Pauline comes the response.

Is everything ok?

Yes. She just wants extra time to rest.

I look at the time, it's not even 9:00 A.M. I'm thankful to Pauline for giving me an early heads-up, but I'm also worried. What kind of new meds have they put Collette on?

When I arrive at West Seventy-eighth Street, an umbrella at my side, the clouds blanketing the sky with a heavy foreboding gray, Stephen yanks open the door to greet me.

"What time is it?"

Dumbfounded, I look at my watch. "Twelve?"

"What time are you supposed to be here?"

"Ten, but Pauline sent me a text saying Collette wanted to rest."

He scowls.

I look for any sign of Pauline to appear and back me up. She can vouch for me. But she's not around.

Stephen backs away from the door and lets me in. "No one said anything to me," he says, folding his arms. "I wasn't told Collette needed to rest."

I dig my phone from my pocket to show him the text messages, but he waves it away, motioning for me to follow.

"I wish Pauline would have said something. I don't want Collette to get worried or upset thinking you're not here." He lets his voice trail off as he ducks his head from one room to the next, looking for Collette.

She's not in the breakfast room or the lounge with the baby grand piano. No sign of her in the family room either. Stephen picks up his pace.

We find her in the bedroom. And she's not alone—Pauline is sitting in the middle of the bed with her, the two looking like a pair of giggling schoolgirls. The curtains are open, the lights on, the bed has been made, and Collette is dressed, her hair swept into a loose bun.

"It was the sweetest thing," she says, reaching for Pauline's hand. The women are barefoot, large decorative pillows propped beneath them as Collette turns and watches us come in. "Oh, Sarah. You're here!" She smiles broadly. "Pauline has been keeping me company." She pats the woman on the knee. "It was a lovely start to the day." Pauline is smiling too.

"No sense in you rushing here early if it wasn't necessary," the housekeeper tells me.

Stephen sighs and then retreats down the hall. Collette holds her arms out to me in welcome.

"I'm so glad you're here. Pauline is suggesting we stay in today." She looks out the window. "You're right, Pauline. It does look like rain is coming and we should stay in the play-room instead."

Pauline nods. "No sense in going out all the time." She gives me a look and then her eyes drop to the new prescription bottles beside the bed. She leans against the pillows.

And that's when I see, in the middle of the bed, the Patty doll.

It's propped up, wearing its tiny dress and its still blue eyes staring straight ahead, the doll, dwarfed by the sheer size of the California king and the women sitting on either side.

Collette picks it up and cups it with one hand. Using her index finger, she strokes the doll's hair.

"You know," she says, "this was given to us by Ms. Fontaine, our first nanny." She cradles it to her chest. "Do you remember, Patty? She gave you that family of dolls. The teeny-tiny baby in a pram. A mama and a daddy. And then Ms. Fontaine brought this one home to look more like you, a girl about your age. We named her Patty too."

She hands the doll to Pauline, who handles it like a pro. No grimacing, not like me. How many times over the last twenty years has she been asked to hold that thing?

"Sarah," Collette says. "Will you go with Pauline and Patty and help them straighten up the playroom?" She slides off the bed before looking down at the space beside her. "That's right, sweetheart. They'll be there to help you."

Pauline slides from the mattress and joins me at the door. But Collette calls out, "Wait." She looks at us expectantly. "Make sure to hold Patty's hands."

I turn to Pauline, who holds out her fingers, the tilt of her chin and steady look in her eyes telling me to do the same.

So I do. I copy Pauline and reach out, gripping nothing but air.

As soon as we're out of sight, Pauline and I drop our hands. She walks ahead, leading me to the playroom.

"Wait until you see what she's been up to," she says, pushing open the door.

Sometime last night, it appears Collette came in here with a child's paint set and proceeded to paint, if that's what you can call it. Large sheets of paper are clipped to a board with blobs of acrylic dripped on the floor, red and yellow smeared into the carpet too. The edge of Collette's heel tracked through the paint and trailed it to the window. Six oversize sheets of paper are drying. Large swirling lines and what looks like a house with a sun, maybe a tree. She paints like a child.

While the medication might be tiring her during the day, she's wired at night.

Pauline reaches for a can of carpet cleaner and shakes it before spraying each area, telling me to stand back as she tackles each acrylic blob. She says we'll have to wait ten minutes before rubbing at them with paper towels.

At the bookshelf, I run my hand along the spines: *Little Red Riding Hood* and *Sleeping Beauty*. A hardback version of *Grimm's Fairy Tales*.

"How come there aren't a lot of pictures of Patty?" I ask.

"They don't keep them," Pauline says, shrugging.

I think of my one and only visual of the girl, the single frame that had been partially covered. I have yet to see another photo, a commissioned oil painting or an album filled with pictures of Patty as a baby—an album I'd expected Collette would have asked me to look through by now. I have found no additional picture frames in the living room or den. No family portraits. Nothing of the smiling daughter.

"Why not?" I ask.

"Well, for starters, Collette swears she sees her daughter night and day. She doesn't need a portrait of the girl. We only have the one photo in the parlor, which is the one area of the apartment Alex doesn't go near."

"Why not?"

"That's where they kept her body after she died. Alex doesn't go in there anymore."

I'm stumped. "Why wouldn't they keep more pictures of their daughter? I know it's tragic, but wouldn't he want memories of her at least?"

"I don't know," Pauline says, sighing. "Who knows what goes through that man's head. I've worked for him for years and I still can't figure him out. Maybe it breaks his heart to see his daughter's face. Or he thinks that if the photos are hidden away, his wife will eventually snap out of it. She might come to terms with their daughter's death."

She sighs again. "Nothing else seems to be working except having you. Having a nanny. Wouldn't be my way of doing it, but who am I to say? I've never lost a child, never been through what they have."

I shake my head.

"Everyone has their own way of grieving," she tells me, shooting me a look. "You haven't been through everything here with us."

But not only are there no photos of Patty, I realize, there

are no wedding photos of Collette and Alex. No photos from their honeymoon or of Stephen as a child either. They have tapestries and murals, priceless works of art and one-of-a-kind paintings highlighted in gilt frames, but nothing personal.

"You know," Pauline says. "It wasn't all Ms. Fontaine's idea to give her that doll."

I look up.

"Mr. Bird got her that dollhouse but it was Ms. Fontaine and myself who bought her those dolls. We came up with the idea of the Patty doll together."

She looks at me, then glances away, her eyes tracing the space between her and the dollhouse. After a moment, she pulls the Patty doll from her pocket and places it inside, settling it at the dining table.

"Do you miss Ms. Fontaine?" I ask.

Pauline's eyes rocket toward me. "I hate that she left, if that's what you mean."

"The two of you must have been close. The death of Patty must have brought you together in a tragic way."

"It was hard on all of us." Her lips harden. "But I wish she wouldn't have bailed on us like that." Her hand wrestles with her sleeve, and there it is again, the elastic band against her wrist. "I think they had a thing going on," she says, and it's so quiet, I almost miss it.

"Who?"

"Ms. Fontaine and Alex."

I almost laugh. And then I cough.

Mr. Bird? Having an affair with the first nanny? It seems hard to believe, given the love I still see in the man when he looks at his wife.

But then again, what do I know about Mr. Bird? And I've never met Ms. Fontaine.

"There was something between them," Pauline insists. "I've never been able to confirm it, but it was always a hunch. The air changed in the room when the two of them came together. The mood shifted, enough for me to notice."

"But why?" I ask. "Why would he do that to Collette?"

"I have no idea," Pauline says. "All I know is, Patty died and the happiness was sucked right out of this place. Alex Bird changed, and shortly after, Ms. Fontaine took off with little explanation." She snaps her fingers. "A lovers' quarrel, death of a child, and then poof, she was gone."

CHAPTER THIRTY

=====

The next day, I suggest a walk, but Collette has a bigger idea. She slips her prescription bottle in her purse. "We're calling for Henry," she announces. "He can drive us somewhere."

But Pauline is hesitant. "Maybe that's not such a good idea."

"Nonsense," Collette says quickly. "Besides, Patty needs to get out too. She's excited."

The housekeeper's eyes dart in my direction.

"FAO Schwarz," Collette says. "That's where we're going. We can collect decoration ideas for her party. Patty can let us know what she thinks."

With the phone partially hidden in my hand, I fire off a message to Stephen: *Toy store. One hour, tops.*

He responds with *Keep your eyes on her.*

FAO Schwarz is the biggest and most iconic toy store in Manhattan. We arrive at its Rockefeller Plaza location within twenty minutes, and already, it's crammed with hundreds of children playing with games and crafts. Kids are shouting, and impatient shoves jostle us at every turn. Girls and boys scamper from one floor to the next, taking the curved staircase two steps at a time while their parents chase after them.

Within seconds, Collette's mood turns from glee to overstimulation. She's running from one section of the store to another, her eyes whirling at everything surrounding her. Worry gnaws at my insides as I hurry to keep up.

We're at the top of the stairs when Collette says, "I'm buying the carousel."

My mouth drops.

"For the party. Bridget sent me the info and I called first thing. It's in Boston and they're shipping it here in a few weeks." Her frenzied smile reaches her ears. "I want it put together in time for Patty's party. She can have a few turns on it before showing her friends."

I halt my steps—what friends? Who would we possibly invite? How do you bring children to a party for a child who's been dead twenty years?

Images flash in my mind: a large table filled with cupcakes and goodies, Collette and myself singing "Happy Birthday" to no one, the carousel spinning but empty behind us.

"I'm thinking of a carnival theme," Collette says over the noise. A child runs by squealing. "The kind with toy trains and circus animals, balloons too. We'll have the carousel and carnival music and cake from the bakery on West Eighty-first." She ticks off each item on her fingers, a feverish brightness to her eyes. "I'll want you to get in touch with the caterer. Handle the invitations. There's a party store we'll check out next week. We also need toys for the goodie bags." She's rattling on and I'm starting to wonder if I should be taking notes. "Patty will have to get a new dress, of course." She swings a glance at me and takes in my discounted shirt from the Gap, my skinny black jeans, and winks. "We'll find you something special too."

She heads for an area of colorful wooden baskets teeming with plush miniature elephants, toy lions, and bears. She arranges the items and tells me she's making centerpieces.

While upstairs, we stumble into the baby section next. It's much quieter, stocked with blankets and plush bunnies, soft to the touch. Collette strokes most everything she sees. She picks up a teddy bear and holds it close to her chest.

"Oh, Patty, isn't this the most incredible, softest thing you've ever felt?" She squeezes the bear to her chin before dropping it low, willing her daughter to rub its soft ear.

A boy walks up to Collette. He's three or four years old with sandy blond hair and green, inquisitive eyes. He peers at Collette, who's clutching the teddy bear and singing to herself. He reaches up and shouts, "Teddy!"

But Collette doesn't respond.

The boy repeats, "Teddy! Can I see it?"

It takes a lifetime for her to look down at the boy.

"I want teddy!" he says, puckering his lower lip.

Collette frowns. "This one?"

"Yes!"

"But it's for my daughter. She wants it." She glances at the empty space beside her, then back at the boy. "You can choose another one . . ." She points at the display. There are bunnies and puppies, but no more teddy bears. "How about a sweet panda?"

He stomps his foot. "No, I want the bear." And he turns. "Daddy! She won't give it."

A man appears wearing a windbreaker and a small backpack on one shoulder, a drink thermos sticking out from the mesh pocket. Possibly tourists.

"Hey, buddy. Let's find you something else," he says, placing his hands on the boy's shoulders. He sweeps an apologetic glance at Collette.

But pitiful tears form in the boy's eyes. "I want that one!"

Collette instinctively drops to her knees. Drinking him in, she mulls the child over and asks, "What's your name?"

He releases a sniffle. "Justin."

"Well, Justin. My daughter really wants the bear too. But I tell you what." Her hand reaches out. "I'll buy you whatever you want. Anything on this table." She grabs hold of a panda and presses it gently against his chest. "What do you think?"

The man blinks his surprise. "No, that's not necessary—"

"But I don't want the panda!" the boy shrieks. "I want teddy!"

Another squeeze of the boy's shoulders. Flustered by his kid's outburst, the man tries turning his child away. "Come on, buddy. Let's look at something else—"

"The teddy!" Justin stomps.

"I'll buy you anything you want," Collette whispers to the kid, her face within inches of his.

My eyes lock with the man's, a startled pinch across his cheeks.

I try to usher Collette away. "We should get going, Mrs. Bird." But she doesn't budge.

Brushing the toy against his hands, she tells the boy in a hushed voice, "Come on now, Justin. Take it." They're the same words she used to persuade me to grasp the lock of Patty's hair. My mouth runs dry.

The boy swats the panda to the ground. "Give me the bear *now*!" he screams.

Something in Collette's face crumbles—a look of despair that lasts half a second before flipping to outrage. "Now you've gone and messed it up!" She rescues the toy from the floor and brushes at it with an angry swipe of her hand. "I said I would buy you anything—*so take it!*" She hurls the toy into the kid's hands.

Appalled at his own child's behavior, the intense reaction from Collette, or both, the man grabs hold of his son.

"Let's settle down. Everything's going to be fine—"

But Collette screams, "Your kid's nothing but a brat!"

The man jerks away. The boy lets out a howl.

Shit. My eyes skirt the area for the nearest exit.

I step forward. "Mrs. Bird, let's go. *Now.*" I pull her by the elbow.

She begins to move and the boy drops the panda, his eyes staying locked on what's in her hands. "She's taking it!"

"I'm so sorry," I tell his father, trying my best to move Collette along. "I'm sure they have more in the back. Can you ask a salesperson?"

The man stands in disbelief.

Collette unleashes another jab. "Tell your kid to stop crying! He's had his chance!"

I yank hard until she almost loses her footing. She's skittering but soon finds her balance on those damn stiletto heels she insisted on wearing, and I half-drag, half-pull her toward the stairs.

The boy is still hollering. "This is outrageous," the man shouts after her. "You're a real class act."

Collette shrieks. "Tell your kid to get over it!"

The boy breaks free from his dad and rushes at Collette, tears dripping down his face. He tries to wrench the bear free from her grasp, but she screams—and it's such a high-pitched, bloodcurdling sound that anybody in the store will think someone is being bludgeoned to death. Not a grown woman and a child arguing over a bear.

The father chases after Justin and pulls him away just in time for Collette to do the most horrible thing.

She smacks the man across the face.

The sound of the hard slap pierces the room as his head is knocked back and the skin on his face turns red and then splotchy white where her fingers had been.

An audible gasp leaps from everyone nearby, including me. A repeated loud noise slams against my eardrums until I realize it's my heartbeat.

Collette has assaulted a man in broad daylight, and in front of dozens of people. Over a damn teddy bear.

Before anything else can happen—before the dad can lunge at Collette and before the cops are called—I drag her down the stairs.

My heart pounds as we make it to the bottom floor. Collette is skidding and slipping and doing her best to wrestle herself from my grip, but I won't let go. At some point, she manages to pull wads of cash from her purse—twenties, hundreds, she's not taking the time to count—and throws them in the air, letting the bills cascade from her in a rainfall of money.

"For the bear!" Collette shouts triumphantly as an audience of bewildered shoppers stare at her dumbly.

I whirl my head around to the lunatic grin on her face. She can slap a man in public, but God forbid anyone accuse her of shoplifting.

CHAPTER THIRTY-ONE

===

"What in God's name happened?"

I'm sitting across from Alex Bird, who's seated behind the desk in his study. He looks ready to kill me.

"It's a toy store, for Christ's sake," Mr. Bird says. "*A toy store.* How in the world did that end in such a shitstorm?" He points a long finger in my direction. "What did you do?"

Me? What's he talking about? I'm not the one who assaulted someone.

"You were there less than thirty minutes." He rocks back and forth in his chair until the wheels are rattling against the floorboards. "Why didn't you stop her?"

"I'm sorry. I had no idea—"

"The police were called, did you know that? *The police.*" He rakes his hands through his hair. "And now I've got to deal with that too. Deal with the cops and make this whole mess go away." He yanks drawers open, then slams them, shoving papers from one side of his desk to the other until I'm not sure he's looking for anything in particular. He's so jacked up he wants to do something—anything—with his hands.

He pulls at his tie next, undoing its knot, and tugs at his shirt buttons too. He's so angry it's like he could be choking;

the color of his face is scarlet red, his neck turning a deeper purple. Mr. Bird slams another desk drawer.

Whereas Stephen keeps his study tidy and devoid of paper, a minimalist's approach, Mr. Bird's office looks like a bomb went off inside. Stacks of paper are piled everywhere, notepads and scribbled notes and folders bound together with clips. Either it's always this messy or Mr. Bird came in here last night and wrecked the damn place.

Spit forms at the corners of his mouth. His eyes flash. He's waited until I returned this morning to scream at me.

"An absolute nightmare," Mr. Bird says. "What in the hell was she thinking? Throwing a fit over a damn teddy bear—we have a thousand more toys like that at home. Why does she need another one?"

I don't dare tell him it's for Patty's birthday party.

"The man is thinking about pressing charges, did you know that?" I sink lower in my seat. "Charges! *Against my wife!*" He's shaking. "The store manager said they're considering issuing an official complaint. They don't want Collette to return to their store ever again, which, after what happened, is fine by me." He cuts through the air with both hands. "She's not going *anywhere*."

I shrink where I sit, not knowing what to say.

His cold, steely look shoots at me from across the desk. "Stephen said we would start allowing small trips. That you would be there every step of the way. How could you let this happen?"

"I was just trying to help—"

"Bullshit!" He slams his hands on the desktop. "You could have stopped her. You could have gotten her out of there."

The heat rises in my neck. "How was I supposed to know something like a bear was going to set her off?"

Another slam of the hands. "Everything sets her off, Sarah. *Everything.* Don't you understand that yet? Haven't you noticed?"

"I'm sorry," I say again and grip the armrests of my chair to keep my cool.

Mr. Bird won't let up. "You were with her. You should have gotten her out of the store the moment she started to lose it, not wait for it to spiral out of control."

It's my turn to glare at him. But he holds out a hand. "I thought I made it perfectly clear you had to stop this kind of thing from happening. I told you how important it is that our family name be protected, that nothing can get out." He lowers his voice in a threatening grumble. "I'll do everything in my power to protect this family."

"But what about her?" I shout. "What about *her* needs?"

He rises to his feet. "How dare you speak to me like you know anything? You don't know a goddamn thing about what we've been through or what she needs."

"I know she needs serious help. A proper hospital. Every day, she's falling apart."

"You let me handle that," he snaps. "I've been dealing with this a lot longer than you. You've been here a week and you think you know what's best?" His arm whips out and he knocks a stack of folders from his desk, papers and notebooks sweeping to one side and landing on the floor. He ignores the mess, but I jump.

"We all know the best thing for her is to stay home," he says. "With a nanny. Stephen convinced me a few outings could work. He said it would be good for her, that I could trust her to be with you. I caved. And look where it's gotten us . . ."

But I'm not to blame! I want to shout. *You're* the ones who let her believe she still sees her daughter. *You're* the ones keeping her in this fantasy world and doing this to her—not me.

I can't be the only one who knows this is wrong, that this charade can't go on forever. And when the truth is exposed, when Collette finally realizes her daughter is dead, she'll be destroyed. The heartache will rip through her soul and she'll spiral into a dangerous tailspin. Slicing her skin and running out in front of a car will pale in comparison with what she'll try next.

And whose fault will it be then?

CHAPTER THIRTY-TWO

———

I leave the apartment, pushing past Malcolm so he can't see the tears welling up in my eyes.

At the subway, I choke back my anger and wipe more tears from my cheeks. When I return home, I rush toward Jonathan for a hug at the exact same time he says, "I got a job!" But the smile on his face drops the moment I fold into his arms.

"Whoa," he says, his body tensing. His arms wrap around me in a tight hug. "What's going on? What happened?" He pulls away. "Are you hurt?" I mumble no, my mouth pressed against his shoulder. "Are you okay, Sarah? You're scaring me."

I stand back. "I'm sorry."

"What happened?"

I rub my eyes. "What were you saying? You got a job?"

"Yes, that wine bar in SoHo." He shakes his head. "But never mind. What happened?"

I don't know where to begin. But I can't keep it a secret anymore. Not from the only person who I know will be on my side.

"There is no little girl," I tell him.

He doesn't say a word, only scrunches his face in confusion.

"The girl," I tell him. "Patty. She's dead."

Still, Jonathan only stares.

"There's no one to nanny," I explain. "There never has been." And before I know it, the words are rushing out: the girl's death, Collette's illness, the fake nannies. What the family wants to hide.

It's nearly impossible for Jonathan to comprehend right away. He looks at me intently, wheels turning, eyes shifting, as he takes in every word.

I drop to the futon mattress, exhausted. I've blurted out what I promised and signed a contract never to do, but I'm at my breaking point. I need to let Jonathan in—I can't do this on my own. If I'm going to share my life with him, I need to come clean.

Jonathan monitors me as if he's seen a ghost. I cradle my face with my hands.

"So it's all made up?" he asks.

"All of it. I would have told you sooner but they made me sign a contract. They threatened to sue us both if I ever told. All of the nannies have been under contract not to speak to anybody."

"Wait . . ." Jonathan raises a hand. "*All* of the nannies? How many? For how long?"

"The last twenty years."

"Sarah . . ." He's rubbing his head, struggling for the right words. "This is . . ."

"Severely messed up?"

"Yes." His eyes race to meet mine. "And you've been going in every day and doing what? Pretending?"

"Yes." I tell him everything: the make-believe games, the housekeeper and chef and doorman, Malcolm, who I'm almost positive knows. The stepson, who organized the interview. The ghoulish birthday party I'm supposed to be helping to plan. The dress-cutting incident, Collette's drunkenness. Alex Bird yelling at me about the toy store disaster.

"Holy shit," Jonathan breathes when I'm finished. But that's not all. There are so many other details I'm preparing to tell him when my phone buzzes in my back pocket.

Three more buzzes, a string of messages coming in one after the other.

Oh, please don't let it be Alex Bird. Or Collette.

It's Stephen.

My dad lost his cool but he's calmed down now.

It's going to be okay.

I snort when I read this, unable to picture Mr. Bird in any way, shape, or form calming down.

Not to mention these messages are coming from Stephen—I'm still not certain if I can trust him.

The next text reads: *We'll see you tomorrow.* When I don't respond, he says: *Don't forget you signed a contract.*

My heart sinks inside my chest.

"We need to track down the former nannies," Jonathan says that night. "Get them to talk. Find out what happened, how they got out."

I'm still sitting on the bed, my phone thrown against the pillow, avoiding Stephen's texts. "The first nanny took off when Patty died," I tell him. "That was twenty years ago, so God knows where she is now. The second nanny died—" His eyebrows shoot sky-high. "No, nothing like that. It was an accident. She got hit by a cab in the middle of the street."

"Jesus," Jonathan says. "So what happened to the next nanny?"

"She only lasted a year and took a different job."

"What's she doing now?"

"She's a paralegal, I think."

"We have to find her."

"*We?*"

"Yes, we." He squeezes my hand. "I'm here to help you."

"I don't want you getting pulled into this mess."

"I love you. We're getting married and we're going to spend the rest of our lives together. So, yes, absolutely I'm going to help. Don't even try to stop me. There's got to be something this other nanny can tell us."

I shrug. "I have no idea how to find her. Her first name is Anna, that's all I know. I'm not even sure if she's still in New York."

"Well, let's find out," he says. "We need to know what she went through."

CHAPTER THIRTY-THREE

———

I'm holding a bag of clothes and two paperbacks. They're mine but Malcolm won't know that. "Pauline asked that I bring these back to Anna," I tell him.

"Anna, the last nanny?" he says. And then he averts his eyes to watch someone pass us on the street.

I lift the bag higher to my chest.

"I've got to return these. Pauline said something about her taking a different job but staying in New York?"

Malcolm watches a cab drive by, barreling down the street before turning on Columbus. "Anna . . ." he says slowly. "I haven't thought about her in a while. I wonder what she's been up to."

I shrug. "I have no idea, but I'm sure she misses working here."

He smirks. "Sure." His eyes drop. He clears his throat. "I have no idea where she is now. It's a shame, really. I liked her—" He smiles in my direction. "Oh, I like you too."

"Thanks," I say awkwardly.

We stand for a few moments, the pair of us watching the empty street.

"So," I say to him again, jostling the bag. "I've got to get these back to her, I'm sure she'll want them. Any chance you know where she lives?"

Malcolm thinks for a bit. "She was out in Brooklyn before, or maybe it was Queens? Hell, she could have moved to Hoboken after quitting this place, I honestly don't know." He pauses. "My buddy sure misses her though."

"Oh?"

He laughs. "Yeah, Judd. He used to come by and bring me sandwiches from his food stall over at the Grand Bazaar. Anything left over he'd pedal this way. I miss that. And he loved coming by to catch a glimpse of Anna. She's real pretty. Judd would try to chat her up, as if she was ever going to give him the time of day." Malcolm lets out a laugh. "She was blond and thin, just like Mrs. Bird. I swear, they could have been sisters. Super pretty . . ." He grins. "It's a damn shame she left."

"And now you've got me," I say, trying to joke.

Malcolm smiles. "It's a good thing Judd doesn't have his food stall anymore or he'd be pulling up and asking for your number too." He winks. "He even got as far as asking Anna out on a date. She said no and he was crushed. She told him she had a serious boyfriend and, in fact, I'm pretty sure they got married." He looks at me. "When you look her up, try checking out her new married name, Cewenski."

Oh, the power of Facebook. Say what you will about social media, but the ability to connect easily through technology absolutely comes in handy, especially at times like this, when you're looking for a former nanny who now has a very uncommon last name.

I find her. She's the only Anna Cewenski listed in the New

York area, and just as Malcolm said, she's recently married. Her profile page is set to public and features a ton of wedding photos: Anna and her new husband posing under trees, in front of altars, and inside gazebos.

Malcolm is right about something else too. She's a ringer for Collette. Thin, blond, and pretty. A twenty-something version of Mrs. Bird. I can see how people would have thought they were sisters.

I start typing. My first message is short and brief: *Hi, Anna. My name is Sarah Larsen and I'm a nanny for the Bird family. Can we meet?*

It's pretty vague, and after sending it, I worry it might have been too vague. She won't bother answering.

The weekend goes by without a response.

I open Facebook Messenger about a hundred times with no success, the days creeping by until I'm concerned she may not have Messenger at all.

I look her up on LinkedIn. Maybe I can track her at the office instead. But no dice, and I'm back to square one: waiting on Messenger to ding.

And then it does.

We can't talk comes the response.

That's it—nothing else.

While she's still logged in to Facebook, I type a new message, my thumbs flying across the screen. *I don't want to cause any problems but I'd really like to talk. You're the only one who understands.*

I throw in: *I don't know what to do.*

It takes a long time for her to respond, and I hold my breath, my phone gripped in my hands, waiting for a new message to appear.

What comes next is a single line.

I can't.

I want to throw the phone across the room.

I need help, I tell her. *The Birds are crazy, you know that.*

She responds, *I'm surprised you're reaching out. They won't like it. Please be careful. Don't let them know you've contacted me.*

Anna, I start to write, but she's already typing a new message.

They were supposed to stop after me. They said I was the last nanny. I should have known.

Another message pops up—I've got her hooked.

They wanted me to move in. Kept saying I could be a big sister for Patty.

Pauline got me out of my contract. Stephen promised they would get Collette proper help. No more pretending. No more nannies.

I should have known they would lie.

CHAPTER THIRTY-FOUR

===

I was in the shower and missed Jonathan's calls—all nine of them—and now my phone is blowing up again.

Squeezing the towel against my chest, I pick up. "Jonathan? Are you all right?"

I hear loud breathing. "Sarah?"

My stomach clenches at the strain in his voice. "Yes, I'm here. What's going on? Are you okay?"

"I don't know . . ." There's the sound of more breathing—is he running? He utters words I can't make out, his mouth pressed against his phone as he speaks.

"Jonathan, what's going on?"

He curses something unintelligible, followed by something crashing as if he's kicked over or thrown something.

"Jonathan, you're freaking me out. Where are you?"

"I'm heading home." My breath calms for a second.

"How far away are you?" I stare at the door. Dropping the towel, I reach for a pair of sweats and a shirt.

"I'm on Ninth, almost home." He's huffing and I can tell he's on the move, picking up the pace and barreling down the sidewalk.

"What happened?"

"It's bullshit! I lost my job at Allegro." Allegro is the Italian wine bar his buddy hooked him up with. "They said they found stuff in my locker, but it's not mine. I swear, Sarah, it's not. Someone planted it. It's a setup."

"Setup? What stuff? What are you talking about?"

"Cocaine," he says.

There's a roar in my ears. *"Cocaine? How?"*

"Not how," Jonathan says, "but why? It doesn't make sense. Why would someone put that inside my locker?" Something else crashes in the background and I think he's smashed a trash can.

A dizziness shoots through my head. With my hand against my temple, I ask, "What makes you think someone did this on purpose?"

"There was a guy in the restaurant earlier, a table by the window. He had all kinds of files and was meeting with someone, spreading out these drawings. Some architecture firm. It's got to be them—"

"It's got to be who?"

"The Birds!" he shouts. "Do you think they know you told me?"

I stop in my tracks. "What did the man look like?"

"Young. Our age."

Okay, so not Mr. Bird. Maybe Stephen?

"Short. Blond curly hair."

Okay, not Stephen.

"They were at the table for an hour or more. Never ate, only drank. It wasn't my table so I didn't talk to them, but I know the family you work for are in commercial real estate. The Bird firm—"

"Did I tell you that? I don't remember saying that."

"You didn't have to, I looked them up. Their company owns a ton of properties around the city. It's too much of a coincidence, Sarah. Alex screaming at you like that. Think about it. You tell me their big secret. We track down Anna. Then somehow cocaine mysteriously appears in my locker the same night someone from a property firm visits the new restaurant I'm working at? It's them! *They know*."

Panic seizes my heart.

"Somehow they're on to you—on to us. They're trying to scare us."

I hear a slam of the building's main door, followed by the distinct hollow sound of footsteps beating in a stairwell.

Jonathan's almost to our apartment door.

The key rattles and the door swings open. He drops his phone to his pocket and I hang up too.

"They wouldn't punish you, only me."

"I made some calls," he admits. "After you told me what happened, I couldn't let it slide. I knew I needed to find out more about this family."

My eyes bolt open. "Who did you call?"

"People at their firm. The front desk at Bird and Associates."

"*Why?*"

"To find out what they know about the family."

I want to cover my ears.

"What did you think they would say?" I ask. "Oh yeah, sure, our boss is a nutjob? The man who pays my salary is a complete psycho? His whole family too?" I throw out my hands. "Jesus, Jonathan. There's a gag order. I wasn't even supposed to tell you and now you're calling their office?"

Jonathan lets a rush of air fall from his mouth. "I was discreet about it. Come on, Sarah, give me some credit. I posed as a reporter wanting to write about the man behind this massive firm—"

"And you didn't think that would get back to him? That people wouldn't say there's a reporter asking around for background?"

"I was only trying to help." He marches to the sink and fills a glass with water. He gulps the water down steadily.

My fingers claw anxiously at my sides. Someone at the firm must have tracked his calls. They know who Jonathan is, that he is not a reporter but my fiancé, which means they know I've spilled. I've told him everything—broken my end of the contract.

I went to work today and sat beside Collette. Played game after game of Chutes and Ladders with Patty. I thought I'd been in the clear, the police phone calls and toy store complaints handled and contained, at least for now.

But all afternoon, Alex must have been digging into Jonathan.

Still, would he really go so far as to track him down at a restaurant and have someone slip drugs into his locker?

And now Jonathan's been fired. Even worse, they could arrest him.

My heart leaps. "What about the manager? Did he say he was going to press charges?"

"No, thank God. He took the coke and is probably using it himself, that shitbag."

"Jesus," I breathe again. I can't stop shaking.

Is this what Mr. Bird intended? Besides getting him fired, did he also hope to send Jonathan to jail and leave me alone, even more isolated and scared?

I'll do everything in my power to protect my family, he'd said. He meant it.

CHAPTER THIRTY-FIVE

====

Stephen finds me the next day. He corners me near the parlor so I can't get by.

"This is a shit show," he says. "We never had this many problems with the other nannies. Hell, Therese lasted fifteen years without so much as a hitch."

I suck in a ragged breath. I'm on two hours of sleep, the very thought of returning to the Birds this morning setting my teeth on edge. Jonathan had barely slept either.

"That disaster with my stepmother . . . and now"—he gives me a hard look—"the mess you're caught up in." He leans in close. "I heard about your fiancé, Jonathan."

My eyes snap open, a bitter taste forming in my mouth.

"I'd watch out for a guy like that." He wags a finger. "Drugs? Not something you want to get caught up in."

Goosebumps flare up and down my arms.

"He's damn lucky they didn't call the police and have him arrested. That much cocaine?" He whistles. "That's a serious offense."

I can't breathe. My voice comes out in a whisper, my heart beating an erratic drum. "Why would you do that?"

Stephen holds up his hands. "Wait, now, hold on. What are you suggesting, exactly? Your fiancé is the one you should be worried about. We just heard about it," he says. "We have eyes and ears everywhere. Someone told us. I'd be very careful what you accuse us of, if I were you."

He leaves me standing alone, my knees shaking.

At home, Jonathan is sitting at the table with his laptop; an empty coffeepot on the burner, and a can of Red Bull tossed in the recycling bin.

He's hunched at the computer, jaw tightened, and bearing the look of someone who isn't backing down.

I slide my bag to the floor. His stubbornness, his drive to fix what's wrong, his fierce need to protect us are usually among the many things I love about him.

But I don't know if he can fix this. I don't think he understands how much danger we could be getting ourselves into.

"That second nanny," he says, quickly scrolling the mouse. "The one who lasted all those years?"

"Yes."

"I found something."

I head directly for the fridge and find a beer. Something to calm me.

"You said her name was Therese, right?" He squints at his laptop. "They told you she died?"

I step closer to the table, an unsettled feeling blooming in my chest.

"It took me a long time," he says, "but I found it. Police blotters and city reports. A listing of car accidents from several years ago. A woman who was struck down by a cab at West End Avenue and Seventy-second." He looks up. "That's five or six blocks from the Bird place, right?" I nod. "She stepped out while the traffic light was still green and a cab hit her traveling more than fifty miles an hour. There were witnesses. Several people were interviewed, including two women who had been walking with her." I feel a rise building in my stomach. "One of the women is named in the article. Collette Bird."

His eyes shoot up to meet mine. "She said, quote, 'It was a horrible accident and it happened so quickly.' Another woman, who they don't identify except to say she is an employee of Collette Bird—" It must be Pauline. "The other woman says, 'The cabdriver was going too fast.'"

Jonathan scans a few more lines. "But another bystander told police they thought something didn't seem right. Quote, 'The woman was walking ahead of me, but then she fell to one side as if she'd been shoved.'" I swallow the beer down, hard. "This gentleman, unfortunately, isn't identified. Other people told police they couldn't confirm she'd been shoved since they only noticed her after the accident."

I take another gulp of my beer. As I sit in the chair opposite Jonathan, one phrase repeats in my head: *as if she'd been shoved.*

"Police reviewed security cameras," Jonathan continues, "but there were too many people on the street and they covered what happened."

Why didn't Pauline tell me this part? When she'd told me Therese died, why didn't she tell me she and Collette had both been walking with her when it happened? Why leave that part out?

They were there. They saw everything.

She lied to me.

CHAPTER THIRTY-SIX

Collette is crying in the hall, a ghostly sound. It echoes off the walls and travels mournfully down the corridor. Her sobs pause before picking up again. A hollow wail. She sounds like a wounded creature.

I poke my head out from behind the door. I've been in Patty's bedroom arranging the books as Collette requested. She wants them in alphabetical order. "That way," Collette told me, "when Patty asks for a book, I'll know exactly where to find it."

Pauline and Collette had been in the living room cutting up pieces of craft paper for Patty's birthday party. The image of Collette wielding another pair of scissors is something I could do without, and I'm glad to be in another room. But today something has gone wrong.

Her cries send a tingle down the back of my neck.

I step cautiously out into the hall.

Collette is no longer in her jeans and blouse; she's wearing a white nightgown.

The silk material is so thin I can see her ribs sticking out, the small roundness of her breasts, and the oblong nipples pressed against the fabric. She's barefoot, her hair swinging past her shoulders, her face bare and wiped clean since I saw her less than an hour ago. Her eyelashes, naked and blond-white, disappear against her eyelids. She's cried the makeup straight off her face.

The cut marks on her body are healing. Several of the longer, zigzagged slashes down her arms are turning pink. I can't see her belly, but I'm confident there are slash marks there too.

Someone walks up behind her, and I think at first that it's Pauline, here to shush Collette and escort her to bed. But it's not the housekeeper. The long, quick strides belong to a man.

"Collette," Mr. Bird says and he spins her around. "You must get ahold of yourself."

But Collette's voice only drips with accusation. "You . . ." she says, pointing a manicured finger in his face. "Why won't you spend time with Patty?"

He doesn't answer.

"You never play with her. You're always working. And now look at you." She beats her small fists against his chest as he stands still. "You're home from work for once and you won't even visit the playroom. She wants to show you the party decorations." More sobs erupt. "She's so excited, Alex."

He pulls away. "I have to get going."

"But she's so excited," Collette repeats, wiping her tears. "Why won't you give her five minutes—just five minutes, that's all. You used to give her so much time . . ." Her voice begins to fade. "Remember that, Alex? After she was born. Remember those days?"

But Mr. Bird sounds weary. A tenderness takes hold in his eyes. "I'm so sorry, Collette. I've got to go."

She stares at him, then laughs, heartbreak and tears mixed in with the sound. "Why bother? You've broken my heart, Patty's too. She's hiding in her playroom now, crying. See what you've done?"

Mr. Bird turns his back and leaves her in the hall.

She looks pitiful—lost and alone in this massive apartment. My heart tugs and I step out from behind the door.

She turns to me, tears falling down her cheeks and running to her neck, a drop seeping against her gown and spreading a quarter-size stain above her breast, a wet mark against the white. She reaches her arms for me.

"Oh, Sarah," she says. "Thank goodness you're here."

"Do you think someone pushed Therese?"

My eyes whip around to Jonathan. He's tossing his keys on the side table, the door closing behind him.

"I can't stop thinking about it," he insists. "Something's not adding up right."

I can't stop wondering about it too, but I'm thinking we should just drop it. I don't have that much longer with this job and we should get through it the easiest way possible, instead of digging into the past. We've already had enough problems with the Birds.

"We don't know if that's what happened."

"What? Just like we don't think they put coke in my locker?"

My face startles.

"And something else that bugs me, the way their daughter died."

"It was a tragedy, Jonathan. Nothing more."

"I've talked to a few of their neighbors," he says.

My heart freezes.

"You went to their apartment?"

"I wanted to find someone who knew Patty when she was alive."

"*Why?*" I ask. "That was twenty years ago. They'll say yes, there was a girl, and yes, she died. We already know this."

"But what if she died under mysterious circumstances?"

I'm losing my patience. "She had some sort of disease, an infection. It was horribly scarring. It was a long time ago and they didn't know how to cure it back then."

"What kind of disease could that be? Something that scarred her face and body to the point they refused to let her be seen? Closed casket and everything? No wonder the woman went crazy."

"There were skin blisters," I tell him. "I looked it up after Pauline told me."

"What kind of skin blisters kill a kid?"

"Open sores that can lead to sepsis, loss of bodily fluids. The child can stop eating and breathing."

Jonathan scratches at his neck and chin. "I don't know, it just doesn't—"

"What are you trying to say? That's not how she really died?"

"No." He's pacing. "Yes . . . maybe . . . I don't know." He sits down with me, his eyes darting from one side of the room to the other, his brain churning. "It just seems weird."

"Everything about these people is weird."

"Don't you want to know what happened to Patty?"

"No one killed her," I tell him sternly. "They loved her too much." I meet his eyes. "Let's think about this for a second, okay? Why kill a girl and then spend the next twenty years pretending she's still alive?" I shake my head. "That's not what happened."

"Well you can't ignore what might have happened to Therese. There's something wrong there, I know it, and you know it. And the other nanny quitting on them like that . . ."

I rub the bridge of my nose. "I told you. Pauline helped get her out of that contract because the family promised she would be the last nanny."

"But she wasn't, right? They didn't stop."

I sigh. Jonathan's eyes won't leave my face.

"No, they didn't," I tell him.

CHAPTER THIRTY-SEVEN

It's nearing midnight and Jonathan hasn't come home yet. He said he would be meeting up with friends at a bar and asked me to join them. After everything we're going through, I guess he wanted to let off some steam. I needed the quiet time to myself; our conversation from earlier left me weary and rattled.

When the doorbell buzzes, I instantly drop the remote.

It buzzes a second time. Swinging my legs off the futon, I shuffle to the intercom panel on the wall. With my finger jammed against the button, I say, "You okay, babe? You lost your keys?"

A pause.

"Ma'am?" an unfamiliar voice says in return.

I flinch and pull my finger away from the wall. I push the button again. "Who is this?"

"Ma'am," the voice repeats, a deep baritone. "New York City PD. Can we come up?"

I'm not buying it—Jonathan's paranoia and Stephen's warnings have got me on edge—and I rush to the window to get a better view. I'm not going to buzz just anyone into our building.

I see two figures below. Slamming my hand against the

window frame to rattle it loose, I lift it up just an inch, enough for me to call out, "Can I see your ID?"

The two people outside my building are dressed like New York City police officers—one male and one female in stiff black jackets and black pants. Looking up, they locate the sound of my voice and spot the open window.

"New York City police," the male officer repeats, holding up his badge. The woman does the same.

"What is it?"

Another pause. The female officer speaks this time. "I think it's best you let us up."

I move back to the intercom panel and buzz them in, my breaths getting shorter. It's harder to squeeze the air into my lungs.

Within seconds, the officers appear at my door and I'm thinking: the Birds sent them. They've had complaints from the neighbors about Jonathan asking questions. They've sent the police to warn us.

"Can we come in?" the female officer asks.

I let them in. One look at their faces and a sick feeling grows deep inside my stomach.

"What is it?" I ask. "What happened?"

"I'm sorry to have to tell you this . . ." the female officer begins.

And I suddenly know what they're about to say. The reason they're here.

This can't be happening.

"Jonathan?" I stumble back. The male officer reaches out to hold me even though I shake him off to take another step.

Maybe, I think, if I make it to the other side of the room, what they're about to tell me won't be true. Jonathan will come walking through that door any minute and this will all be a big mistake.

But that's not what they're telling me, and my world bottoms out. The floor opens up to swallow me whole, a cataclysmic boom and rip in my universe.

Covering my ears with my hands, I stumble again, but this time find enough of my footing to reach the edge of the bed, my knees buckling so I can sit. They're talking in a fishbowl, I can't understand them—don't want to hear what they're saying. I'm telling myself they've got it all wrong. They've screwed up big time. ID'd the wrong person. It can't be Jonathan, must be someone else.

They found him in an alley.

A syringe in his arm.

Someone found his body.

Their voices sound as if they're underwater. The walls are spinning around me.

"Do you have anyone you can call?" one of the officers asks. "We need to get in touch with his family too."

"Is there anyone who can sit with you?" asks the other.

I'm covering my face with my hands. My breathing is labored, shallow.

Shut up, shut up, *shut up,* I want to scream.

I think I'm shrieking, but I'm not. Only breathing— desperate attempts at gulping air.

"We need to get ahold of his parents," the female officer says, flipping out a notepad. She lowers her face to me. "Ms. Larsen?"

I'm crying, a dam breaking open inside my head. "I don't understand. You mean . . . Jonathan . . . ?"

Jonathan is dead.

Did the Birds have something to do with this?

The female officer drops to her knees beside me, her hand on my back as I rock and wail. I push her away—I don't want her to come near me. I don't want either of them in the apartment anymore, and I beg them to go.

When the door shuts, I search for my phone, my hands trembling. I call Amelia, but I'm crying so hard she can hardly understand what I'm saying.

"Jonathan . . ." I sob something about a syringe and how they found him dead and I need her to come quickly. I don't know how to tell his family.

Amelia is hysterical too. She arrives at the apartment within minutes, her eyes wild and red and matching my own. And we fall to the floor, holding each other because we don't know what else to do.

CHAPTER THIRTY-EIGHT

Overnight, my world goes gray. I don't know how else to explain it except that colors drain from everything I see. Noises are sucked out. There's only a hum and a throbbing ache where happiness and laughter used to be. Everything I touch is now cold and hard—nothing has texture. I want to lie on the floor and shrivel up.

I sleep, but only to avoid everything because it's the only way I can hide. Numb the pain and knock myself into a black, sleep-heavy oblivion.

I'm empty inside. The emptiness is so overwhelming, it's exhausting, and I never understood before how that can happen. The grief and heartache literally take my breath away until I have no energy to do anything else. The simplest of tasks are unimaginable. The grief erases all emotions except sheer, excruciating pain.

This is how Collette must have felt when Patty died.

Jonathan's parents travel from Philadelphia to view his body. I didn't call them, at least I don't remember calling them. Everything has been a big hazy blur. I don't remember who I've spoken to, who has called, although I'm sure there have been visitors. Stacks of food go to waste on my kitchen counter. Someone forced me out of the clothes I've been

wearing since the police were here—was that Amelia? I look
down at the soft green top I'm wearing, the jogger pants, the
drool that has collected down the front of my chest, the
wrinkled material at my waist, and I think that must have
been days ago. It's time I change out of these clothes too. But
I don't.

Jonathan's parents coming was one of the most painful
experiences of my life. They asked me if they could take
some of his things. I remember staring at a picture of the two
of us at Coney Island, Jonathan standing behind me, his
arms wrapped around my waist, both of us smiling like two
schoolkids for the camera. The mother reaches for one of
Jonathan's favorite shirts with the Philadelphia Phillies logo
on the front and brings the shirt to her face, breathing him in.

We'd talked about having the wedding in Philadelphia
since I didn't have any family left and most of Jonathan's
family and friends are still in the area. He wanted me to meet
his dog, Wilson. He said he wanted to take me to a skating
rink near his home where he could teach me to skate. He told
me he'd hold my hand.

But none of that is going to happen now.

The thought of attending his funeral service is enough to
make me want to rip off my skin. It hurts too much. I don't
know how I'm going to survive losing him.

First, my parents. Then the devastation of losing Aunt
Clara. And now Jonathan.

His parents asked me questions too, in scared and horri-
fied tones—did I know he was using heroin? Was this something that had been going on for a while? Why didn't I try to
stop him?

I told them no, that's not right. You've got it all wrong.

That's not Jonathan. He would never. But I'm hysterical through all of it, not sure if I've convinced them.

After they left, I turned off the lights and crawled back into bed.

At some point—is it Thursday, Sunday? I have no idea anymore—Collette and Pauline appear in the apartment. At some point I must have sent them a message about Jonathan, about why I wasn't coming into work, but I honestly can't remember. Collette may have tried calling too. When she and Pauline arrive, I don't want them here but can't find the strength to tell them to go. At first I recoil, but Collette is loving and kind and wrapping me in hugs while Pauline makes me endless cups of hot tea and sits quietly with Kleenex and blankets they've brought.

Collette is crying too.

I stare at the woman: Does she have any idea what her husband might have done to the love of my life?

Am I losing it to think it was them?

But she doesn't know anything—of course she doesn't. She sits by my side and lets me rest my head in her lap while she strokes my hair. Pauline takes my hand and squeezes gently. They let me cry some more and then they let me sleep. I have no idea how long they stay, but when I wake hours later, they've left a note. Collette tells me they'll be back in the morning to check on me.

At 7:00 A.M., the doorbell is buzzing. I don't answer and pull the covers over my head. But loud knocking pounds on the main door outside, and then footsteps echo up the stairs. Someone has opened the door for them; I hear Collette's voice outside my door, followed by someone else's. One of my neighbors has let them in—do they know what's happened? My fiancé is dead. Today is his funeral.

I don't want to move—at first, I refuse to—but Collette and Pauline practically lift me from the bed and guide me to the shower. It hurts to stand up. I've been in the fetal position for days with the apartment in darkness and it hurts my eyes to have the light turned on. The water feels like acid on my skin.

Pauline is helping me get dressed when Amelia appears at the door. I remember her being here yesterday—or was it three days ago?—the pair of us saying we would attend Jonathan's funeral together. We'd take the train, and after returning to the city, she would stay the night to make sure I wouldn't be alone.

She clutches a small duffel bag.

But Collette is backing her toward the door and speaking to her in hushed tones. She places a hand gently on Amelia's shoulders and tells her it's unnecessary, that she doesn't need to worry, because she and Pauline are here now and able to take care of me. They will take care of everything.

Amelia cranes her neck. She shoots me a worried look and I know what she's thinking—she doesn't know these people. Her one and only encounter with Collette was watching her lose her mind at the restaurant, costing both me and Jonathan our jobs.

Amelia says something to Collette in return. She's protesting, I can tell that much, but Collette is reverting to that singsong voice that always gets her what she wants.

She returns Amelia to the hall. Hands her cash and tells her to use it to buy a train ticket.

"We'll take Sarah comfortably in our car."

But Amelia says, "Sarah . . . ?" And she looks in my direction to make sure I'm okay.

I tell her, "It's all right," and give her a small smile. And then Amelia is gone.

Henry drives us. The apartment I share with Jonathan disappears behind us as we move along the city streets, then out of Manhattan toward Philadelphia. The drive will take two hours.

I look out the window blankly at New York City, the place I once thought magically exciting and full of hope. The place I found Jonathan. It's all turning to gray. Gray streets. Gray buildings. Even the skyline and once dazzling skyscrapers are large and ominous and threatening to crumble and crash around me.

As much as I'm beside myself thinking there's a possibility Collette's husband had something to do with Jonathan's death—every time the thought enters my brain I want to throw up or scream, or both—I can't bring myself to fight the family right now.

Because honestly, I need Collette's help to get me through this day. I'm too tired and overwhelmed to do anything for myself right now. I just need someone to hold me up, make sure I don't fall to my knees. She's the only one I know who understands how crushing a loss like this feels.

But I seethe. How could he? How could Mr. Bird do something like this to the man I love—if this is his doing?

Does Collette have any idea who she's married to?

I cry thinking about Jonathan, overcome with grief that I'll never see him again, that I won't wake in the mornings to find him next to me in bed. No more nights sharing Chinese takeout or watching him at his laptop, scrolling through end-less news headlines or ESPN scores. No more sharing coffee mugs or breakfast before work. The bagel shop around the corner.

No more planning our wedding. No changing my name to Mrs. Romero.

No chance for ice-skating lessons at the skating rink.

The chance for our little family to grow together—my own family after I've already lost so much.

CHAPTER THIRTY-NINE

━━

I don't remember much from the funeral except the feeling of Collette and Pauline on either side of me, holding me up.

Afterward, they fold me into the back of the car again, and before I know it we are returning to West Seventy-eighth Street, the women helping me up the elevator and bringing me to one of the guest rooms, where Collette says I can stay for as long as I'd like.

I watch Collette. The room darkens as she pulls the curtains and moves past my bed. I raise my head again, but exhaustion washes over me. My eyes are heavy and all I want to do is sleep. Shut everything out. Lie here and sleep and no longer feel the pain, even if that means staying in the home of the man who might be responsible for my grief.

"Stay here for as long as you need to, sweet girl," Collette says before quietly stepping out of the room. Collette is on my side, she's not going to hurt me. For now, we will help each other through our terrible ordeals.

I pull the covers over my head, willing sleep to come.

I think I stay there for days, although I can't be sure. Days and nights run together and it's hard to keep track, especially when the curtains are always closed. Collette and Pauline bring me food, and occasionally, they manage to get me to eat a few bites. Just like at my apartment, they encourage me to shower. They comb my hair, and Collette brings me a new lip balm. It's vanilla-scented, she says. One of Patty's favorites.

Other times, I ask them to leave. I tell them they don't need to hover, that I can do it myself. But then I go back to sleep, and when I wake, Collette is there again, checking on me from the doorway. She blows me a kiss.

I wait for Mr. Bird and Stephen to return from their business trip. Collette says they've been gone a few days.

What convenient timing, I think, although I'm still not sure how I'm going to be able to face them when they appear.

A few days later, I'm eating part of a sandwich Pauline has brought me, and Collette considers this a success. "Progress," she says. "You're gaining your strength." She coaxes me out of the guest room to watch a movie in the living room. I sit on the couch, a fog clouding my head as the movie plays. I have no idea what it's about, can barely pay attention to the words let alone the story line, but at least I'm sitting up. I'm no longer in the fetal position.

I'm wearing leggings and a shirt, although I don't recognize them as mine since I haven't brought a stitch of clothing with me, not even a toothbrush. But apparently that's all been taken care of. Collette has bought me brand-new everything, from shampoo and deodorant to new underwear. But these clothes look like they've come straight from her closet.

I'm no longer their employee but someone they must take care of—they insist upon it. Often, I hear Collette speaking to Patty. She'll ask her which movie she wants to watch next. We sit through *Cinderella* and *Pinocchio* and *The Lion King*. Freddie brings us tea and hot chocolate in that same rainbow mug. Pauline moves around us quietly, lightly dusting or wiping at countertops before checking to make sure I'm all right.

Another day passes and I'm thinking the men must be coming home soon—they can't stay away forever. What will I say to them? Will I be able to confront them? They'll deny everything, I'm sure. They'll tell me I'm making it all up in my head.

I look around, my throat choked with tears. Fatigue washes over me again, followed by that now-familiar helpless feeling.

I'm wearing Collette's clothes. I'm staying with her around the clock. She's loving that I'm with her.

Despite everything—what I know, what Jonathan warned me about—I'm doing exactly what she wants. What she wanted with the last nanny too.

Without realizing it, I've moved in with the Birds.

CHAPTER FORTY

It's strange, but I find I'm enjoying staying with Collette. I know I should leave, should tear out of here, but I don't have the energy to move. And it's comforting being taken care of by someone else. I'm too weary to leave this apartment, because then what? I go back to my tiny apartment, where everything reminds me of Jonathan? The French press he used to make us coffee. The pots and pans with the bright red handles in which he cooked our first dinner together. The extra pillow he used to prop up his head as he checked his phone for emails.

Amelia has texted me I don't know how many times, asking me if I'm all right, asking to come see me, wondering how I am.

Sarah, please let me know if you're ok.

We're all thinking of you. Thinking of Jonathan xx

Two days later: *Sarah, are you there?*

You don't have to talk but please text me so I know you're good.

Another message: *Should we be worried?*

I'm okay, I text her. *Thank you for checking on me.*

She immediately messages back.

Where are you? I've been to your apartment so many times. Are you still with that family?

Yes.

Do you need anything? Are you okay?

I'm good. They're taking care of me.

No need to tell her anything else. Like how frightened I am of the moment Mr. Bird will arrive home, or that Collette and Pauline have become my unlikely lifelines right now.

Can I come see you?

I ask Collette.

"My friend," I tell her. "The one you met at my apartment—Amelia. She wants to visit."

Collette looks up from her magazine. "Here?"

"Yes, here."

She reaches for my arm. "Not right now, sweetheart."

I stare at my phone, then back at Collette. "Only for a few minutes? I think she's worried about me."

Collette smiles. "That's kind." And she rubs her fingers over my hand. "But Alex will be coming home soon. Let's not have any visitors."

She closes her magazine and rises from the couch. But my heart seizes.

"He's coming home tonight?"

"Soon," she says.

Icy fear locks inside my chest. Collette doesn't notice the altered look on my face, the panic I'm swallowing as she continues curling her blond hair around one finger. She sashays toward the kitchen and calls over her shoulder, "I'm making hot chocolate for me and Patty. Want some?"

But I can't speak. I don't answer. She says something about bringing me one anyway.

I watch her disappear behind the door. My phone drops to my lap, Amelia's question left unanswered.

Just as Collette said, Mr. Bird returns that evening from his business trip, Stephen too. Neither of them looks surprised to see me, their sad little houseguest, which means Collette has already told them I'm here.

My heartbeat slows to a crawl as the men set down their bags and greet Collette with a kiss, hug Pauline, and then say something to me about condolences for Jonathan.

I don't move, the air an arctic blast inside my lungs. I'm unable to take a full breath until they leave the room.

If Mr. Bird had a hand in Jonathan's death, he doesn't show it. Neither does Stephen. Both of them, blank faces.

I suppose, in Mr. Bird's mind, my being here in his home with his family is proof I'm not running to the cops. He must think I'm easy to manipulate. Unable to fight on my own. Letting the enemy take care of me because I have nowhere else to go. Maybe he's right.

I depend on Collette and Pauline now. They're the long-lost mother and aunt I've been doing without for so long. I've missed that kind of support system.

Collette is returning to me, whispering in my ear and telling me everything is going to be all right. She hands me a sketch pad, brand new. A world of possibilities, she says. She encourages me to draw and create and take my mind far away from here.

"Design me a new outfit," she says. "A line of dresses. Something for Patty too."

And Mr. Bird is already turning away. His silence is no longer threatening. He's unbothered, unfazed. Seems surprised when Pauline mentions something to him about heroin in a dark alley.

And I'm starting to wonder if he had nothing to do with Jonathan. Maybe it was someone else.

And I sink against the sofa, my brain in turmoil. The mind games in this place.

CHAPTER FORTY-ONE

I hear her—Patty.

Tinkle-bell laughter of a girl. I hear her as clear as any-thing, the sound so small and joyful it reverberates off the walls.

A few days later, I see her too. The wisp of her blond hair as she runs around the corner. The small frame of her body as she scampers into another room.

I'm going mad. The girl is dead—*she's dead*. I know this. Collette is the one who invents her in her head, not me.

She's getting to me. Alex being home, his very presence and my paranoia, is seeping into my core.

This whole place has taken over my senses.

I'm grieving. Jonathan's death is too much to handle. But *seeing Patty?* I know I'm a wreck, but I can't be losing my reasoning too, my ability to know real from imaginary.

But there's no explaining what is happening to me now. I'm seeing things that aren't there. Patty skipping down the hall. The patter of running feet. Dolls moving around in her playroom. But I'm not the one touching them.

I haven't been right lately—my head isn't right. My fiancé is dead. I watched his family bury him in the ground. There is no one left for me to go home to. That's enough to make anyone go off the deep end, right? I mean, look what happened to Collette.

I just need more rest. I'll sleep this off until I can't hear her anymore—can't see her. I'll shut my eyes and shut out Patty.

But I wake up, and there she is.

Blond ponytail coming around the corner, the impish grin. The gentle skid as she slides along the floors in her socks. She's running from one room to the next, her head thrown back with laughter—her mom too—the pair of them cuddled together on the couch watching a movie. I *see* them. I smell her strawberry bodywash too. The sweet tang of it.

But I'm only imagining things, right? Collette ran the bathwater earlier and dumped a bottle of strawberry bodywash into the tub like she does every time. That's what I'm smelling, not Patty. The scent lingers down the hall and follows me everywhere.

It's not Patty. She's not here—*dammit, she's not.*

I shut my eyes, plug my ears, and tell myself she's not in the room. She's not asking me to play with her dollhouse. I'm not following her to the playroom. I'm not opening the door. But when I turn around, I'm there. In the playroom. My legs and body have brought me here. My head is in a whirl and everything is foggy, but I'm stepping across the carpet, kneeling at the dollhouse, and lifting the Patty doll as she tells me to.

I'm sitting at the table for a tea party. Listening to Patty tell me about her birthday, the friends she'll have over, the fun times we'll have. I'm listening to every word, bringing a teacup to my mouth.

She's calling me Sissy. She says she's happy to have a big sister, and I'm nodding and letting her hug me, her strawberry-scented hair pressed against my cheeks until all I want to do is choke and cry, crawl out of the playroom because it doesn't make any sense—this can't be happening.

I'm spending hours in the playroom and barely realizing it. The days are flying by. We spend all our time in here now.

Something strange is happening too—something else I don't understand. I'm no longer cringing when I hold the Patty doll. It no longer frightens me. And before I know it, I'm stroking the doll's hair without anyone asking me to. Like Collette, I'm clutching her in my hand.

I wake up to find Patty's lock of hair, the one Collette gave me, next to my pillow. I don't remember putting it there, but there it is. Every morning. I breathe in the strawberry scent of my own hair too.

After a few more days, I'm hurting. My body is aching and feverish. I can't explain it—Collette can't either. I languish in bed and feel sick to my stomach as Collette tucks me under the covers and tells me to get some rest.

Eventually she wonders if we should call for a doctor. "Not the family doctor," she tells Pauline firmly.

The housekeeper brings a washcloth for my head and then the fever breaks and I'm beginning to feel better. My body doesn't ache as much. The nausea is subsiding. My need to sleep or sit in a daze for hours on end is dissipating. Collette tells me my grief for Jonathan has weakened my immune system.

I hear Collette whispering to Pauline. She tells her she hopes I haven't gotten Patty sick and wonders if we should stay apart for a few days to make sure Patty doesn't fall ill too. But she doesn't. The little girl doesn't stay away. Sure enough, Patty finds her way to me.

CHAPTER FORTY-TWO

The moment I step into the kitchen, Freddie minimizes whatever he was looking at on his computer and turns away.

"Are you feeling okay?" he asks, and I halt in my tracks.

The fact that he's spoken to me, acknowledged my presence, is strange. The last couple of weeks he's been setting an extra place at the table for me dutifully and without comment, barely looking in my direction, which has been par for the course since I started working here anyway. But *now* he wants to talk?

I stare at him for a long, steady minute before clearing my throat. "I'm all right," I tell him.

"Are you sure?"

I clear my throat again, an uneasy feeling blooming inside my chest, and search for the right words. "I'm tired. Grieving. It's been a really rough time." *Like you care,* I want to add.

But he throws me a cautious look. "Do you have other people you can talk to? Another place to stay?"

"You want me to leave?"

"Don't you want to leave?"

I look down at the floor. "No," I say, and then look up. "Not right now, I mean."

"Don't you want to be with your friends?"

I think about Amelia. She's texted a few more times, and each time I've told her not to worry. She hasn't been sending as many messages anymore.

"What about staying with your family?" Freddie asks.

"I don't have any family left." If he'd bothered to get to know me, he would have known this.

To my surprise, he looks sympathetic. "I'm worried . . ." he says and stares down at the same bowl he's been drying for the last couple of minutes, the towel going around in circles. He folds the towel tight in his hands. "Something isn't right again."

My eyes flinch. "Again?"

"Something with all this." He makes a face. "I've been watching this family for years and they never think I notice. I stay quiet, do what I'm told, but I notice things—I overhear things." He gives me a wary look. "I also don't try to stop any of it, I know, and I could. And for that, I'm sorry."

I step closer.

"What is there for you to be sorry for? You work in the kitchen. I'm here to be a fake nanny. Your job has nothing to do with me."

"Oh, but it does. And now look what's happened. They've got you living here too."

"It's not permanent," I say quickly. "Only until I figure out what to do next."

"And when will that be?" He raises his eyebrows, a warning tone creeping into his voice. "They won't want you to leave. You can try, you can tell them you're ready, that you're feeling better, but they'll find ways to keep you—it's what they always do."

It's what they always do.

"I'm only here until the birthday party and then my contract is over."

He stands still.

But something alerts me, something he said earlier. "Why did you ask if I'm feeling okay? Did you mean feeling sad about Jonathan or something else?"

"Something else," he says. "Besides emotionally, I mean. Have you been feeling sick?"

"You know I've been sick," I snap. "I had a stomach bug. I haven't been eating much. I'm still . . ." I hate repeating the word. "I'm still grieving. But I'm getting better. Don't you think I seem better today?"

Freddie dismisses my question. "What about seeing things? Wanting to sleep all the time? Strange dreams?"

By strange dreams, does he mean sobbing in my sleep, drenching my pillow in tears as I remember my last moment with Jonathan, how he'd left to meet up with friends and I'd stayed home instead. My last words being *Don't stay out too late.* But at least I kissed him goodbye. He'd squeezed my hands twice: once for I love you and the second for I'll be thinking of you.

I squeeze my eyes shut. Thank God we had that moment one more time.

"I've been upset," I tell him. "My fiancé *died,* remember? They think Jonathan OD'd on heroin—"

"Except you don't think he did."

It's my turn to raise my eyebrows.

"What's happened in the past, to Anna and Therese, even to Patty, never sat right with me. Never. And now Jonathan."

A shiver takes hold of my body. "What are you saying?"

He holds my look. "I don't like how your fiancé died. Something isn't right and you know it isn't," he repeats. "Someone got to him, Sarah. Someone did that to him." A tremor I've never seen before darkens his face. "And I'm afraid if you're not careful, you're going to be next."

CHAPTER FORTY-THREE

I can't shake what Freddie said. What's happened in the past. His suspicions about what happened to Jonathan, about the fate of everyone else.

Does this family hurt anyone who asks questions, and did they go after Jonathan? Did the same thing happen to Therese? Was she pushed—and by whom?

Not Pauline, that wouldn't make sense. She wouldn't kill another member of the household staff. What purpose would that serve?

I think about Collette. Killing her beloved longtime nanny doesn't make sense either.

Is it possible Mr. Bird paid someone to shove her into oncoming traffic? It couldn't have been Stephen. He'd been only a teenager at the time. Maybe Alex worried she was done keeping their secret, so he silenced her forever?

And what about the way Patty died? Freddie seems to think that was suspicious too, just like Jonathan had. But I still have my doubts.

Mr. Bird is a monster, Collette is beyond insane, but they wouldn't kill their own child.

Something strikes me at that moment, and I stop myself just outside the piano room.

Stephen. Just like his dad, he comes off friendly enough, but once he's tested, once he gets angry, he's more than capable of—how had he put it?—bringing down the hammer.

Did Stephen kill his own sister?

The thought has never occurred to me until now. But that can't be right. He was what, twelve years old when she died? He wouldn't hurt his baby sister. I've heard the way he's talked about Patty. As for his parents, she'd been the light of their lives. He could never do anything to hurt her because then he'd be alone. But he'd also be the remaining child. The one to inherit everything.

Was this his way of getting his father's attention to himself? And, eventually, all the money?

I lean against the wall, the thoughts making me dizzy.

If Stephen could have pulled off something so heartless at such a young age, I have no doubt he'd be capable of killing to keep his secret. Did Therese catch on to what he was doing, and Stephen made sure she would never tell a soul? All this time, poor Collette and Pauline have been thinking it was a senseless tragedy.

Or did Alex kill his own daughter? I remember what Pauline let slip several weeks ago—that she thought Mr. Bird was having an affair with Ms. Fontaine, the first nanny—the one who ran off in the middle of the night. Did Therese find out and he silenced her because she was trying to blackmail him?

Would he go so far as to kill Jonathan also? Did he pay someone from the office to plant cocaine in his locker? And when that wasn't enough to scare him off, did he have someone follow my fiancé instead, drag him to that alleyway, and pump him with enough heroin to make his heart stop?

Could they have done this to him?

I blink back the tears, searing pain returning to my chest as I look around at the priceless art and shined-to-the-brink marble floors. This apartment is a glass prison—and I've been *living* in this prison, willingly. Staying in the very home of the people who could be responsible for killing my fiancé. *What have I done?*

I suddenly want to run. Grab my things. Go straight to the police.

I rush for the nearest corridor, the one that will take me to the front door and the elevator beyond. I won't stop to say goodbye to Collette. I won't explain myself to Pauline— I just need to go.

But I hear someone behind me and I freeze.

It's Mr. Bird. He's in the hallway, the two of us locking eyes.

"Where are you going?" he asks simply.

For whatever reason, I don't answer, only backtrack, my feet slowly inching across the floor.

He watches me carefully, his eyes intense, but then turning soft. "If you're thinking about leaving, please don't." And he clasps his hands together, almost pleading. "Please don't go. We really want you with us."

I look down, avoiding his gaze.

"I know this is a difficult time for you . . . I can't imagine. But you being here, it's helping Collette so much, you must see that. You must know she's thriving being able to care for you." Our eyes meet again and a tremble of emotion fills the back of my throat. "You're giving her purpose."

He pauses on the word *purpose*.

I think about everything Freddie told me, the questions

lingering between us. What he's seen in this house and what he thinks is happening again. And what Mr. Bird is implying now, that by suffering in my own grief, I'm giving Collette something to focus on.

"I have to leave at some point," I tell Mr. Bird. "I can't stay forever."

"No, of course not," he says, his eyes flickering with an understanding that all but disappeared the last time we spoke. He'd been slamming his fists on a desktop and accusing me of allowing Collette to spin out of control in a toy store. "You'll be strong again soon. You'll be able to move on."

"But until then . . . ?" I say.

"It will be best if you stay here. It's good for you, we can be here for you. And," he adds, "Collette needs you too."

"And then I'm leaving," I say firmly.

He nods, a little slowly I notice, but at least it's a yes. "Until Patty's birthday," he says. "She'll want you here to enjoy the big day."

I nod, hoping every word of this is true. But then he adds, "Because if you leave too soon, she'll fall apart." He steps away. "And we won't want you bearing that guilt for the rest of your life, now will we?"

CHAPTER FORTY-FOUR

—

Collette knows something is bothering me. I've barely spoken the last two days and have been hiding in my room until she tells me Patty is begging for me to come out and play.

I cover my ears with my hands as Collette calls through the door. "Patty misses her sissy. Won't you come out for one more game?"

Collette is getting too dependent on me. The longer I stay here, the more she wants me to indulge in her fantasy of living and staying with Patty.

I'm getting too dependent on her too.

But I'm worried. Like Mr. Bird warned, what will happen to her if I leave early? And after I leave the birthday party, will they send her away?

But she calls. She doesn't give up. And the following morning, she knocks on my door. "I think it's time we get you outdoors. All of us," she says, smiling. She means Patty too.

I don't want to, but she practically pulls me from the bed, helping me brush the knots from my hair and telling me to change clothes. I slip on a pair of jeans and a blue blouse she places for me on the chair.

Pauline stays behind in the apartment. It's just Collette and myself. And Patty.

She hands me a pair of sunglasses as soon as we step outside, and I'm grateful. The fresh air and bright sun hit me like a shock wave, but I must admit, it feels good to finally be leaving this place, this wretched apartment, even if it's only for a short while.

I haven't been sleeping. After Jonathan died, I'd slept for hours. But now I lie awake, fearful, desperate to leave.

I've been staring at the ceiling instead. Thinking about Jonathan. Missing our apartment and wanting to go back, to be surrounded by our things again, to clutch his pillow, which I'm hoping still has his smell.

And yet, I haven't left. I still need Collette. Every time I push her away, I find I'm falling back to her again.

We're walking and Collette is holding my hand. She's not swinging it, thank goodness, but gripping it. After so many days kept inside, she knows this is a big outing for me. She directs us to Central Park and calls ahead for Patty to slow down, but never once does she let go of my hand.

I don't fight it, just keep walking. I hadn't realized until now how much I needed a walk in the sun.

"I was thinking about lunch today, the three of us," Collette says. "There's a beautiful place in the park, the Loeb Boathouse. Have you been?"

I shake my head. I've seen it from a distance on summer walks through the park but never sat inside.

"The restaurant is lovely too," Collette says. "We love going there." She gives me a hopeful look. "Do you think you could handle that today?"

I nod, and she looks happier than she has in days.

We walk to the boathouse slowly. It's been a long time since I've stretched my legs and traveled farther than the Birds' hallway.

We stop several times to admire the flower beds filled with lavender and white pansies, and I miss walking the park with Jonathan. I want to be holding his hand, not hers. Collette means well, she wants to see me get better, but I'd rather feel the warmth of Jonathan's fingers against mine, his hand moving to my lower back.

I hate the idea I'll never be able to walk with him again . . . see him again . . .

The tears threaten to spill, but I swallow them back. I must keep walking. One foot in front of the other. I don't want to lose it out here.

Collette tugs my arm gently and insists we move to the other side of the path, which overlooks a grassy area. We watch a small girl chase her dog. Collette calls to Patty to run and play too and the other girl stops and stares, confused about whom Collette is speaking to. But before the girl can say anything, we're off, and moving farther along the path.

I'm exhausted, and when I see the boathouse, I feel relieved. It's a beautiful place. The only venue set on a Manhattan lake with a stone, brick, and wood structure, and white-columned patio seating with views of the Central Park West skyline. Iconic rowboats float nearby. A gentle breeze rustles through the trees. It will be nice to sit down.

I'd walked by this place a half dozen times with Jonathan, but we never made time to stop and eat here. Now I wish we had.

The hostess leads us to a table outside, and as I'm admir-

ing the rows of white tablecloths and glistening water beyond the balcony, something hits me. The strongest sensation
of déjà vu that I've been here before. Sat in this very dining
area. But I know I haven't.

Collette looks at me curiously. "Are you all right?"

I don't answer.

We order our food and eat in silence. Collette tries making small talk. She brings up the weather but I'm not interested.

Mostly, I stare at my food. The pond. The boats. The sun
glistening off the surface of the water.

The way people are walking nearby, enjoying their afternoon. Everything in their lives seemingly perfect. Lovers
holding hands. Families placing boats in the water. Children
playing and scampering in the grass.

On the table, Patty's spaghetti and meatballs goes cold.

CHAPTER FORTY-FIVE

We plan Patty's birthday party. The caterer is booked, the cake ordered. Everything, to Collette's excitement, is coming together nicely.

She thinks keeping me busy will help me through my grief. She says it will do me good to have something to look forward to, although Jonathan is constantly on my mind.

I hear Pauline on the phone with the kids' entertainment center in Boston, where the carousel will be coming from.

"We can't have everything delivered at one time," she tells them. "It must arrive in stages." She's silent before continuing, "That's right. Spread the delivery out over the course of two weeks. Everything needs to come up the service elevator. You'll have access to the back of the building." More silence. "Yes, thank you so much for your understanding. We look forward to receiving it."

She and I share a knowing look and she clicks her teeth. None of us need the neighbors looking on and speculating. We need this to be discreet.

"We have a big day ahead," Collette tells me. "We need to start thinking about who to invite to Patty's party."

I raise my eyebrows. Yes, that one detail I haven't been able to wrap my head around.

"I really want to give the guests enough time to prepare," Collette says. "Make sure they can attend since it's the most special day of the year."

I wait for Collette to bring out a list. A group of kids from the building or a list of kids she's remembering from way back when. But those children would be in their twenties by now. Some of them may even have kids of their own.

She doesn't provide such a list, though, only looks at me expectantly. A minute passes and her stare takes on a more serious expression as I return it, not knowing what else to do. But then I realize with a start what she's getting at, and the top half of my body straightens like a rod. She means for me to figure it out on my own.

But we don't know any kids.

"I'm sure you will take care of this," she says, getting up from the sofa. "Those playdates Patty's been having . . ." *What playdates?* "The group of children she loves spending time with . . ." *There are no kids.* "I'd like Patty to have her best friends join us on this day."

I want to pull the hair from my head. What children?

I can't go down the street and knock on doors, recruiting kids from the neighborhood. The parents would look at me like I was crazy. So many living on the Upper West Side know the Bird family and may even know Patty is gone. They'd start talking, the rumor mill building. No one within a twenty-block radius would send their children to a party when they know the Bird girl is no longer alive. The story would spread like wildfire.

I think about the party planning we've done so far, the steps we've taken. The cake and snacks and decorations that have been ordered.

Is it possible to order child actors? An off-Broadway per-
formance group that we can pay?

But my shoulders slump—that would never work. Those
people wouldn't be capable of keeping their mouths shut.
The party will be too bizarre and too deliciously full of gossip. People would be saying how Collette should be locked
away in an asylum.

I must bring in people who won't talk. But how? And
where?

How have the other nannies pulled this off?

"Okay . . ." I say slowly, but my mind is racing. I look to
Pauline for any guidance. Suggestions on where to get some
kids.

But Pauline lifts our coffee mugs and heads for the kitchen.

"We'll need invitations," Collette says. "I know the perfect place." She eyes me carefully. "You up for another outing? We can head to the invitation store."

Henry drives us, and there, among the invitations, I keep
asking Collette questions. I need her to give me some idea of
what her expectations are. Who do I address them to? Where
should I find these children?

After all, she's hosted this party every year for twenty
years—surely, she can tell me what she's done in the past.
Who she's brought to the penthouse on West Seventy-eighth
and forced to sit around a table and sing "Happy Birthday."
It couldn't have been only Collette, Pauline, and the nanny.

Unless—it's make-believe kids. Collette will imagine their
presence. She'll think we mailed the invitations, when really,
they'll have gone in the trash.

Collette is flipping through books of card stock and talk-

ing excitedly about patterns and layouts, admiring water-
colors and drawings from each artist.

"These children need to come with their parents," she
tells me. "They can't be dropped off like last time. I need
someone escorting the children up to the apartment and
back down again."

I temper my worried look—imaginary parents too?

"And the children need to be dressed nicely," she adds.
"We'll have the carousel for them to play on, but they need to
look handsome. Their Easter best." She gives me a smile.
"You think you can handle that for me, sweetie?"

I stammer but nothing comes out.

She browses another row of card stock. "I don't want you
doing what Anna did last time, that silly girl. No one showed
up—can you believe that?" Her hand rushes to her throat. "I
mean, *no one* came, Sarah. I could have killed her. She said
she'd sent out invitations and then she asked if I could see
the kids, when there wasn't anybody there. She kept pointing
and saying, 'But they're right there. Can't you see?' But there
were *no* children. It was so confusing. We had to make up
something to Patty about the party being rescheduled or else
she would have been devastated."

So, there it is. Anna's mistake had almost become my
own. I'm going to have to find real kids at a real playground.
I'm going to have to convince their mothers to show up. How
in the world am I going to get this done?

I open Google Maps on my phone and scroll thirty, then
forty blocks north of West Seventy-eighth Street. Soon, I'm
hovering above 125th Street in Harlem.

Collette holds out one of the sample books with a design

for an invitation card. It's pastel with a train circling the track, lions and zebras waving from the open compartments. Hanging from the caboose is a smiling clown. And stenciled above the train, the words *You're Invited!*

I take one look at the card.

The floor shakes and an unsteady feeling rushes over me. A violent heave in my stomach.

I throw up.

CHAPTER FORTY-SIX

"What's happening?" Collette steps back, looking in shock at the vomit-splattered book, which she immediately throws from her hands, the rest of my vomit dripping to the floor. A small amount smears across my cheek.

The saleswoman comes running, hands clamped across her mouth when she spots me—the disgusting mess and stench—and spins on her heel, disappearing to the back, presumably to fetch a washcloth or paper towels. I survey what I've done. She's going to need a janitor-size bucket and mop.

I hunch my shoulders to keep the vomit from dripping onto my clothes—Collette's clothes—a cashmere sweater I'm thinking she'll never want back.

"I'm so sorry . . ." I say, the stench flaring my nostrils.

I have no idea where that came from; the nausea hit me so violently. I'd felt fine up until point-five seconds before I projectile-spewed across the invitation design Collette had been showing me. The train with its smiling animals, now ruined.

"I'm sorry," I repeat, embarrassed. I haven't thrown up in public in years and certainly not in a fancy shop with lush,

padded carpet and Brahms Symphony no. 4 playing on the
sound system. To my horror, splatters of croissant and raspberry jam, remnants of our breakfast, have landed within
inches of Collette's designer boots.

The saleswoman returns. She's rushing with a stack of
paper towels, the expression on her face between a scowl and
frown of concern. The smell is revolting. Her precious sta-
tionery book isn't salvageable. The carpet will have to be
shampooed. More than likely, she'll need to close up shop
for the rest of the afternoon.

Collette moves fast too, fawning over me with paper towels and doing her best to clean me up. She begs the saleswoman for a bathroom, and the woman points. Collette
walks me in the direction carefully, gingerly wrapping her
arm around my shoulders.

"Are you all right, Sarah?" she asks as soon as she shuts
the door. "What's happening? Food poisoning? The stomach
bug? Do you need to see a doctor?"

"I'll be fine." I lean forward to splash water on my face.
Next, I rinse my mouth and spit in the sink.

"You poor, poor thing. I'm so sorry you don't feel well."
She plucks several tissues from her bag and looks at me in
the mirror. "You're so pale."

I stare at my reflection too. My eyes are sunken, the color
drained from my cheeks, and I'm clammy, my forehead
prickling with sweat.

"Let's get you to a doctor." She pats my back. "I'll take
you."

Within minutes, we're walking out the door with Collette
calling to the woman to invoice her for everything that's ruined. "We'll take care of the cleaning bill."

Outside, we wait for Henry to pull up. I feel faint and my body wobbles. I sway forward until I'm tipping back, then lean my hips against Collette for support.

I'm sleep deprived, that must be it. Except for the croissant Collette forced me to have this morning, I've barely been eating either.

Inside the car, I lean my head against the cool glass, doing my best to shut out the throbbing in my head.

The car stops. We haven't traveled far before Collette is shuffling me out again. A nurse appears, and I'm vaguely aware of them placing me in a wheelchair and guiding me into a building. We're rolling down a hall.

My head lolls to one side, I'm so damn tired. The nausea has subsided, but if I could only stop the pounding in my head . . .

"Where are we?" I ask, but my voice is muddled, my mouth filled with marbles. My tongue, thick and limp against the back of my throat.

"The doctor," Collette says. She walks by my side, the nurse pushing me in the wheelchair as we pass a series of closed doors.

The family doctor—the one Collette hates so much? She wouldn't.

I want to ask, but I don't. My head droops and my eyes close again. The wheelchair comes to a stop and the door closes. The nurse lifts me to a table so I can lie down, and immediately, the lights dim. The women's voices disappear into an echo. The last thing I remember is Collette squeezing my hand, and thinking of Jonathan, I wait for the second squeeze. The one that will tell me he's thinking of me. But it never comes.

———

When I wake up, I'm in a darkened room, but it's no longer the doctor's office. I'm surrounded by soft sheets, a large comforter. Silk printed paper on the walls and flowing drapes.

I've returned to the Birds' apartment but I'm not in the guest room. Something is off, I can feel it. Something's different.

I'm lying in Patty's castle bed.

I try sitting up, but pain ricochets through my head, nails hammering into my brain, and I cry out, wincing. I look around. The curtains have been pulled—Patty's pink curtains. A single lamp is left on in the corner. A scattering of toys, figurines, baby dolls, and princesses line the shelves.

I roll to one side, hoping I can prop myself on my elbow and lower my feet to the floor, but my head screams the moment I shift my weight. Dizziness swirls in my eyes, stars burst, and I lie back, my arms and legs deadweight.

I blink several times to will the pain away. The room is empty, the apartment quiet. With the curtains drawn, it's hard to tell what time it is. How long have I been sleeping? Is it still the same day or have I slept until the next morning?

I look down—I'm no longer in the cashmere sweater. The pants Collette loaned me are also gone. I'm in a nightgown, an old-fashioned thing that's buttoned right up to my throat with long sleeves cinched at the wrists and embroidery across the bodice. Under the covers, flowing white cotton rests at my ankles.

She's put me in a nightgown—the style, of a child's nightdress, going back decades.

Collette doesn't come. Pauline doesn't either. The minutes tick by until I'm dozing off again, and when I wake, I'm almost positive night has fallen. The room seems darker. Additional hours have slipped by without me knowing it.

I fumble again, wishing I could get out of this bed and remove the nightgown. Find my way down the hall.

The door opens.

Light ripples into the room, causing my eyes to slam shut. The brightness is blinding.

Someone is walking toward the bed—I can't make out who it is at first. They're one big shadow.

It's Mr. Bird—and I flinch. I want to kick at him, tell him to back off. He's walking in here to threaten me. To tell me about Jonathan—

But the shadow stops moving, and I blink again to adjust my eyes to the light. A face forms. The outline of a jaw. Square shoulders.

It's not Mr. Bird—it's Stephen.

CHAPTER FORTY-SEVEN

What does he want?

I pull my leg back. If he gets too close, I'll knee him where it hurts. I won't let him touch me, won't let him grab my arms. But my leg is stiff and I'm not sure if I can kick anything.

Stephen doesn't yell. Instead, he lays a hand to my forehead. He checks for a temperature and pulls back.

"You're going to be fine," he says.

I scoot as far away as I can. But he throws aside the comforter and pushes an arm beneath my shoulders. Tucking his other arm beneath my legs, he whispers, "I'm getting you out of here."

My heart skips a beat. Alarm sounds in his voice. The way he's holding me close, almost protectively.

"Stevie?" I whisper. "Stephen," I say, correcting myself. "What's happening?"

He keeps moving but holds me close. It's unlike any way he's ever acted toward me before—well, if you don't count the first time we met and he'd been so kind. But that was before I knew what he was made of, before I knew what his family was all about.

But something is different—*this* Stephen is different. What am I missing here?

My eyes strain against the light. Dizziness shakes me as I'm yanked from the bed, but I have no choice but to let him carry me. He's not taking no for an answer and I press my head against his chest, feeling weak, as Stephen carries me out of the room.

We move slowly, the hall stretching a mile long. Another harsh strip of light attacks my eyes as we cross into the foyer. The front door, and freedom, only a few steps away.

He reaches for the doorknob, but fumbles, his hand trapped beneath my legs. He pauses. He doesn't want to let go and have me fall, but there's no choice, and I shift my weight, drumming up the strength to stand. Pushing against his chest, I force my legs to drop until I'm on my own two feet, wobbly, but upright for now.

Stephen checks the hall for anyone who might be coming, but no one is. He turns to me.

"I can get you in a cab. You can stay at my place."

"I'm not going anywhere with you."

"Why not? You can't stay here anymore."

I give him a look. "What are you doing?"

"I'm helping you get out."

"Why?"

"Because something's not right. Something's making you sick."

"What's happening then?" My eyes narrow. "Are you guys poisoning me?"

His eyes jerk open. "No! We would never do that."

"Jonathan," I tell him. "He didn't do drugs. He would

never touch heroin. And that night when he got fired from his job—" I point a finger at him. "One of you planted it in his locker."

Stephen looks cautiously down the hall. He lowers his voice. "I didn't have anything to do with that. Putting that in his locker, that was my dad's idea. We couldn't have him poking around and asking questions. He was calling up the firm, Sarah."

My mouth drops open. I want to scream.

"He was calling up people and asking questions *about Patty,* for Christ's sake. Half the people who work there don't know there was a child twenty years ago. And I told you from the beginning—you have to understand how discreet we need to be."

Heat races to my neck. "Jonathan didn't trust *any* of you people. He was so right! And now look what you've done. You killed Jonathan . . ." My voice wobbles and trails off. The images are still haunting my mind. The needle in his arm. The lonely, dark alley where the police found his body. He'd been all alone.

But Stephen pleads. "That's not what happened, Sarah. Please believe me. My dad wanted to frighten him, not hurt him. We would never take it that far."

"You really think I'm going to believe you? Please." I push to get far away from him. "You're as guilty as your dad. You did this to Jonathan."

Stephen recoils. "No, that's not what happened. You have to believe me."

But I can only stare at him—the damn good actor. Of course he is. The whole family has been practicing their lines for years. They're professionals at this point, every one of them.

A noise comes from down the hall and it makes us jump. Our eyes race to see what it is. Someone's coming.

Is it Pauline? Collette?

Mr. Bird?

Whoever it is, they're moving fast and it's too late for me to escape.

CHAPTER FORTY-EIGHT

Stephen reaches for the door again, and my heart hammers in my throat. If it's Mr. Bird, he's here to stop us. He won't let me leave, even if Stephen says he's taking me to his own apartment.

But it's Collette—she's leaping in front of us like a wild woman, surprising us both until we're staggering back, her arms holding steady against the doorframe and barricading our only exit. Her breath is ragged, her eyes flashing a look I've never seen before. Her chest is heaving as she says, "Wait!"

Stephen throws up an arm to shield me, but I shove it away. I don't want his help anymore. I'm doing my best to stand on my own and take another step.

"Get out of the way," Stephen tells his stepmother, and the tone in his voice confuses me. I've never heard him speak to her that way before.

Collette's eyes rip in my direction. "Don't let him take you, Sarah—*please*. You can't leave me."

"I need to," I say. "I've been here long enough." I point at the floor-length nightgown to prove my point.

As I move to the door, I feel dizzy and my knees start to buckle again.

No, no, no. Don't let them see I'm weak.

Stephen turns on Collette. "What are you doing? Forcing her to stay in Patty's room? Dressing her up like this?"

"I'm not forcing her to do anything," Collette says. "I'm taking care of her. I brought her to someone—"

"What, Dad's doctor again?"

Collette looks stunned.

Turning to me, Stephen explains, "Pauline called. Told me you were a mess, that you got sick at the store, that Collette brought you home and was keeping you in Patty's room. You've been knocked out for hours." He looks me up and down, then searches my face. "Has anyone given you anything? Do you remember what the doctor gave you?"

I try to think. Everything after the store, the ride to the doctor's office, how I ended up in Patty's room, is a blank haze.

He turns once more to Collette. "Have you been drugging her?"

Her eyes bulge. "What? How can you say something like that?"

I'm confused too—how can he say that about Collette?

"Did you give her some of your pills?" he asks.

"What?" she shrieks. "Why would I do that?" She's staring at us both, waving her hands. "Sarah," she says, grasping my arm. "I'm not slipping you anything, trust me." She glances at Stephen too. "I promise."

"Then what is happening?" I ask, dizzy again. A hand clutches my stomach. "And this nightgown." I lift the material. "Patty's room. Why am I in there?"

"Pauline was stripping the sheets from your bed. We wanted to get everything cleaned. Your clothes too." She shrugs. "Patty said she doesn't mind."

I stare blankly at her.

Collette looks at Stephen. "You're under a lot of pressure, I know you don't mean what you said. I might not know everything that's going on, but something is different in this house and I think you can feel it. Things are changing. They've been changing for months." She glances at the rest of the apartment and shivers.

I want to shiver too.

"Who would want to hurt Sarah?" she asks. "Pauline adores her. And your father would never do such a thing."

If she only knew what her husband said to me . . .

"Sarah," she says, her eyes turning soft. "Come back to bed. You must rest. There's no one back at your apartment to take care of you." And she steps forward, caressing my cheek, her hand smooth and warm to the touch. My knees buckle. "But I'm here. I will always be here for you."

Stephen tries again. "Let her rest at my place."

But Collette waves him off. "She must stay here." She holds my hand in her own. "With me. I'll protect her. She's too weak to be out there alone."

I close my eyes to her singsong voice, my mind growing hazy. I'm so tired. So, so tired . . .

I'm sick and I know I must get better. Collette is the only one who can take care of me. And if I leave, what will happen to Collette? She needs me, like Mr. Bird said. I must help her with the birthday party or she'll fall apart.

I press my hand against the wall. I'm too tired to do anything else but sleep . . .

And I turn toward the room—my guest room and not Patty's—wanting more than anything to lie down and get some rest. By tomorrow, I hope, I'll be good as new, and within days, we'll have Patty's party and I can cut ties with these people. It will be for the best for Collette and me to separate.

She holds my hand and walks me back to my room.

CHAPTER FORTY-NINE

——

By the next day, I feel better. The day after that, stronger still.

No more vomiting since that incident at the invitation store. No more aches or feeling dizzy. And most important, no more seeing or hearing Patty. The only time I go in the playroom is when Collette tells me to, and as soon as I can, I find reasons to head back out again.

After I'm fully recovered I spend the next few days helping Collette with final party planning. Hours are expended on arranging and rearranging decorations. Elephant plush toys mixed with giraffes and bears. Miniature wooden train cars and streamers and banners strung together. Children's place settings and juice cups arranged on the table.

I keep a notepad in my hands and scribble down everything Collette tells me, last-minute instructions and phone numbers for the caterer and florist and bakery. Numbers Collette wants me to call the day before to confirm everyone's delivery time.

When the invitations arrive, Collette says, "Now you need to invite ten children."

I manage to find six children and their mothers at a playground in a quaint section of Harlem on the corner of Lenox and West 140th Street. I've never been here before. Collette and I have visited multiple playgrounds but never this far north.

And now, here I am, sitting on a park bench beside the jungle gym and the mothers are staring and laughing at me. They ask if I'm crazy. They wait for me to tell them it's a joke.

I hand them some forms. "All you have to do is sign this."

Of course, I don't call it a gag order. I don't want to scare them with the severity of the confidentiality clause, but I also don't want them to arrive unprepared. I'm sure as hell not going to risk these women coming in blind the way I did. The Birds misled me, but I won't do the same to these women. They will need to be prepared, and they might also need to prepare their children. We can't have anyone freaking out that day.

But the guilt—it's hard ridding myself of it.

I explain to the women they can't share this information with anyone. They are not to tell a soul, not even their friends.

It's a long shot, I know, but then I bring out the money. Five hundred dollars apiece. I promise another five hundred a week later—I'll be long gone by then, but they don't know that. Stephen will send out their payments, but he doesn't know that part yet either. He's given me cash to pay for most of the party services, not wanting credit card transactions to show any evidence of the Birds throwing a child's birthday party. I'm using the extra money to pay each mother and child to attend.

The women stare at the cash in their hands. They consider the promise of more money to come—the offer, tempting. I watch them review the single-page document in their hands, the write-up I thought would be the simplest way to explain.

I let the women know the event will last less than two hours and ask them to arrive by 3:00 P.M. They will need to wear their Sunday best, especially the children. I remind them Collette will be imagining a birthday girl who isn't there and their kids will need to ignore anything strange the hostess says. It will be confusing, I admit, but if everyone does their best, we'll get through this together.

Finally, after an interminable wait, and to my relief, the women agree one by one. Money has once again spoken. They sign the form and promise to arrive.

But it's only six children and not ten as Collette wanted. I tell myself that's good enough.

CHAPTER FIFTY

With the guest list secured, a flurry of activity follows. T minus two days until the party.

We order balloons from the store on Columbus. Select cookies from a bakery on West Eighty-first, and remind the caterer to bring macaroni and cheese and toast points as well as petits fours and tea for the mothers.

And the hammering—did I mention that?

Carousel pieces have been arriving by the truckload. A team of men clang metal and use drills with the parts taking up most of the dining hall: brightly colored posts and animals whose heads are topped with red caps.

When finished, the carousel is spectacular. The workers complete their task with just enough time to turn on the lights and let it whirl several rotations before deeming it good to go. They pack up their tools and leave, wishing Collette a wonderful party but never once asking why they didn't meet the birthday girl.

After they depart, Collette is nearly drunk with happiness. She watches the carousel as it plays a fun, melodic tune, the animals moving up and down and in a circle, lights blinking overhead. On the platform are a horse, a unicorn, a bear, and a tiger. A gold post in the center leads to a circus tent roof displaying a painted mural of angels surrounded by roses and stars. Each animal has a handsome saddle. The horse and unicorn show off colorful manes. The bear wears a crown; the tiger, a friendly smile.

The hairstylist, Bridget, had been right to suggest such a wonder. And Collette is the only person I know who could pull off this feat in her dining room.

She stares at the carousel, her eyes glowing as she insists Patty go for a spin.

"Which one do you think Patty should ride?"

I shrug. "How about the bear?" I suggest.

Transfixed, she sways to the music herself, a dreamy smile spreading across her face. "The bear is a wonderful choice," she says. "But they all are, don't you think? Or the unicorn." She winks. "Looks like fun . . ."

Collette waits for me to move toward the carousel, but I don't. She wants me to ride with Patty, but I'm not in the mood. The thought of riding alone while Collette stares is unnerving.

She clucks her tongue and spins on her heel before walking away.

The carousel continues turning in slow motion with animals gliding and music playing. No one is riding it other than the pretty blond girl Collette sees in her head. And suddenly, it's disturbing—the empty carousel. The flashing lights beckoning to no one. The music, forlorn and eerie. The animals, watching and taunting. The tiger's teeth, sharp and pointy and no longer friendly.

———

On the day of the party, I wake up with a solid knot in my stomach. I take a couple of deep breaths.

I don't know why I'm getting so worked up. I just need to get the event over with and then I can finally leave.

Before leaving my bedroom, I pause to calm my nerves. I fill my mind with words from Aunt Clara, and my heart with her guidance, and wish so much that I could pick up the phone and ask her if I'm doing the right thing.

I take another deep breath.

In the dining room, I find Collette decorating. Only two hours before the party begins, and I know I should be assisting since she looks like she could use all the help she can get. She's jittery. Her calm from when she'd been caring for me the past few weeks is replaced with frenetic speed and agitated movements.

"Everything must be perfect," she says.

I watch her frantically clean things Pauline has already tidied, spastic energy rattling through her voice as she says, "Her birthday is so special. We have to make sure everything is perfect." She's repeating the same sentiments over and over, and I'm no longer sure if she's telling me or herself.

She rushes from one task to another, wiping at a spot on the table, her eyebrows scrunching at a solitary blemish.

I want to pull her aside and tell her that everything is wonderful. It's all going to be fine.

Treats and goodie bags are laid on the table. The caterer has come and gone; the balloons have been delivered and scattered across the room. There's nothing more for Collette to do, but she's unable to sit still. She's busying herself with the centerpieces, her hands adjusting each decoration.

I busy myself too, checking each place setting: spoon and

fork. Napkins lined up. Everything straightened for the one hundredth time.

And at the far end of the dining hall, the carousel keeps turning. The carnival music keeps playing, a frightening tune.

I glance at my watch. The kids will be here soon.

CHAPTER FIFTY-ONE

Malcolm calls, announcing the group's arrival, and I ride the elevator down to the lobby and greet the mothers as if we're long-lost friends. They smile with the tiniest tinge of disbelief in their eyes—anticipation of this most unordinary day I've promised them.

But I'm also breathing a sigh of relief. They're here. They've made it.

Just as I did on my first day, the children are ogling Malcolm's fancy coat. One of the boys reaches out to touch the shiny gold buttons at his wrist and Malcolm smiles and indulges them, instantly putting the children and mothers at ease.

They take in the lobby, the children's mouths dropping open at the sight of a room unlike anything they've likely ever seen: plush carpet of crème and burgundy, a crystal chandelier bouncing light above their heads.

We move to the elevator. It will take two trips to transport all the mothers and children. One of the kids looks at the panel of buttons as I tell him number twelve, the top floor, and he squeals, "The penthouse!" The children giggle as the doors close and the elevator lifts.

The kids bump into one another with the kind of excitement children have when finding themselves somewhere new, somewhere fancy.

In the foyer, they stop and stare, but I don't let them linger, only lead them down the hall to the dining room like the Pied Piper, handing out red lollipops as the children rip off the wrappers and jam the candy into their mouths.

They make loud exclamations when they see the carousel. "No way! Look at that!"

The children immediately want to run and play. Several of them scurry loose, breaking from their mothers' grips and rushing forward.

"Soon," I tell them. "We need to sit at the table first."

Pauline appears. I ask her to direct the mothers to the parlor and tell them to relax while the children play; they'll find petits fours served on china plates and hot cups of Darjeeling tea. Pauline leads the women away without a word. The children stay behind and seat themselves at the table.

Several of the children cast worried glances as the French doors close, but then they remember the lollipops in their hands and continue to chatter. Collette enters the room and grabs their attention. She smells divine and is fawning over them like their fairy godmother.

She's wearing a brand-new dress with diamonds strapped around her neck. Enormous earrings dangle on either side of her chin. The children stare in wonder, their faces lighting up. And in return, she's thrilled to see them. She points to the balloons, hands out candy, and tells them about the birthday cake.

The children's chatter is mounting, then quieting, then rising again as they grow increasingly restless. They're dying to climb on the carousel, and I can't blame them. The ride is tantalizing, the bright flashing lights with carnival music beckoning to them. The children sit and stare while declaring which animal they're going to ride first.

But Collette is starting to look anxious. She keeps whipping her head to the door as if she's looking for someone— and I know who she's looking for. She's waiting for Patty. She's told herself the child is still getting ready.

CHAPTER FIFTY-TWO

═══

I should have known to stop Collette after we sang "Happy Birthday." One of the girls piped up, "Where is the birthday girl?" And I should have answered for her.

I should have distracted the children with more slices of cake or announced rides on the carousel when Collette turned to the door and said, "Here she is." Whatever their mothers had tried explaining to them, the children are still confused.

And when Collette leans forward and whispers to no one in the chair, when she says, "Happy Birthday, my sweet darling," and leans down to give the invisible child a kiss, the children's eyes grow wide as saucers. A few start giggling as they watch Collette blow out every candle on the cake.

But then Collette is telling the kids to run off and play, and they don't have to be told twice. With the attention span of preschoolers, they've forgotten to ask who on earth she is talking to.

In the excitement, one of the boys knocks over a centerpiece. Collette looks upset about keeping it upright. She brushes the glitter that's fallen from its place.

And that's when I hear him. Mr. Bird.

The unmistakable booming sound of his voice. *"What in the hell?"*

I stop dead in my tracks. So does everyone else.

He stands at the entrance to the dining room. His cheeks are bright red and the sides of his mouth puff air as he surveys the room.

What is he doing here? I didn't think he would show up. From what I understood, he never attends the party. But here he is, glaring at the children and looking like he wants every single one of them to disappear.

I'm confused—I thought he'd be thrilled to see we've pulled it off, the party he told me he wanted. He said, *Throw Patty the most spectacular party*. He asked me to stay and help. And I did. Mr. Bird has known every detail of the planning as for days Collette has talked about nothing else at dinner. Mr. Bird has seen the men assembling the carousel each morning as he walked out the door for work.

What did he think—that no one was going to come here and ride that thing? That they paid for an entire carousel to sit in their dining room and never be used?

Collette whirls around. Pauline does too, and she drops a plate, her skin blotching red from her neck to her cheeks. Pauline is staring at me, and then at Mr. Bird—she's panicked.

But why? He wanted this—I thought this was okay—

He marches toward me, and I instinctively back up.

I look to the carousel, to the kids who are still playing, before Mr. Bird bellows in my face, *"Sarah!"* The kids freeze and the parlor door opens. Alarmed, one of the mothers pokes her head out.

Stephen runs into the room next, his eyes opening wide when he finds a room full of kids. And he skids to a stop, his stare taking in the ridiculously ornate carousel spinning in the background, the party decorations, and balloons. The children he's never seen before.

Suddenly I understand I've messed up. Royally.

Nausea roils through my stomach. I know where I went wrong.

Anna didn't invite kids to the party because she knew better. Collette had been upset about no one showing up, but Anna lied and told her the children were standing right there. She tried to make her believe when there had been no one.

I thought I'd done well. I thought this was what the family wanted—what Collette wanted.

But I've screwed up and Mr. Bird is screaming at me and it's too late to fix it.

Because I broke the rule the Birds stressed above all: I told someone else. I'm not supposed to let anyone into this apartment to observe how Collette acts around her make-believe daughter. And now I've brought into this building twelve strangers who've all seen Collette.

Confidentiality agreement or not, they will talk. I was stupid to think they wouldn't. They won't be able to help it.

Did you hear about that family on West Seventy-eighth Street? Last name Bird?

How could I be so stupid?

If I could dissolve into the wallpaper, I would. If I could press myself into the wall so hard I disappeared and never have to face this family again, I would do it right now.

I'd been so close to pulling this party off without a hitch. I'm so close to getting the hell out of here.

I turn to Pauline—*why didn't you warn me?* I want to cry out. *Why didn't you tell me not to let the kids in?*

But in the last few days, I'd failed to share my plans with the housekeeper. Stupidly, I didn't think it was necessary. Still, when I brought the group to the door, why didn't she stop me? Why didn't she say, *Are you crazy? You can't bring kids to the apartment no matter what Collette demands. We've got to get them out.*

She should have protected me from this disaster, but she didn't. She didn't even give me a warning.

I stare at Pauline now, my heart racing, my piercing eyes asking all these questions, but she doesn't say a word. Only lets her chin quiver and shrinks back, furiously snapping the rubber band on her wrist. She's scared to pieces and doesn't know how to help me.

I'm on my own.

=

CHAPTER FIFTY-THREE

Mr. Bird shifts his eyes to Pauline. "Make these kids leave."

Pauline does what she's told. It's no small feat—not a single child wants to leave the carousel.

"But we haven't gotten our goodie bags yet!" they holler. "I want another ride!"

The rest of the mothers are stepping into the room, and Pauline shoots them a look to tell them they can't be here.

"All right, party's over," she says as cheerfully as she can. "Time to go. What a wonderful afternoon." She does her best to smile while pushing the children and mothers toward the door handing out the goodie bags.

Then she walks to the carousel and pulls the power cord. The music shuts off and the carousel stops midspin. The kids let out a groan.

The mothers claim their children, each of them glancing once more at the room, at us, and especially at the furious man in the center of it all. Pauline squeezes the group out the door until they're spilling into the hall.

The sounds of the children drift away, the commotion quieting with a discernible slam of the front door.

Pauline returns to stand beside me. But she's shaking, and I give her a wary look.

I survey the room—the five of us. The tension in the air is so palpable, I feel like my heart is about to burst. Mr. Bird stands a few feet away while Collette is on the other side of the table. She hasn't said a word but looks devastated—she doesn't understand why the party is over. Why the children are gone. Why the carousel is no longer spinning.

It's a miracle she hasn't thrown a fit yet. It's a wonder that the moment Mr. Bird said to get rid of the kids, she didn't tell him to stop. I'm shocked she isn't yelling and crying about how upset Patty is. But she doesn't move, doesn't speak, just stands frozen.

Mr. Bird draws a long and heavy sigh before he speaks. He says my name again, but this time, it's a low grumble. He's trying to get his breathing under control. But his eyes harden. "What were you thinking?" he says. "How could you bring those strangers into our home?"

I drop my head, instantly feeling ashamed. "I thought that's what Collette wanted."

He stares at his wife, then back at me. "It's not your job to give Collette whatever she wants. Didn't you know this would be the worst possible thing you could do?" He moves closer until he's literally inches from my face, his teeth grinding. "The stupidest, most reckless, most asinine thing you could come up with? I mean, *what were you thinking?*"

I whimper. "You told me to throw a party."

"But I didn't say for you to bring people here. I thought you understood how catastrophic that would be." He whirls away again, his hands rising to his face. "What are we going to do?" He fires off a look at Stephen. "Those women. We need to track them down. Pay them whatever it takes. Or . . ." He looks away. "Shit. They're going to talk. We know they will."

"No, they won't," I insist. "I told them we'd pay them more to stay quiet."

Mr. Bird rears his head back in laughter. "You stupid, stupid girl. You have no idea how this works."

Collette speaks up at that moment, her voice quiet and small. "What do you mean pay these women?" She moves around the table and reaches for Mr. Bird's arm. "Alex, what's going on? Why did you stop the party? We were having such a wonderful time." She looks at the rest of us. "I don't understand what's happening." And she turns back to her husband. "You're scaring Patty." She puts an arm around a chair and leans to one side to comfort her child. "It's okay, sweet girl," she tells her. "Everything is going to be okay."

"Oh, for Christ's sake, *there is no Patty!*" Mr. Bird screams.

Collette stiffens.

I freeze.

Pauline's hands cover her mouth as she gasps, the entire top half of her body heaving. Stephen's eyes bulge and he falls forward, then stumbles back, reaching to grip a chair beside him.

The air is caught in my windpipe—I'm almost certain I shrieked. My mouth hangs open. My hands rise like Pauline's to cover my mouth.

"What?" Collette gives a nervous laugh. One of disbelief and confusion. "Why would you say that?" She sits beside Patty, her eyebrows furrowing as she stares at her husband as if he's truly gone mad.

Mr. Bird groans and spins in a tight circle. He pulls on his face until he's rubbing at the skin, the sides of his mouth turning pink. He shuts his eyes.

Again, Collette says, "Why would you say that? Why

would you say such a horrible thing in front of our daughter—and on her birthday?"

"Collette . . . this has to stop."

She flinches. "What has to stop?" Her eyes race from me to Pauline to Stephen. "What is he talking about?"

I see how Mr. Bird is looking at her. He's about to tell her the truth. He can't keep this charade up any longer.

After twenty years, it's becoming too much.

He must be thinking about next year and the year after that. More nannies. More birthday parties to arrange. More voices to silence. It's getting out of control and he knows it.

Collette is getting out of control. He can't fight it. The look on his face says it's time for her to know the truth.

=

CHAPTER FIFTY-FOUR

"Collette," he says. "I can't carry on like this anymore."

She doesn't move.

"It's over." His voice is fraught with anguish. In an instant, he appears to age a decade.

Mr. Bird falls back a few steps. He kicks a plush giraffe that's fallen to the floor. Swinging out an arm, he knocks down one of the centerpieces too; the stuffed animals and toy trains Collette spent hours putting together tumble across the surface.

Collette cries out.

Another sweep of the arm and he's toppling a row of juice cups, knocking a plate with half-eaten cake to the floor, the strawberry icing landing on the marble with a *plop*.

Collette jumps from the chair. "Stop that!"

He hits a toy train with the back of his hand, a teddy bear too, not caring that juice and cake are spilling down the length of the table.

"Stop that!" she shrieks again. "You're ruining everything. You're upsetting Patty."

He spins around. "How many times do I have to tell you? *There is no Patty*."

She leaps back. But then she rushes forward again, smacking his arm and shoving at his chest, her eyes filling with tears. "Why are you saying this? Why are you acting this way?"

He raises his hand and I brace myself. Pauline sucks in her breath and clutches my arm.

But Mr. Bird lowers his hand to hold her. "Collette," he tries again. "Patty isn't with us anymore."

She points to the chair. "She's right there, Alex, next to you. Don't you see? What's wrong?" She throws out her arms, her glare landing on every single one of us. "What's wrong with all of you?"

"She's not here," Mr. Bird says again.

"Yes, she is!" She points a second time. "Patty, tell Daddy you're right there. Jump into his arms. Tell him he's being silly." She clicks her teeth. "I don't know why he's acting this way but I'm sure he'll snap out of it." She levels a steady gaze at her husband. "I'm sure he's just had a long day and doesn't mean what he's saying. He's going to apologize."

"You've got to stop doing that."

"What? Talking to our daughter?"

"That's not your daughter."

"You're being cruel."

"*Look,* Collette." He motions at the floor. "Look at the space you're pointing to. It's *empty*—don't you see? There's no one there."

Her voice rises to a shrill. "Have you gone crazy? Dammit, Alex. Open your eyes!"

"Patty is dead!"

And Collette shrieks.

Pauline shrieks too, her knees buckling.

Alex Bird grabs his wife's arms. She's falling toward him, but then realizing who she's falling toward, she rears back to strike him. He holds her close in a bear hug, preparing for her to kick and thrash and scream, which she does.

"Patty is gone," he says, but this time, he says the words more gently. She's writhing but he's not letting her pull away. "Don't you remember? All those years ago?" He closes his eyes while Collette looks as if her own eyes have been peeled wide open. She's turned stiff—shocked beyond anything. The man she loves is gripping her in an embrace that's more like a wrestling move and he's whispering such terrible things to her.

"It was such a long time ago," Mr. Bird says. "She got sick. There was nothing we could do. It broke our hearts."

"Stop saying that," Collette whispers.

But she doesn't blink. Her electric blue eyes stare at something on the wall. The color drains from her face.

Mr. Bird squeezes her to his chest, but she resists.

"She was sick but then she got better," Collette tells him.

"No, she died, and we buried her, and it was a terrible, terrible thing." He cries softly now. "But you wouldn't believe it. You kept insisting that you could see her. You refused to accept that she died. You've been doing this for years."

"No, I haven't. You're lying."

"I'm not lying."

She doesn't answer. He's rocking her.

A single tear drops from her eyes. I can't tell if she's finally comprehending the harsh reality or just terrified of the horrendous things Alex is saying.

"I don't believe you," she whispers. "You've done this be-fore. Telling me Patty is gone." And this time, she breaks free. "Oh, you don't think I remember? You told me that Patty wasn't here anymore, that she wasn't in her room even though I could see her and Therese could see her. You said I was crazy. Why, Alex? Why would you say something like that about our daughter?" Another tear drops, and then an-other. "What kind of a father would do such a thing?"

"Because it's the truth. Patty died twenty years ago—you *have* to come to terms with this. No more pretending. She didn't make it to her fourth birthday. We buried her on a Sunday. You've been making her up in your head ever since."

He looks around the room. "And now it's gone too far. You've been hosting a party like this every year, except one thing never changes." He looks at her. "She's always turning four. She doesn't get older. Haven't you noticed that? Every year, even with a new nanny, our daughter remains four years old. The rest of us get older but Patty doesn't. I mean, look at Stephen." She spins to fix her eyes on him. "He's not a kid anymore. He was twelve when she died and now he's a grown man. Everyone has been moving on, but not Patty. Come on, Collette. How do you explain that?"

She steps away, her hands covering her mouth.

"Today was too much." Alex Bird glares at me next. He also stares at Pauline. "People came to our home and saw all of this." He swings his eyes back to Collette. "And now they know about you, about your sickness—"

"I don't have a sickness!" she screams.

"Yes, honey, you do. You're very sick." And he says this with such sadness even my heart breaks. "You've been sick for a long time, but we thought we were helping you. We've worked so hard to protect you from the truth and now"—he shakes his head—"I can't do this anymore—none of us can. This has gone on for far too long. It has to stop."

Collette backs away. "No . . ." Her eyes well with tears. "I don't want to hear this. I don't believe you. You're making it up." She points a finger. "How could you?"

"I only did this because I love you."

"Shut up!" she screams. "*Shut up!*"

"It was the only way we knew how," Mr. Bird continues. "But it's our fault. We messed up but now it's over. You have to understand." He looks around at the table and balloons, the silent carousel. "There is no child here. No Patty." He looks to the rest of us. "None of them see Patty either."

"Yes, they do!" She rushes to Pauline. She desperately grips the housekeeper's arms. "Tell him you see her, Pauline. Tell him you see Patty."

But the housekeeper is crying, her chin wobbling. She looks to Mr. Bird, then back at Collette, not knowing what to do, what to say. "I . . . I don't know . . ."

Collette shakes her. "*What?* Dammit, Pauline! Tell them you see her."

"No . . . I'm sorry . . ." The housekeeper's shoulders crumple.

Collette grabs my arms next, her breath inches from my face. "Sarah, what about you?" Tears stream down her cheeks. "Tell me you see my Patty. Tell me you see my little girl."

She points at an empty space, and my shoulders slump like Pauline's. "I don't see her, Mrs. Bird. I'm sorry."

She hurtles toward her stepson. *"Stephen!"* she screams. "Please tell me you're not falling for this shit. You see your sister, don't you? You see Patty." She holds his head in her hands, her fingers splayed on either side of his jaw, and looks deep into his eyes, willing him to say the words she wants to hear.

But he can't do it. He can't speak. He's shaking too, tears flowing from his eyes.

"Stephen?" she whispers. "Tell me you see Patty . . ."

He starts to say something but stops. She squeezes his face tighter, begging him with every ounce of her being.

He nods.

And I gasp.

He *nods*.

"I see her," he tells Collette. "I see Patty."

She drops her hands and whirls toward Mr. Bird. "You see? Whatever this is, whatever you think you're doing, *you're wrong*."

Alex Bird stares at his son. "Stephen," he warns him. "Tell her the truth."

Stephen wipes at his nose. He's staring at the floor.

"Stephen!" Mr. Bird shouts. "Tell her you don't see Patty. That she's dead. We lost her a long time—"

"I won't," Stephen says, his eyes jerking up. "I won't do that, Dad."

"Why not? *Dammit,* Son. Tell her the truth!"

"I am!" he cries. "I am telling her the truth. I *do* see Patty." And he points a steady finger.

At me.

I shrink back. What's he getting at? What does he mean?

But he doesn't drop his hand, only continues staring at me, tears pooling at the corners of his eyes.

"Patty's right there." And he looks at his parents, a pleading, desperate look, before sliding his eyes back to me. "She's been right here. Right in front of our faces. She's been with us this entire time."

CHAPTER FIFTY-FIVE

I press my back against the wall.

He's delusional—he's got it wrong. Or else he's still trying to preserve the lie for Collette's sake. He doesn't think she can handle this.

But Stephen keeps staring, his eyes not dropping from my face. He holds his gaze until my neck and cheeks are burning.

Pauline steps away, shocked. Collette and Mr. Bird stare too.

"What are you talking about?" Collette asks.

"That's Patty," Stephen tells her.

"Don't say that!" she screams. "Your sister is only four. Stop making things up."

"I'm not making it up." He turns to his father. "Patty didn't die twenty years ago. She lived. She grew up." He points at me again. "I'm telling you, that's Patty."

No one moves. No one knows what to say, but Mr. Bird speaks up. "Stephen, you don't know what you're talking about."

Pauline steps closer again. She's the first one to stare at me up close. "It can't be." She shakes her head. "That's impossible."

But Stephen repeats, "It's her. I know it is. Sarah *is* Patty."

My heart wants to explode inside my ribs.

Mr. Bird and Collette won't stop staring.

Impossible.

You're all batshit crazy.

No way in hell.

That's what I want to tell Stephen—what I want to tell all of them. They've got it wrong and I need to get out of here.

Stephen's eyes are red. The saddest expression grips his face. But through his tears there is also hope. The tiniest of smiles. He's pointing and staring and believing his words are true.

But he's wrong, I keep repeating.

He must be.

I'm not Patty.

Their daughter is dead. They buried her. There was a coffin and a funeral.

A closed casket . . .

And something in my heart turns over.

They never got to say goodbye. They weren't allowed to see her body . . .

But that's impossible.

I back away, but there's nowhere to go since I'm already pressed against the wall. Pauline is sandwiched next to me, her mouth gaping, trying to understand what this means.

Two months ago, I'd never heard of the Birds. We'd never crossed paths.

I saw a flyer, a job posting. Stephen put it there, but he posted flyers in other buildings too. They interviewed several nannies—right?

I stare at Stephen. Of everyone he spoke to, did he pick me on purpose?

But Patty is dead, I repeat. I've got to get a grip. Stephen is just as delusional as his stepmother. He doesn't want to believe it either; he wants so much to believe his sister is alive. All these years of pretending have gone to his head too.

"I found an email to Freddie several years ago," Stephen says.

Freddie? I think about the chef, the man who'd barely spoken to me until a few days ago.

"He was in the kitchen. He walked out to get something but left his computer logged in. I was nosy," Stephen says. "Saw an email about a funeral and I remembered him asking for time off to travel somewhere. I wondered if that was what it was for." He looks at me again. "The funeral was for a woman named Clara Larsen." The sledgehammer in my heart hits deeper. "And when I clicked on the link for the obituary, I saw a picture and it was her. The same nanny from all those years ago. I was just a kid, but I remember her—Ms. Fontaine. Except she'd changed her name to Larsen, just like Sarah's, and was living in Virginia Beach."

I shake my head. "No . . ."

But Stephen keeps going. "Freddie was here when Patty died. He knew Ms. Fontaine. He must have kept in touch with her after she left."

Beside me, Pauline is whispering to herself.

"He knew about her funeral. He knew she had been caring for a child, a child who is now about the age Patty would've been if she had lived."

Alex Bird breaks in. "What are you saying? How could Freddie . . . how could Ms. Fontaine . . . ?"

"Turns out, after we were told Patty died, Ms. Fontaine moved to Virginia Beach with a girl. She raised her as her own, claiming she was the girl's aunt and was caring for her after her parents died. She changed her name."

I don't think I'm breathing anymore, the air is locked inside my throat.

Ms. Fontaine.

Clara Larsen.

Aunt Clara?

Aunt Clara had lived in New York City. But she told me she worked for an insurance company. We moved to Virginia after my parents died. We moved there . . . twenty years ago . . .

I find my voice. "This doesn't make sense," I say, every word trembling. "If Patty didn't die, she would be twenty-three, turning twenty-four." I stare at him. "I'll be twenty-six soon. How do you explain that?"

"She forged a new birth certificate for you," Stephen explains. "She made up a fake birthday and fake parents." He points at Mr. Bird and Collette. "*Those* are your parents."

Collette is crying—she's distraught and confused. Her hands are squeezed tight over her mouth as she sobs. Mr. Bird's face is pinched and pale. He's speechless, unable to stop staring at me and simultaneously looking terrified.

"No," I tell them. "That's not right. My parents died in a car crash. Aunt Clara raised me."

"Yes, she raised you, but she wasn't your aunt. I hired a PI. He traveled to Virginia to investigate, but you'd changed so much, we couldn't tell if you were Patty. But then you moved to New York and I couldn't believe my luck. I followed you for a while . . ."

My eyes grow wide.

"You seemed to be doing okay, you'd found a good guy." I

wince at the memory of Jonathan. "But you were in horrible debt and struggling to make ends meet. I thought I could help you out financially while finding a way to bring you here so we could get to know you. Find out if you're really her." He gives me a look. "I put that flyer in your building for a nanny. We needed a new one after Anna left, and Collette was becoming inconsolable again. I knew we had to do something. You showed up for the interview and I couldn't believe it, the plan was working out perfectly. I convinced Collette to hire you." He gives his stepmother a sympathetic look. "I said you were the best candidate and she agreed. She felt like the two of you had a strong connection, and no wonder." He looks at us both. "You're mother and daughter."

Collette is crying. She reaches out but then pulls away again.

"Stop!" I slam my hands over my ears. "She's not my mom!"

"That first day you sat down with me," Stephen says. "Do you remember? We had tea. You didn't want to eat but you had tea and that's how I got a DNA sample and sent it off to a lab. We matched your DNA to Patty's lock of hair." He looks to his dad. "I didn't want to say anything to you until I knew for sure . . ." He looks at me again. "The results came back a perfect match. You're Patty."

I'm going to be sick.

Mr. Bird's chin is shaking. He's searching the room for answers, his eyes flicking this way and that. "But how?" he asks. "How on God's green earth did this happen?"

"Patty was sick, there's no doubt about it," Stephen says. "Ms. Fontaine snuck her out of the building. She must have been working with the doctor—remember how we used to think they were close, and at one point, you thought they were having an affair? I was just a kid, didn't know enough to pay attention. I just knew Patty was here, the doctor got really worried, and then she was gone."

"The closed casket . . ." Mr. Bird says.

"He never let us see her. We never got to say goodbye."

Mr. Bird blinks, his eyes bulging until they look as if they could pop from his head. "But he told us her condition . . ." Their conversation is whirling around me. My hands spasm. "We should have asked more questions," Mr. Bird says. "We should have demanded to see her."

"You wouldn't let me!" Collette shrieks. "You said she had to stay in that room!"

"The doctor told us that!" Mr. Bird says. "How was I supposed to know he was lying? He said she had to be kept separate from us, that we wouldn't want to remember her that way."

"You didn't let me see her . . ." Collette whimpers.

"We didn't know," Stephen tells her.

"And he was working with Ms. Fontaine?" Mr. Bird asks. "He made up this lie and helped her sneak Patty out—but why? Why would he do something like that and lie to us about our daughter dying?" He's pulling at his face again. "I want to find this doctor. Strangle him with my bare hands. Sue him for every penny he's got. We'll make sure he never practices medicine again. I'll kill him—"

"Except he's dead," Stephen says.

Mr. Bird stops in his tracks.

"I had the PI look him up too. He retired and moved out of the city. Died at his home in Connecticut."

"*Fuck!*" Mr. Bird bellows. He looks wildly at Stephen. "And Ms. Fontaine is dead too."

"Ms. Fontaine—Clara Larsen," Stephen says. "Yes, she's dead too."

I'm still trembling.

Aunt Clara . . . I think again. This can't be true.

She worked for the Birds? She wasn't employed by an insurance company but was a live-in nanny?

She *stole* me? She took me to Virginia Beach?

Why would she do something like that?

She told me about her love affair, the man she'd left behind in New York. Was he the doctor? Pauline thought the nanny had been up to something with Mr. Bird, that they were the ones having an affair, but she had it all wrong. The affair had been with the doctor. The man who helped Aunt Clara remove a child from this home.

My head is spinning, the last twenty years of my life coming into question. Everything I know, a lie. All those memories: Aunt Clara caring for me, teaching me to ride a bike, helping me with Girl Scouts, soccer, studying for my SATs . . .

She told me my parents were dead. She was the only family I had and she loved me. She cared for me with all her heart.

But if my parents aren't dead, if Stephen is correct and my parents are right in front of me—*Collette and Alex Bird*—and he's my brother—

Then this family is mine.

CHAPTER FIFTY-SIX

━━

I can't stop shaking.

"I know this is a lot to process," Stephen says.

The weight of his eyes is heavy upon me—Collette's too. She turns to Mr. Bird, but there's no response.

Then she faces me slowly, her voice cracking on the word, *"Patty?"*

"No." I back away.

She moves toward me. Tremulous. Uncertain. With every step, Collette looks torn between wanting to believe it's true and terrified to find out it's not.

I glance warily at Mr. Bird and note the shock written across his face. I'm the ghost of a daughter past and he has no clue about what to do.

Collette tries touching my hair. "But I don't understand . . . how have you gotten so big?"

I slam my back hard against the wall and drop to one side. "Get away from me!" I eye my only exit from the dining room, but my feet are clumsy. I'm stumbling and forcing myself to slide against the wall until I'm moving only inches. "You're all crazy."

Once again, Collette looks at Mr. Bird. "Is it really her?"

Mr. Bird speaks up, but he focuses on Stephen. "I don't

understand how this could happen. How Ms. Fontaine could get away with something like this. Sneaking our child out of this house and raising her five states away? How would we not know about this?"

"The doctor helped," Stephen says. "He must have been in love with her."

"But she was sick!" Mr. Bird avoids looking at me as he says, "She was so ill. Removing her from this house would have caused her to get worse. She could have died . . ."

"She wasn't as sick as we thought."

Mr. Bird's eyes fly open. "What do you mean?"

"I think Ms. Fontaine faked it all. She faked how sick Patty was—I mean, remember how much access she had to Patty in her room? All those long days and nights by her side as her nanny. I think she made us think Patty was sick, convinced that doctor to tell us she was dying. Then he helped carry her out of the house. He told us to have a closed casket. We never got to see them putting her in there because there was never a body." It's Mr. Bird's turn to cover his mouth with his hands, the blood draining from his face. "We had a funeral for no one. We buried an empty casket."

Mr. Bird steps back. He reaches for a chair, finds nothing but air, grapples for Collette's arm and holds on to her instead.

"This can't be real. It can't be true." He's sweating. "*How?*"

"Ms. Fontaine was much cleverer than we realized," Stephen says. "Incredibly clever. She loved Patty so much she wanted her for her own. She wanted to take her away from us and raise her—"

"Ms. Fontaine took her?" Pauline says. Her eyes dart around the room. "*She* did this?"

"Yes, she took Patty from our family."

Pauline searches my eyes next, the puzzle pieces clicking in her head. "*You're* Patty?"

I shrink again. *I don't think so,* I want to tell her . . . *God, I surely hope not . . .*

Then comes a chortled laugh. So odd, so strange.

It stops me cold, the eerie sound. The laugh that's coming from Pauline.

Stephen's eyes wrench up. Mine do too.

Pauline laughs again. "You think *Ms. Fontaine* is the clever one?" Her face cracks into an uncomfortable smile. "Are you kidding me? That woman was an idiot." She breaks away and moves closer to the window. "She might have taken Patty, but that's about the only thing she was capable of."

Stephen gives her a startled look.

Mr. Bird stares at her strangely too. "Pauline, what are you talking about?"

"You give that woman too much credit, is all I'm saying." Pauline lets out another chuckle. "You've done well, Stephen," she tells him. "Figured out so much on your own. Good job." She raises her eyebrows. "But I hate to tell you, you're wrong about a few things."

Stephen's face turns white and he looks cautiously at Pauline, the woman he thought he could trust, his right-hand woman in this household—me too. My heart hammers hard.

"Yes, Ms. Fontaine loved Patty and I'm sure she wanted to raise Patty on her own. But please don't insult me by thinking she did this by herself."

"Pauline," Mr. Bird says steadily. "You'd better tell us what you know right now."

"Ms. Fontaine didn't do all of it!" Pauline shouts, a darkness striking her eyes. "She doesn't get the credit!"

I jump.

"Ms. Fontaine found out what I was up to. She was suspicious and I couldn't have that." She takes turns looking at each of us, how we're fixated on her words.

She takes it slow, a strange but excited smile on her face.

"I couldn't stand how obsessed you were becoming," she tells Collette, and Collette flinches. "Like the only thing that mattered in the world was Patty. She was the only person you wanted to spend time with." Collette balks but Pauline keeps talking. "It was too much. She was the center of your universe. She was all you could think about, all you could talk about. All day, it was Patty this and Patty that."

Collette shouts, "Are you insane? She was my daughter!"

"You were obsessed and it wasn't healthy. Ms. Fontaine didn't think it was healthy either, the way you were constantly hovering over her. You never had time for me." Collette gasps. "You stopped wanting to be with me."

"But she was *my daughter*," Collette repeats. "How could I not want to spend time with her?"

"You weren't with *me* anymore," Pauline says, angrily.

"What did you do, Pauline?" Mr. Bird asks. "What did you do to Patty?"

But she only stares at Collette. "I missed being around you, Collette. You used to depend on me for everything. When Patty came along, I was forgotten. Ms. Fontaine became your closest helper. You didn't need me anymore." She raises her voice. "So I fixed it. I took care of it on my own."

"You were in on this with Ms. Fontaine? *You* hurt Patty?" Stephen asks.

She smirks, the coldness of her smile reaching into the rest of the room, giving me chills.

"I needed to get rid of Patty." She looks at me, and I instinctively recoil. "Or at least, I thought I did. I thought it worked." She returns her gaze to Mr. and Mrs. Bird. "I poisoned her. Slowly at first, only a little bit in the beginning and then more and more." She makes a face. "Ms. Fontaine, that busybody, started noticing things. Questioning things. Talking to the doctor. I guess"—she shrugs at me—"she thought she was saving you by taking you from this house. But she had it all wrong—she thought it was Collette who was making her sick." She laughs. "She thought Patty's own mother could do such a thing. Boy, how she got that one wrong. But, Collette"—she looks at her—"you weren't well. Drinking again. Ms. Fontaine thought maybe you were depressed, or you weren't thinking clearly and were slipping something into Patty's food."

She looks at us all. "But it was me. I did it." She turns to me with an ice-cold look. "But it seems it didn't work. I failed to get rid of you permanently. And now you've come back."

CHAPTER FIFTY-SEVEN

═══

Mr. Bird hurtles forward like he wants to hit her. Strangle her. Throw her out the window.

But he only shakes. Collette sobs and Pauline laughs. She turns her back to us and moves toward the center of the room.

"I thought it would be my secret forever and no one would find out. That was a shame, really. Because all this time, all these years, I really wanted you to know how smart I can be too." She gives Stephen a creepy smile. "But the day is here. I just couldn't sit here anymore and listen to everything you were saying about Ms. Fontaine, giving her credit, when really, you should have known she was an imbecile."

My blood boils—she's talking about Aunt Clara.

"But she managed to get Patty away from you," Stephen says. "Collette wasn't the one making her sick. She got that part wrong, but she did save Patty's life. Ms. Fontaine's plan worked. I hate how she did it, but she did save Patty."

"And look how that turned out." Pauline laughs again. "You brought her back. You did all that work, spent all that time chasing her down—and for what? To return her to this apartment so she could get hurt again?"

"But you didn't know . . . how could you know it was her?" Stephen says.

"I didn't know." She gives me a wide-eyed look. "Until today, I had no clue. That was a big surprise. I didn't see that one coming." Her eyes snake up and down the length of my body and I will her to look away, my breath releasing the moment she turns back to Stephen. "But you brought her into this house and got her tangled up with Collette again, and I didn't like that either. Once again, Collette was getting too close. Too dependent on another nanny. Just like she did with Therese, just like she did with Anna. I had to get rid of each of them."

"What did you do to Therese?" Collette whispers.

"She had to go," Pauline says. "Fifteen years was a long time for me to sit on the sidelines. So I pushed her."

Collette shrieks. "*You?* You're the one?"

Pauline shrugs. The gesture so cold, so simple. "I pushed her into traffic. It was easy. You didn't see it—no one did. She died and it was done."

"Jesus . . ." Stephen whimpers.

"And Anna?" Mr. Bird asks.

"Well luckily she wasn't much of a problem. She had her own boyfriend, her own plans. She quit before you got too attached. But then, this one." She glares at me. "She couldn't handle you correctly." She clicks her teeth. "She couldn't take care of you the way I knew I could. She got in the way."

Pauline stares at me again and a chill runs down my spine. "And then that Jonathan of hers, asking questions and poking around. I couldn't have that, especially when he was looking into Therese's death. He was getting carried away. Too bold. I got rid of him too." A crack opens inside my chest. But she smirks again. "I made it look like an overdose. He thought I was there to talk to him about you, to make sure you were okay. I convinced him to go for a walk."

"You killed Jonathan?" I ask, the pain tearing its way from my heart to my head. "How could you? He didn't do anything. He was only trying to help . . ."

"He was getting in my way. It had to be done."

My knees go weak. Blood throbs in my ears.

"And then you," she says, her eyes remaining locked on mine. "You became a big emotional wreck after he died. Pitiful. And Collette was at your constant beck and call. She devoted all her time and attention to you."

I think about Pauline's messages weeks ago when she'd been telling me to arrive late. The excuses she came up with for me to leave early. She hadn't been trying to help me. She'd wanted me out of the apartment so she could be alone with Collette.

Having me move in had been all Collette's idea—and Pauline hated it.

"You killed Jonathan," I say to Pauline. "You put cocaine in Jonathan's locker."

"No, Mr. Bird is responsible for what went in his locker," she tells me.

I swing my eyes wildly to his.

"I did that and I'm so sorry," Mr. Bird answers quietly, and for this, he sounds remorseful. I glare at him, but it's way too late for an apology. "I wanted to quiet Jonathan. Keep you here longer. You staying here would keep my wife from hurting herself." He winces terribly. "I'm so sorry."

"You see, I'm not the only bad one," Pauline says, smiling. "But none of it was enough to get rid of you—and, oh, did I want to get rid of you. Have more time with Collette. My true love." She smiles at Collette before returning a calculated grin at me. "And now look at you. Patty." She once again looks me up and down until I feel my soul lying bare. The chill returns to my bones as I contemplate everything she's done to me—*for years*. "It's like it all came back full circle," Pauline says. "You coming back into this house all grown up. And me, here." She puts a hand over her heart. "Trying to be rid of you again."

CHAPTER FIFTY-EIGHT

==

I take off.

I find my feet and run as fast as I can out of the dining room.

Aunt Clara loved me, I know she did. She did what she did to protect me, to keep me safe. But the lies are a lot to handle. She's not my real aunt. Only my nanny. My parents aren't dead. She raised me to think I had no other family.

I spin around the corner, fighting my tears while thoughts of Aunt Clara clamor in my heart. But those thoughts are consumed by my driving fear of Pauline—the woman who's too close right now. The woman who has admitted to poisoning me when I was a young child.

I need to get away.

The woman is obsessed, there's no doubt. She's upended our lives so she could be alone with Collette, wanting nothing more than to be with the lady of the house, the one person at the center of her universe.

She tried killing me—an attempt to rid Collette of her own child.

She killed Therese.

She killed Jonathan.

If she had her way, she'd get rid of me again now. Maybe permanently.

I'm racing down the hall, my heart leaping from my throat as I fight to keep down the bile that rises, my choking screams, desperately wanting to get as far away from this hell on earth as fast as I possibly can.

Stephen is calling after me, "Sarah!" Then, "Patty!" But I don't stop. I'm tearing toward the front of the apartment and he can't stop me.

"Please don't go!" he shouts. He's running too, a raspy breathlessness breaking through his voice as he approaches.

Finally, I reach the front door. But Stephen is behind me.

"You remember me, don't you?" he says. "Tell me you remember."

But I don't—and I don't want to. I only want to leave.

"You called me Stevie, remember?" I feel a lurch in my chest as I rip my eyes away from him. "That night you were sick, you called me Stevie. You have to remember, Sarah. When you were a little girl, you called me Stevie too. It was the only name you had for me. You remember, I know you do."

I want to squeeze my hands over my ears and shut out his voice.

"Patty . . ." he whispers.

I fling the door open and spot the elevator. I can make it there in seconds, I just need to move.

But something makes me stop.

No, no, no!

He's playing mind games—this whole family is. I don't have to put up with it anymore.

But there it is again—*his* name. A sound.

Stevie . . .

It's the sound of my own voice. Just a squeak. Me as a little girl calling out as I run toward someone. A boy who's older than me with reddish blond hair and a playful smile, his arms opening wide and ready to give me a hug. He hugs me close and I know he loves me.

Stevie . . .

My childlike voice calls out to him again.

But it can't be . . .

And yet, I'm reaching for my brother. I'm peering into his face and hugging him close.

I'm three years old, which makes him about twelve. He's taking my hand and leading me toward the dollhouse—*my* dollhouse. We're sitting down and playing and he's showing me my brand-new doll, something the nanny and house-keeper have gifted me. But I'm coughing. I don't feel so good and Stevie is handing me a cup of water. But I don't want to drink it. I don't like eating or drinking anything anymore— everything tastes funny and I'm too little to understand why. The soup they feed me tastes funny too.

But it's not my mother handing me the spoon. And it's not my nanny, Ms. Fontaine—the woman I will eventually grow up to call Aunt Clara.

It's Pauline, the housekeeper. She's telling me my mommy has gone down for a nap. She's feeding me soup and bringing the spoon to my lips, saying, *Patty, one more sip. Your mother will be so pleased.*

I'm too young to know what's happening. Too young to explain how I'm feeling to Stevie because he wouldn't under-stand it either. He's only a kid like me.

And then I hear them—Pauline leaves the room but Ms.

Fontaine and the doctor are staying behind. They're whispering in the corner, smiling at me reassuringly but also trying to hide the looks of concern on their faces. They're making plans. They're worried about my mother, and they have no idea it's Pauline they should be worried about instead.

They tell me I need to leave my home and I don't understand why. They say I can't stay here anymore.

I love Ms. Fontaine. She will take care of me, she always has, so I go with her. The doctor covers up for them and we disappear. She tells me to call her Aunt Clara and lets me pick out a new name too. She tells me it's a fun game and I choose the name Sarah.

I freeze. I no longer want to burst out the door.

Stephen's voice is coming back to me—he's older now. I turn to face him. We're standing in the foyer. The elevator is only a few feet away.

But I remember . . .

A woman. I'm holding a woman's hand and she's beautiful. A radiant blonde.

We're sitting together and humming. A scent of strawberry bodywash envelops us both as she holds me close.

The dollhouse—*that* dollhouse. I instinctively dropped to my knees the first time I saw it in Patty's playroom, and now I know why. I used to sit before that dollhouse and play with it for hours.

I'm clutching the Patty doll to my chest, but something's different. The doll's hair was different back then—it was a synthetic, odd color, not the soft blond hair she has now. The hair my mother cut from my head as a keepsake.

My mother. Collette.

The beautiful woman. Chanel No. 5 and creamy red lipstick.

Bedtime stories snuggled up with her in the castle bed. My father, Alex Bird, kissing me on the forehead.

And then it's me and my mother lying in bed. She's stroking my hair and humming another song.

Patty and Collette.

Mother and daughter.

I am Patty.

Collette is my mother.

I see her now. Collette is walking toward me. She's coming up from behind Stephen and entering the foyer. She's no longer crying but holding something in her hands. A plate with a slice of cake. She's smiling and looking at me lovingly, a glazed expression taking over her face. She clutches candles too.

I can't breathe. Can't move. She places one candle after another into the cake, the candles sliding through the frosting, strawberry, the flavor that had been my favorite when I was a child.

I count the candles. But there are only four. She's not adding any others.

Collette pulls a lighter from her pocket. She lights each candle, the cake plate balanced carefully in one hand, the glow from the candles lighting up her beautiful face.

She calls to me, softly. "Come here, Patty. Come close to Mommy." Holding the plate, she says, "It's time to make a wish. Blow out your candles."

Every muscle in my body locks tight.

My mother is here before me—my actual mother—except everything is messed up. Collette is still locked in time.

The four candles. The glazed look. She's unable to see me as a grown woman, even now.

"Happy fourth birthday," Collette tells me.

CHAPTER FIFTY-NINE

Pauline is handcuffed and led out of the Birds' apartment to a patrol car below. She's confessed everything to us and the police officers are wanting to interrogate her.

The rest of us sit, shell-shocked. We've moved into the family room, the door to the dining room and the silent carousel closing behind us.

A pair of police detectives sit across from us and ask a litany of questions. Mr. Bird does most of the answering, and I find myself turning away every time he so much as looks in my direction. The detectives ask me several questions too, but I struggle with what to say. Stephen takes over and fills in the gaps.

"We had no idea," Stephen tells them.

And Collette? She's in a chair in a corner of the room, still smiling that strange smile of hers. I want her to stop—it's unnerving. Yet part of me is fighting the urge to run toward her and place my head in her lap.

Freddie hands her a cup of tea. But we lock eyes for a second before he disappears back into the kitchen. He knew about Aunt Clara, about her dying. Did he come to the funeral like Stephen suspected? Is that why he acted so odd toward me when we were introduced, did he recognize me?

But I don't get a chance to ask Freddie any of these things—not yet—because the door to the kitchen swings closed and he's leaving me with these people. These people I don't know, whom I don't trust.

Collette in the corner, smiling eerily and thanking her lucky stars she's reclaimed her long-lost daughter.

She is . . . my long-lost mother.

I've been in her presence for two months. Playing board games on the floor. Watching movies on the couch. Taking "Patty" to the playground and caring for the ghost of her child when that ghost had been right in front of her the entire time.

It's unimaginable—a scenario beyond Jonathan's worst suspicions. If only I could tell him what's happened.

Mr. Bird can't stop staring. He's answering the detectives' questions but steering clear of the cocaine incident in Jonathan's locker, I notice, and my blood boils. How the man continues to lie and dodge bullets is beyond my comprehension.

His face is a whirlwind of conflicted emotions too. He's terrified of me, but he also wants to beg my forgiveness. Will I ever be able to call him Dad? When the dust settles, what will we say to each other?

I feel as if my soul has been separated from my body. My brain too. The conversations swirl around me. Collette stares maniacally—and I tell myself this isn't happening. It's someone else's mess now since I'm leaving. Patty's birthday party is over and I can go soon.

But Stephen's and Mr. Bird's eyes are shifting to me every few seconds and I have the doomed, sinking feeling that I will never be able to go—unless there's something I can do about it.

I have parents now. A brother. I have money.

All of this is mine.

But I don't want any of it.

My mother is insane. My father and brother are manipulative assholes. Stephen knew exactly what he was doing, especially when the DNA results came back. So why act like such a monster? Why threaten me into silence and talk about me and Jonathan in such a horrible way? That last-ditch attempt at rescuing me from Patty's bed, a little too late.

If that was his way of trying to get back on my good side, of keeping me around, of having his little sister return to his life, he's royally screwed in the head. He knew how vindictive his father could be, how threatening, and he didn't do anything to stop him. They never defended Jonathan.

But in Collette's messed-up way, she meant well. She cared for me and was terrified I would leave, but she cared for me nonetheless. Especially after Jonathan died. But she wasn't someone I could depend on, her emotions were too erratic.

She thought she could depend on Pauline—the whole family did. And look how terribly that turned out.

She could have killed me. She tried to kill me before as Collette's daughter.

She killed my fiancé. She also killed Therese.

If I'd stayed as the nanny, she would have tried to get rid of me too.

Oh, in the beginning, how I'd thought this was going to be an easy gig. If only I could go back to that day two months ago and throw out that flyer. If only I had never seen it, if someone else had taken it from the bulletin board instead.

Would Stephen have returned to the apartment and posted another flyer until he finally got my attention? Probably.

His selfish plan for bringing me back into the house has cost me so much. Sure, he regained his sister, and perhaps one day Collette can be made well again. But what about me? I lost Jonathan. I'm not sure how I feel about Aunt Clara—that one hurts. Not to mention finding out I belong to this crazy family.

I wish I'd carried on working at Hearth instead of coming to this place. We could have made ends meet, Jonathan and me. We would have struggled, but we would have found a way.

I should have tossed that flyer in the trash and never spent a single moment wondering about this family. I never should have assumed their world would be so much better than mine.

The family that warned, *Special conditions apply*. Their need for utmost discretion. They'd meant it, and I'd fallen for it.

Alex Bird is walking toward me now. He's crossing the living room and sitting beside me as the detectives turn their attention to Collette. She's still sipping her tea in the corner and hasn't spoken much, unable to peel her eyes away from me.

I want to push Mr. Bird to one side. Shove him to the floor. He let his wife carry on like this for far too long. He bullied Jonathan and planted drugs in his locker. He blamed me for every misstep.

I jerk my body away from his, but his voice is soft. Low, like he's trying to be tender, or maybe just pretending—I don't know anymore, don't care, still have no idea who to trust—as he stretches his hand toward me and says, "I'm so sorry, Patty . . ." I flinch. "Sarah," he corrects himself.

He pulls back his hand. It's too soon for hugs or consoling, for any sort of father-daughter relationship. I'm not sure if that can ever be possible. He leans forward instead.

"Sarah, I realize this has been a lot—"

I glare at him.

"It's a lot for us too . . ." His voice breaks. "Finding out who you are. What Pauline has done . . . all of it. It's overwhelming."

I grit my teeth but keep my voice to a whisper. "I want nothing to do with any of you."

He shakes and then tries to recover. "Your mother?" He nudges his chin toward Collette. "She needs you."

"She doesn't *see* me," I tell him. "She only sees Patty, age four."

"We'll help her."

"You've done a shit job of that already."

"We'll provide for you and your mother for the rest of your lives."

"More money?" I twist away again, willing him to leave, not wanting to feel his breath close to my skin. "I don't need anything more from you."

"Don't say that," he pleads. "We're family. You're *our* family."

"I'm fine on my own."

I stand abruptly. There's enough jerk in my stance to catch the detectives' attention, and they pull their eyes from Collette to study me. Both are giving me a wary look as they try to guess my next move. Am I about to jump off the deep end?

Maybe I am.

Staring hard at the detectives, I point to Collette and say, "This woman needs help."

The detectives don't move an inch.

"She needs serious medical attention." I hiccup, the tears flowing from my eyes now—*dammit, Collette*—at the hurt and anguish my mother has gone through. What she's done to herself. What no one has been able to give her until now. I wipe at my eyes. "There's no way she's going to get better if these people remain involved. She needs to see a doctor." I gesture at Alex and Stephen. "They've never been able to properly take care of her."

Mr. Bird protests, but I wave my arm to silence him.

"These men, what I could tell you," I continue. "The threats they've made against me. The drugs they stashed in my fiancé's locker. Their culpability when they stood by and let that woman"—I shudder thinking about Pauline—"how they let that woman do what she did right under their noses. Twenty years ago she tried to hurt me and she would do it again now."

One of the detectives cracks a smile, and it's not one of those mocking grins where he's undermining me. Where he's going to get paid off by Alex Bird to drop my accusations. No, he's smiling because he's realizing the ammo I'm sitting on. The details I'm willing to spill about the uber-wealthy Mr. Bird and his glass castle. How I'm willing to shatter it and let everyone see this family for who they truly are. The other detective, I'm not so certain.

I cross the room until I'm standing before the detectives.

"This isn't the kind of family I want to belong to," I tell them. "I'm not staying with these people a second longer. I'll tell you everything."

The other detective, the one who's more cautious, darts his eyes from me to the Bird family as he asks, "Are you sure, Ms. Larsen?"

"I'll be fine on my own."

But behind me, and so eerily out of touch with what's happening, with reality, is Collette's voice. The words send a chill over my body as I hear her announce wholeheartedly, "That's my girl."

And I turn to her, expecting to see the familiar glazed-over look in her eyes, the confusion, but there's something else. The flicker of wheels turning, her eyes locked on me—is that recognition?—but I can't be sure because the light in her face only lasts half a second. It was there briefly, and now it's gone.

But I think I see Collette. And more important, for the first time, I think she sees *me*. And something stretches between us, over time and space and every year we were separated. The understanding that only a mother and daughter can feel. We've made a connection.

I walk straight out of that room and leave the Birds, the detectives too. Slamming the front door, I head for the elevator, all the while wondering if that was my mother's way of telling me to move on, her way of saying goodbye.

Her way of telling me that while she's still trapped in her cage, I need to get the hell out of there.

ACKNOWLEDGMENTS

===

When my sister lived in the East Village, we walked everywhere. To me, it's one of the best ways to see New York City and explore every neighborhood. I'd sometimes find myself on the Upper West Side looking up at the buildings, particularly the penthouses, and trying to imagine what these families are like and what their apartments looked like. Is everything wonderful? Do they love their lives? But what if everything isn't wonderful? What if the family is hiding something? And on the street, looking up, my imagination would run wild thinking about some of the tragic stories that could be going on behind those walls.

That was the spark behind the idea for *Nanny Needed,* and for that, I am appreciative to my sister and our parents for every one of our long walks through Manhattan. We saw a lot! And you never know when a story idea will hit.

I'm most thankful to Nicole Angeleen, who I befriended through our mutual agent, Rachel Beck. *Nanny Needed* is dedicated to you for your support and your drive for reading the first version of this manuscript and coming back with the exact comments I needed to hear. Nicole, you made me turn this book around in more ways than one with your honest feedback and suggestions. I still laugh about the comment bubbles you left, your track changes, and how we killed off an entire POV. Because of you we made this book what it is today.

I am super appreciative of my agent, Rachel Beck, who has been championing me and loving this book since the first time I told her about it. After your first read, your excitement was electrifying, and your passion for this project is what helped sell *Nanny Needed* to Bantam, Penguin Random House, in less than a month. How thrilling! And literally the same week you gave birth to your second child! Rachel, you are an amazing agent and I'm so glad we are working together. I'm also super appreciative of Liza Dawson and the entire team at Liza Dawson Associates for your help with this book.

Huge thanks to my editor, Anne Speyer, at Ballantine Books. I still remember our first phone call and how your excitement for this book shone as you described the storyline as *Gossip Girl* meets *Rebecca*. When I heard that, I was hooked and knew you were the editor I wanted to work with. Thank you for your reviews and careful guidance as we explored each relationship Sarah encounters, particularly the emotional tug-of-war she feels toward the tragically flawed Collette. You have taught me so much about my writing—sometimes less is more!—and I am honored to continue working with you.

Thank you to my friends, readers, and all the authors I've come to know along the way of publication and promotion. You've been sharing and loving my work since my debut, *The Stepdaughter,* and then my second book, *The Missing Woman.* Thank you for reading my subsequent work and for cheering me on with *Nanny Needed.* Your support means so much to me as I continue writing and sharing my news with you. Readers and friends, you are everything.

To my family. Wow, do you remember when I first told you I wanted to start writing again? Remember all those weekends when I locked myself in my room or asked you to babysit the kids so I could work? To my parents and sister, who never doubted me, thank you. You let me talk endlessly about my writing and listened while I rambled about everything I was working on. You always told me to keep trying. To my sons, who have been so patient and will leave me alone so they can make their own waffles in the mornings, thank you. Boys, I love you. Thank you to my stepsons, who listen to me at dinner when I talk about my writing. You guys are so fun and supportive. And to my husband, who has been the biggest champion I could ever ask for, my biggest confidant. You continue to give me the space and time, the support and love for every book I'm writing, for every part of this journey. You are my number one fan, and I am yours. I love you.

The author of *The Stepdaughter* and *The Missing Woman*, GEORGINA CROSS worked in television news and then spent nine years in business development for an aerospace and defense contractor before joining the local chamber of commerce as the workforce director. She now writes full-time and lives in Alabama with her husband and their combined family of four sons.

georgina-cross-author.com
Facebook.com/GeorginaCrossAuthor
Twitter: @GCrossAuthor
Instagram: @georginacrossauthor

ABOUT THE TYPE

This book was set in Sabon, a typeface designed by the well-known German typographer Jan Tschichold (1902–74). Sabon's design is based upon the original letterforms of sixteenth-century French type designer Claude Garamond and was created specifically to be used for three sources: foundry type for hand composition, Linotype, and Monotype. Tschichold named his typeface for the famous Frankfurt typefounder Jacques Sabon (c. 1520–80).